T0357351

# ISABELLA NAGG
## AND
# THE POT OF BASIL

ALSO BY OLIVER DARKSHIRE

*Once Upon a Tome*

# ISABELLA NAGG
 ◆ AND ◆
# THE POT OF BASIL

A Novel

OLIVER DARKSHIRE

**W. W. NORTON & COMPANY**

*Independent Publishers Since 1923*

Copyright © 2025 by Oliver Darkshire

Illustrations by Sophie Grunnet
Half-title illustration "Pot of Basil" by Daniel Pyrah

For information about permission to reproduce selections from this book, write to Permissions, W. W. Norton & Company, Inc., 500 Fifth Avenue, New York, NY 10110

For information about special discounts for bulk purchases, please contact W. W. Norton Special Sales at specialsales@wwnorton.com or 800-233-4830

Manufacturing by Lakeside Book Company
Book design by Brooke Koven
Production manager: Louise Mattarelliano

ISBN: 978-1-324-10591-6

W. W. Norton & Company, Inc.
500 Fifth Avenue, New York, NY 10110
www.wwnorton.com

W. W. Norton & Company Ltd.
15 Carlisle Street, London W1D 3BS

10 9 8 7 6 5 4 3 2 1

*for my sisters,*

*Amelia,*
*who started all of this long ago by asking me for a story,*
*and (therefore) is to blame*

*and Isobel,*
*who once tried to convince the entire family that*
*I pushed her down the stairs*

# PROLOGUE

I T WAS late summer under a pale green sky, and the wizard Bagdemagus had decided to retire. Not right now, perhaps in a decade or two, when the ache in his bones had really settled in. He felt the itch, the same way he'd felt it when he'd first picked up the book of practical magic commonly known amongst wizards as the *Household Gramayre*. He hadn't known that strange, subtle itch for what it was, back then. Now he could recognize it as a sign that it was time for something new. Wizards didn't die of old age. They were too suffused with Gramayre for that. No, a wizard changed. They took on new shapes, new forms, until one day you never returned. It was in their nature, just as the sun was pushed across the sky by a gigantic beetle, and as goblins returned to the valley each year at the first mischievous whisper of autumn.

The valley was tucked away below the village of East Grasby, and Bagdemagus wandered it freely, deep in the heart of the crag that would soon blossom with wild goblins and their treacherous fruits. He'd tried to banish the goblins for good, when he'd first come into his power, but some magics were too old and buried too deep. Instead, when all power and works had failed him, he'd reluctantly done exactly what his wizardly predecessor had done, and contained the problem instead. A spell encircling the valley, fencing the goblins inside to ensure neither they nor their enticing wares could work evil in East Grasby.* The goblins were harmless enough as long as they stayed in their market until winter, when the cold caused them to wither away.

As he walked, and with extreme care, he scattered mandrake leaves behind him. Most people didn't know of the mandrake's special properties, because they didn't care to listen to the old folk tales. The people of East Grasby didn't listen much to anyone. To each other. To their surroundings. To any of the lectures he gave on the matter when someone turned up at his door with mandrake poisoning. As a matter of principle, and professional curiosity, Bagdemagus listened all the time. There wasn't much else to do when you kept your own company, unless you counted the grimalkin, which Bagdemagus didn't. He spent so much time with the feline creature that he almost considered it part of him, much in the same way as the *Household Gramayre*. Spells and memories all folded into each other until you couldn't tell which was which anymore. It was going to be hard to leave it all behind.

It was often the case that Bagdemagus became so caught up in his own inner dialogue that he failed to notice what was right in front of him, and today was no different. Gaze turned firmly inwards, he stumbled across something heavy in front of him. Catching his balance, he stepped back onto the mandrake leaves, scuffing the line. Cursing blithely, he turned to see what had tripped him.

The body was headless. Large, strong, and oddly contorted, as if it had died in some distress. Unfazed by the sight (Bagdemagus was old, older than anyone gave him credit for), he warily reached down to assess the state of decay. Less than a day old,

---

* The spell required a circle, an oval, or a reasonable attempt at either. The important thing was the spirit of a circle—nature abhors a polygon.

perhaps killed the previous evening. He couldn't state the exact cause of death, not without opening the *Gramayre*, and there were spells in the books that even he feared to cast. What worried him most was the fact that it had been left unwatched. Having been abandoned without a vigil or burial rites, the corpse was almost certain to wake as a licce, tirelessly seeking out some last vengeance or obsession. A body didn't need a head to be dangerous.

He inspected the wound. Jagged. Clumsy. The head had been severed in a hurry, or by someone unfamiliar with the workings of the body. A murder, then. It wasn't the first one in East Grasby and it wouldn't be the last.*

The grimalkin sidled out from behind a rock, all extra toes and crooked teeth. It looked nothing like a cat in any meaningful sense, but that was still the closest word one could use to describe it. The creature was something like an assistant, a deputy librarian, and a tutor all rolled into one. The grimalkin liked to nap on a particular rock when Bagdemagus did the goblin-mandrake ritual, because it was an excellent sunbathing spot, and they rarely ventured down into the valley together except to perform this specific rite.

"Gosh," the grimalkin said, dryly, indicating the body. "Well, it's not goblin. I suppose that's a mercy." It sniffed the corpse. "Not watched. It's going to turn. We'll have a licce on our hands before sundown."

Bagdemagus sighed. "Have to do everything myself," he grumbled. As if he'd have accepted help from anyone, which he would not have.

---

* There had been a time, several wizards back if the grimalkin was to be believed, when the people of East Grasby had indulged in seasonal festive homicides as a way of evenly spreading the death out across the year in a controlled manner. The sacrifices were eventually replaced by civic town meetings, which satisfied the same visceral urges.

Reaching into the depths of his mind, where the spells he had memorized that morning were drifting about, he sifted through the jumble of words and incantations until he came across a spell of burning. It was an unruly thing. Fire always was. It wanted to escape, and you had to be wary lest it catch onto something inside you and burn you out from the middle. With the spell on his lips, eyes burning like coals, he made to touch the body.

"What on earth are you doing?" The grimalkin's sour voice cut into his concentration. He paused.

"What does it look like? I'm burning it before it gets up again."

"We don't have the whole body." The cat had that superior expression it leveraged whenever he knew something the wizard didn't. This happened often.

"What difference does it make?" He was irritable now. The spell slipped from his grasp and vanished from his mind. Bagdemagus wondered, briefly, where it went.[*]

"If you don't burn the whole thing," said the grimalkin, "particularly the head, you won't kill it. You'll just end up with some very alive bones, unless you have fire hot enough to burn those too. Which you don't. Because I know all your spells." Smugly, it waved its tail. "You'll have to bury it until we find the head, and then we can get rid of it all at once."

Sighing loudly enough to make a point, Bagdemagus delved for another spell. This time, slumbering under some cobwebs, and next to where he'd left his list of favourite celery memories, was the Cant of Terrestrial Gerrymandering. He retrieved it. It

---

[*] It went to a small carpenter's shop in the city of Verdigris, which happened to be built on a nexus of magical energies. Several times a week, mislaid spells manifested in the foyer, driving the owner to distraction and his insurance premiums through the roof.

had been a while since he'd memorized it, but it was still good. Under his careful guidance, the spell worked the same way it always did, opening a sizeable pit in the earth into which a body (or several bodies, if you squeezed them) could be placed. With a kick, he heaved the dead man into the newly formed grave. Six feet under, that was the key. Licce might be strong, but even they struggled to reach the surface from there.

"I suppose we should find the head," he said, "before it gets into trouble." He looked around, but it wasn't anywhere in sight.

"Seems someone made off with it," said the grimalkin. "Or it rolled away. Either way, we'll be at this all day. We don't even know which way to start off in."

"We could ask the tinderbox," said Bagdemagus, idly. "We only used two questions, remember?"

"Absolutely not," the cat said, firmly. "Stop suggesting that. I lost an eye last time, Bagsy, in case you forgot."

"Alright, alright. You keep looking after it for me, then." He scratched the famulus around the ears.

Standing up properly, he pulled up his trousers, which were always falling down just a little. "We'll look for the head later," he told the cat, which helped to scoop the dirt back into the grave. "It can't have gone far. And the rest of the corpse is safe down there. No one comes here, and no one would be stupid enough to dig in the goblin market, not unless they want to be weeviled." He sounded almost wistful. He hadn't turned anyone into a weevil in years.

"Can we stop at the river?" The cat seemed to have brightened in mood now that the body was gone. "You know the one. I want a fish. Then maybe some witch backgammon?"*

---

* The parlor game/extreme sport known as witch backgammon is very similar to regular backgammon, except the stakes are the kind you might be burned at.

The river. That would be nice. He could sit down for a while, rest his back (which had developed an ungodly twinge from all those nights under the stars). Finding this head could wait, it was of little urgency now. Besides, a licce didn't speak. A head could cause little trouble on its own, unless it bit someone and they got gangrene. He finished scattering the mandrake leaves and picked up his bags.

Yes, a sit-down. Some nice fish. And then, in a few short decades, he would retire.

He was halfway down the path when all thought of the rogue head slipped from his memory altogether.

Twenty years passed before Bagdemagus decided to finally retire. In that time he never quite got around to remembering the headless body, buried six feet under the ground in the goblin valley.

Deep below the earth, dead muscles twitched.

# 1

## THE STONE

ENRIC NAGG was already face-down in the mud, and it wasn't yet noon. Picking himself up slowly, he glared at the ugly rock towering above him and went back to snipping leaves from the plants gathered at its base. There was nowhere else on Nagg Farm to gather mandrake leaves, because nowhere else was cursed. Not as badly as the Nagg Stone anyhow, which was the kind of ill-starred landmark you could feel looming over your shoulder when you saw it on a map. It had large stains that on a sunny day gathered to look a bit like a smirking face, and this wasn't the first time Mr. Nagg had taken out his frustrations on the stone, a mistake which always left him with a stubbed toe and nursing a bruised ego as he struggled back onto his feet.

Wiping his own brow, Mr. Nagg cut the final bundle of leaves and stowed them in his satchel, making sure not to touch them with his bare skin. Everything about a mandrake was poisonous, from root to crown, and its practical uses were specific to words ending in -cide. Every year, Mr. Nagg came down to the cursed rock and harvested enough poisonous leaves to perpetrate the kind of banquet hall atrocities you heard about from travelling bards. In smaller doses, it could make people anxious, malleable, or uncertain, but that was the kind of thing you could only find out through measured experimentation. Yes, Mr. Nagg was a poor gardener in all other regards, but he belonged to a lineage of self-taught experts on the mandrakes, and was well aware of their dangers.

Having got what he'd come for, and determined to get the last word in, he risked another small kick at the standing stone, which caused him to lose his footing and end up right back in the dirt. He gargled a howl of rage into the muck. Nothing went right around the Nagg Stone. Local opinion differed as to exactly how it had ended up in his family's possession. The common tale, passed down to Mr. Nagg from his grandmother, was that a witch had hexed the monolith after developing a bunion in its vicinity. Whatever the reason, it was a blight on his lineage, and he resented it bitterly.*

Crawling away from the field on his hands and knees, he checked his haul again. He'd charge the wizard double for this. Maybe triple. He wasn't getting any younger, and his knees weren't creaking any less. Bad enough the sorcerer had refused to remove the stone; that he had Mr. Nagg fumbling about in the dirt on his behalf was even more humiliating. "One man's curse is another's boon," he'd said, which sounded to Mr. Nagg like the kind of riddlesome nonsense you'd expect from a geriatric who smoked the herbs from his garden in a colourful and pungent rotation.

Not every village had a wizard, nor did every wizard belong to a village, but they frequently gravitated together. Attempts to study this phenomenon usually ended in failure, due to a lack

---

* Schemes deployed to evict the stone over the decades had led to ruin. Ebeneezer Nagg was trampled to death when his draft horses went feral. Hazel Nagg was knocked senseless by the rebound of her own pickaxe. Cedric Nagg died of a cold, which was attributed to the stone as a matter of principle, even if no one could prove it.

of academic consensus on what constituted a wizard, how many houses made a village, and which units of measurement to use.* In the case of East Grasby, the village (for want of a better word) consisted of scattered farms and moorland cottages, and the sage Bagdemagus was their pellar.

Mr. Nagg was still crawling when he got to the edge of the field, and onto the dirt trail that led away from the farmstead and onto the moors. He only bothered to drag himself to his feet when he came face-to-face with a nasty-looking centipede. He didn't like anything with the wrong number of legs. More than one leg, fewer than five, that was the natural number of legs. Except for three. Three was also bad.†

The walk from the farmhouse on the border of East Grasby to the cottage belonging to Bagdemagus was a long one, and took the better part of the morning, even moving as quickly as he dared in the treacherous undergrowth. The trip wouldn't be worth it if the wizard didn't pay quite so handsomely for the mandrake leaves. The Naggs relied on the annual sum, as the Nagg farm produced nothing else of value. If he'd been a daring man, which he was not, he might have tried to harvest a

---

* This disagreement could be traced back to the founding of the abbey at Gerard's Cross, the stipulated area ceded by royal writ for this purpose being precisely 1,200 acres. Things became complicated when the monks insisted on using a traditional furlong, or the length of field a team of oxen could plough without resting. As the monks calculated exactly how much land they could purloin for their purposes, they made some unethical and deeply sorcerous amendments to the chosen oxen's stamina. For centuries after the fact, mutant oxen drove carriages off the road near Gerard's Cross, but the abbey was very rich indeed so it was chalked up as an overall success.

† It reminded him of his aunt Eunice, who had used her walking stick to emphasize her vituperations with sharp jabs to the listener's abdomen. She was eventually eaten by a wolf, which was unrelated to her poor temperament but nevertheless proved cathartic to all who knew her.

precious mandrake root or two, which were worth many times what the leaves fetched, but he recalled the warnings from his parents—removing the root from the soil caused it to emit an unearthly shriek that dragged the listener to madness and death. The leaves were safer. He'd once been told that a virgin could pull up a whole mandrake without perishing, but he didn't see what good that was to anyone, because a virgin was just as like to stumble across a unicorn or get carried off by a scaled monster as help with the crops. No, Mr. Nagg was at peace with his lot in life, which was to occasionally bring some poisonous leaves to a wizard, and collect his unreasonable fee.

The ragged stone wall surrounding Bagdemagus's hovel was knee high, and getting shorter every year as the elements wore it down. It was covered with trinkets, charms, and scrawled symbols, each of which Bagdemagus insisted was essential for the protection of the cottage, though they were often blown away in mild winds or eaten by curious wildlife. The wooden door, battered around the edges, was unlocked. This wasn't unusual. Bagdemagus didn't really understand how locks worked. Nor did he grasp the point of private property, or the concept of theft. The toadlike structure was stuffed to the brim with strange wooden furnishings, comfy chairs, and hundreds of boxes containing dried ingredients and tools of the trade.

Looking around the cramped room, Mr. Nagg sighed audibly. No sign of the wizard. This wasn't unheard of, as the mage would often wander from place to place for days at a time before finding his way back to the hut, but it put Mr. Nagg's nose out of joint. He'd brought all these horrible leaves here, just as he did around this time every year, and for what? To trudge back home, empty-handed. Was it too much to ask that the wizard be present when a visitor arrived? Couldn't he have looked into the future and predicted a guest? The wizard's absence annoyed Mr. Nagg more than it might have the average person, because

Mr. Nagg lacked a sense of object permanence when it came to other people and their time. On some primal level, deep below thoughts of coins and mandrakes, in the root of his soul, Mr. Nagg didn't really believe anyone else existed when they were not in a room with him, and he found altogether vexing their insistence on wandering off-page to follow plot threads that did not bend to his immediate convenience.

He dreaded to think of the look on Isabella's face when her husband wandered in without the money. He had one job a year, she would say, and he couldn't even get that right. As he put down the bag of leaves on the side, his gaze fell on the *Household Gramarye*.

*The Book of Household Gramarye* is a multipart text as multifaceted as a diamond, and many times as brilliant. Split into twenty-seven volumes, it claimed to know everything there was to know, and a bit more besides, from home remedies to do-it-yourself ensorcellments. Due to the impracticality of parchment production, a village could only be expected to house a single copy of the *Household Gramarye*. Not one but several herds of cattle had to be skinned to craft even a single volume. The margins surrounding the densely packed text of the *Household Gramarye* were traditionally left wide, ostensibly to allow readers to add their own observations (which they frequently did), meaning that no two copies of the *Household Gramarye* were exactly alike.* The farther one strayed from

---

* It should be said, it must be said, that the foremost inconsistency amongst all copies of the *Household Gramarye* was the spelling of the word *Gramarye* itself, a word which has no fewer than seven hundred and eleven recorded spellings, localizations, and regional bastardizations. Amongst folk of letters, the two variants most frequently pitted against each other are *Gramayre* and *Gramarye*. Blood has been spilled on this account. Other less common spellings include *Graham*, *Greem*, and *Glob*. All are pronounced "Grammar."

the city of Verdigris and its scriptoriums, the less common complete copies of the *Household Gramarye* became. In lieu of partial copies, incomplete sets of the *Gramarye* resided in the minds of those who passed down memorized fragments from generation to generation.

The East Grasby copy of the *Household Gramarye* was, naturally, in the care of Bagdemagus. This was generally agreed on to be the best solution, for no one was better versed in its contents, nor as widely feared as the diminutive hedge wizard, and besides it left everyone else more time for the things that were really important, such as looking at the sky and wondering aloud if the weather was about to turn any moment now.

And yet. Perhaps the *Household Gramarye* held the solution to Mr. Nagg's troubles. It was magic, wasn't it? Mr. Nagg could do with some magic in his life. A spell to remove a cursed rock, perhaps? To fill his pockets with riches? He couldn't read himself, of course, but Mrs. Nagg was always poring over whatever scraps she could get her hands on. Maybe when she'd finished cooking and cleaning, she could make herself useful for once. Yes, it was only right that he borrow a volume for a little while. He'd leave the mandrake cuttings behind as payment, and that would be well.

Cheered, he plucked a random volume from the shelf and stuffed it into his bag. His mood was much improved, and there was even a vicious little spring in his step. This was going to be a good year for Mr. Nagg. He could feel it.

# 2

# A VISIT FROM GOBLINS

L ATER THAT evening, Farmer Nagg sat at home, staring at the wall. His dinner, which Mrs. Nagg had thrown together with the grim enthusiasm she somehow found for any activity involving butchery, lay untouched before him. They sat at opposite ends of the broad wooden dining table, and the borrowed book lay equidistant between them, unopened. Farmer Nagg kept sneaking fearful glances at the book, as if he expected it to explode into a pile of snakes at any moment.*

"In a world of pigheaded ideas, Mr. Nagg"—Isabella was mid-rant—"I have never seen anything like this. Theft. From a wizard. Do you want us both to be turned into weevils, Mr. Nagg? Is that what you want for us?"

She rolled her eyes. "I should not wonder if he arrives this very evening to remedy this situation. And I shall be telling him that I had no part in it, you can be sure of that."

---

* Bagdemagus carried a bag of live snakes with him everywhere. He referred to this as the "Wizard's Exit," and used it at funerals, christenings, or simply whenever he saw a good opportunity to cement his reputation as the kind of professional you only solicited when you had no other option.

Mr. Nagg picked at the food, wading through his own thoughts. Rain hammered down on the roof. He'd seen a grass snake on the way home, darting out in front of his path. That meant it would rain for several days yet, if his mother's advice was anything to go by.* Water crept in under the door, as if eavesdropping on the conversation.

A mumbling. Noise at the edge of his awareness. Mrs. Nagg was talking. What was she saying?

". . . all day." She sniffed. "As if we don't be having better things on our minds to be doing, is that not right? Why, I've never been as busy."

He gave her a filthy look, staring daggers at her back as she clattered about the kitchen in a cacophony that set his teeth on edge. What had she been so busy with all day? Torturing dinner? She hadn't even looked at the book, but of course she'd found something to complain about.

Mrs. Nagg set down the last piece of crockery. "He doesn't listen," she said, picking up her pot of basil, and busied herself in the kitchen with some chore that was as loud as it was unnecessary.

Mrs. Nagg considered herself to have a green thumb, Henric knew, and his general dislike of his wife gave him a cynical view of her efforts. She collected snippings and cuttings of plants, going to great effort to house them in a series of inconvenient receptacles such as the bathing tub and the chamberpots. Many of these experiments survived for no longer than a few weeks, as Mrs. Nagg was prone to the kind of suffocating

---

* The *Household Gramayre* noted that "snake-trails may be seen near houses before rain." It also stipulated that "if frogs, instead of yellow, appear russet green, it will presently rain." There was, in fact, an entire chapter of prognostications on the matter of precipitation, blaming rainy spells on the appearance of every animal or phenomenon from red skies to ladybugs. It never really stopped raining in East Grasby.

fits of aqueous affection that would have made her an excellent interrogator. The only exception to this rule was her pot of basil, which thrived in hostile conditions that should have seen it slain several times over.* The herb had a warrior's spirit, and it was the tenacity of the pot of basil that, by Mr. Nagg's estimation, had convinced Mrs. Nagg she was a wonderful gardener. She'd brought the basil with her when they married, one of the few belongings she'd insisted upon, housed in a huge ceramic pot engraved with the image of a frowning face. Mr. Nagg hated the herb almost as much as he hated the scrunge his wife prepared every night,† but something about it made him anxious, and so he'd never worked up the courage to throw it out when she wasn't looking.

The evening was, until this point, a relatively normal one.

Then came a knock at the door. A scratching, biting knock.

Mr. Nagg threw himself to the floor, abandoning his scrunge, and scuttled under the table with the same animal reflex that his ancient forebears had relied upon to save them from tigers and bears. The wizard had come for his book. Cowering against the floor, Mr. Nagg thought about what life would be like for him as a weevil, or a worm. Slower, for sure. Maybe even less stressful. He waited a few moments for the world to descend upon his head, for the skies to collapse, and to meet some unpleasant magical fate at the hands of an

---

* Mr. Nagg had, in fact, tried to assassinate the basil plant on no fewer than five occasions, one time with boiling salt water, but it seemed wrought from steel. Truth be told, its immortality had frightened him a little.

† Scrunge was Mrs. Nagg's signature dish, and she prepared it at every opportunity, because she liked it and held firmly that if Mr. Nagg wanted something else, then he could bloody well make it himself. Scrunge was less a recipe than it was a frame of mind. Anything could be scrunge if you boiled it for long enough.

angry wizard. But no disaster came, and eventually he dared to peek out into the kitchen, which was still there. Tentatively, he extracted himself from his hidey-hole and sat himself back at his food, sparing an annoyed look for Mrs. Nagg, who he noted had declined to answer the door, instead rummaging about in a cupboard for the hideous bristled tool she used to clean the scrunge pot. Perhaps she hadn't heard the knock, or was pretending she hadn't, which he thought was more probable. He wolfed down the last of his meal (prepared by Mrs. Nagg), tightened his belt (crafted by Mrs. Nagg), and got up from the table (cleaned daily by Mrs. Nagg). It looked like he needed to do everything himself around here.

The knock sounded again, and it rang to Mr. Nagg like a death knell. A weevil it was, then. He'd be turned into a bug, and maybe then she'd regret how she'd treated him. Dragging his feet through the kitchen, he stomped to the front door so that his wife would know how inconvenienced he'd been. Undoing the catch, he took a deep breath, ready to start his new life as a creepy-crawly, and yanked open the door.

When a few moments passed and he didn't feel himself shrinking or growing mandibles, he opened one eye.

On the threshold were two spry little creatures, each no taller than Nagg's elbow and jostling for better position in front of the other. They held in their hands, offered to him for inspection, imperfectly round fruits coloured red deep enough to stain the soul.

There were lots of rules to living in East Grasby. Your fence should be mended, your garden tended. Your livestock should be prevented from running rampant. Prudence is what the residents might have called it, if they were keen on talking to one another (which they were not). Amongst these rules, drummed into the residents by long association, was this: Do not eat the goblin fruit. Nuance and reason had long since been occluded by time, but convention was clear—nothing good could come of taking the goblin fruit. Truth be told, this was usually an easy rule to adhere to, because the goblins were so rarely seen outside their market in the valley.*

But it was different when you saw the fruit. It was everything that you never knew you wanted, and it made you hungry in ways you didn't know existed, like a light turning on in the back of your mind.

The goblins waved their fruit, red as blood, held in gracile fingers.

"Come buy," they said in unison. "Buy our lovely goblin fruit. Taste."

The fruit had a gravity to it that drew your gaze. Surely there was no harm in just glancing at it? No one could fault him for taking another look. He was about to lean in closer for a smell when he heard Isabella moving around behind him, and the noise jolted him back to his senses.

"Ah, mischief is afoot, I see," said Mr. Nagg, crossly. Loudly. Guiltily. "Go on, get from here, goblin folk. You aren't wanted here."

The goblins looked at each other, then smiled their broad, skullduggerous smiles.

"Offers," said one.

"Yes, lovely offers. Bargains," the second added.

Mr. Nagg wrestled with his curiosity. An offer? Bargains? He wasn't going to take the fruit, obviously. So was there any harm in listening to what they had to say? He'd shoo them away shortly, and no one would ever know.

---

* Tradition held that the market had once sold many things other than fruit, such as peculiar vegetables and interesting legumes. This isn't relevant to the story, but it does explain why the people of East Grasby retained a healthy suspicion towards courgettes.

The first goblin showed him the fruit again, turning it over in its hands. Goblin fingers were long and supple, designed for seeking and probing, for uncovering secret desires. The fruits reeked of crimson, and were slightly furry in a way that made them seem luminous in the dying light. "You buy one fruit—" the goblin said, in a manner of exaggerated showmanship. "We give two fruit," the second rushed in. The first goblin kicked the second, annoyed, as if some parsimonious script had been deviated from. "One free," corrected the second goblin, resentfully. "Buy one fruit, one fruit for nothing. Nothing!"

Nagg paused. Whether you liked goblin fruit or not, you had to concede this was an excellent deal. His hand twitched towards his coin purse, but he barely had time to look over his shoulder before he was met with an angry-looking Mrs. Nagg, still holding her pot of basil.

"Who is it—oh. Goblins again!" She put down the pot gently, with a more loving glance than she'd ever given Mr. Nagg, and grabbed a broom. "Leave us be, goblin folk! Meddlesome pests! Go on!"

The goblins put their fruit away, reluctantly, and shuffled off the doorstep. One looked back, optimistically, but Mrs. Nagg only waved the broom higher.

As the door closed, Mrs. Nagg picked up her plant and returned to the kitchen table. "It is a poor sign to see them so far from the market," she remarked, darkly. She always got angry when anyone talked about goblins. Mr. Nagg only grunted in response. The image of the goblin fruit remained in his mind. They did look delicious, and besides, there were bargains to be had.

# 3

## ISABELLA ALONE

ROADLY SPEAKING, Isabella Nagg tried not to think about her situation. Her mother would have told her that there was no point crying over spilt milk, and that you should save the tears for something more meaningful, such as if you were trapped in a loveless marriage, and were burdened with an ungrateful daughter to boot. Her mother had cried a great deal towards the end, before she'd finally run away to join a cult who said they could spin straw into gold.

No, crying wouldn't do any good. Isabella knew that from the first five years she'd spent pining for something better, and the next ten she'd spent resenting it when it didn't happen. When the dark thoughts came upon her in the quiet period of the afternoon, she tried to remind herself that her situation was better than most. She hadn't been approached by a roadside hag bearing evil gifts, nor had she been dragged to a watery grave by a slippery horse, or stampeded to death by a nuckelavee. She enjoyed a fate far better than most people were led to expect by parents in this part of the world, who were still of the opinion that three children were best—one to carry on the family name, one to be carried off by a monster, and a spare to nudge the odds a little further in favour of grandchildren.

Life at Nagg Farm was predictable, and there was merit in that. Her husband was not a bad man, she didn't think. "Bad" didn't seem right. He wasn't a good person either, mind, but something ethically agnostic. He occupied that robust yet morally beige space rarely commented on by bards or historians. Mr. Nagg had no interest in right or wrong, just like he had no interest in cleaning up after himself. In any hypothetical life-or-death situation she could care to name, Mr. Nagg would eat a potato until his time ran out, and then be genuinely confused as to why people were angry at him.

He didn't do much at all, really—existing itself was the height of his ambition. He would achieve that as long as she provided food, water, and shelter. He didn't know it, but of all of her houseplants, he was the most difficult to maintain.

Yesterday, top of his list of bright ideas had been to steal from a wizard. In front of her, on the kitchen counter, lay volume IX of *The Book of Household Gramarye*, titled *Of Spiritual Properties and Ethereal Real Estate*. In some ways, it was a kind gesture. He was prone to the kind of gifts* that inadvertently complicated the lives of the recipient. She'd been fond of the idea of Gramayre as a young woman, though the purchase of any grimoire was so far beyond the means of her family as to be comical. She'd long ago allowed her fancies to erode, replaced by a more realistic cycle of laundry and dishes, but she'd often mentioned it to her husband in the brighter years of their companionship, in those optimistic days when she had thought they might share a practical marriage, if not necessarily an enthusiastic one.

She touched the cover of the book with one finger. A book, any book, was a princely gift, but the sympathy engendered by

---

* usually presented in lieu of an actual apology for whatever insult or carelessness had invoked her ire

his effort was eclipsed by her irritation at having another chore to perform on his behalf. It was foolhardy, if not suicidal, to go about stealing things from the wizard Bagdemagus. Though his attitude was usually genial, and his aspect forgetful, those on the receiving end of his temper rarely came away with the same basic configuration of limbs. Even for Mr. Nagg, this had been a terrible idea.

"I shall have to return it." She said it aloud, to the pot of basil on the windowsill. It was her favourite houseplant, her very first, and she talked to it because otherwise she would go days at a time without saying a single word.

"Yes," she repeated, as she often did, because the pot of basil wasn't able to reply, "I shall have to take this book back to the wizard, and hope he is not too angry. I will explain that Mr. Nagg is a fool, which being familiar with him I am sure he must already know, and that will fix things, I expect."

She fetched her walking boots, feeling irritated. There was little chance of making Mr. Nagg fix his own mistake. He would just give her a pitiful look, as if she had kicked a sick dog, and then he'd resent her for scorning his gift. Besides, having caused his daily catastrophe, he had quickly found somewhere else to be. She allowed her anger at Mr. Nagg's carelessness to fester, the way she always did, because in the darkest, smallest, meanest part of her, she knew that she almost welcomed his mistakes. The annoyance was a feeling, and it was better than the monotony to which she otherwise felt consigned.

The pot of basil sat there, as it always did, listening patiently to her natter away. In many ways, it was the closest thing she had to a friend. Though Mrs. Nagg had cultivated a healthy garden of herbs and flowers during her many years at Nagg Farm, the pot of basil was the only thing she'd brought with her into the marriage. It was hers, not Mr. Nagg's, which made it special. She talked to it each day as she pottered about the house, a habit which had started tentatively and was by now a reflex she gave in to without a second thought. "I cannot shake the feeling that this book is the start of trouble," she told the plant. "Dark clouds are on the horizon, you can be sure of that, pot of basil." The basil did not respond, but she envisioned that if it could speak, it would praise her forbearance in the face of great suffering.

"Isabella," she fancied it would tell her. "Good Isabella. Kind Isabella. Do not cry, Isabella. We are together, and all shall be well."

She put her coat on, slowly. But instead of leaving, she cleaned some dishes and folded some sheets from the drying rack. Then, she cleaned the dishes again. Between tasks, her gaze was drawn back time and again to the book on the table. Eventually, she decided to look inside. A peek couldn't hurt. And then she'd return it.

Besides, it was rare to get the chance to peruse an entire volume of the *Gramayre*, especially one belonging to a wizard, which was certain to be well annotated. What if (the thought crept in like an assassin), what if she were . . . good at it?

And just like that, the thinnest of cracks appeared in the dam of realism, of practicality, that she'd so vigilantly built around her enthusiasm, her love, for Gramayre. She realized she was holding her breath. Could she be an enchanter? Just a single spell. Just for an afternoon.

"There's no harm in it," she assured the pot of basil. "No harm ever came of looking."*

---

* This, as any scholar of Gramayre, or ophthalmic herpetology, knows, is not true.

# Mandrake [1] ◆◆◆◆◆◆

*(Mandragora bastardus)*

OTHER NAMES: SCREAMING CABBAGE,
DEVIL'S CARROT, GOBLINBANE,
SORCERER'S ROOT

\* (unknown commentator) its still poisonous once you cook it

† (attributed to Anastasia of Rebolt, transcribed later from the Barrowdown copy of the *Gramarye*) The translation from High Gothic is a poor construal of the late Gothic hypothetical construct, and should read: "hearing their given name, called by the mandrake, and if they found it still true, death invariably followed."

‡ (unknown commentator, thought to be Gregory the Cramped, scribbled hastily) petition to rename the plant *Mandragora flatulatus* denied by Tabernacle

There are lots of uses for a mandrake, assuming you have an entire dinner party of guests you'd like to poison in interesting ways. The difficulty in acquiring it, however, renders questions such as what to do with it, why it smells of guilt, or why it tastes so delightful when braised,\* functionally redundant. Removing a mandrake from the soil is cautioned against except in dire need, for their caterwauling is both tonally depraved (in the same musical tradition as a harpsichord) and lethal to the listener. Though survivor accounts are rare, interrogations of spirits post-mortem all describe hearing their given name called by the mandrake, after which (finding it true)† death invariably followed. Standing downwind at the time of disinterment is not recommended.‡

*from the Gerard's Cross copy of the* Household Gramayre, *a loose insert (parchment, folded widdershins) inside volume VII*, Of Arboriforms and Adelastery

# 4

# THE INTERLOCUTORY ELIXIR

ENSELY PACKED blackletter script filled each brittle page of the volume, accompanied by simple wood-block prints embedded in the text. Around the main script, the wide margins were filled with copious notes in a multitude of hands, each contributing their own corrections, alterations, and opinions to the information within.* Many of the words were alien to her, and over half of the pages had been penned in languages completely foreign to her understanding, though some were accompanied by cramped translations creeping around the sides or bending around corners.

This volume was on the qualities of animals, it seemed, and she came to rest at a page marked "On Brays." Aside from the cursed stone, a network of fallow fields, and the crop of deadly mandrakes, the Naggs had what amounted to a smallholding, on which resided a number of surly, ungrateful animals that

---

* Disagreements concerning the specifics of Gramarye were common. Did a basilisk have six heads, or none? Did it hibernate in the winter, or was it just obscenely well camouflaged? Did it taste good on toast? The field was fraught with lethal inaccuracies masquerading as honest opinions.

caused them nothing but grief.* Numbered chief amongst these was a donkey. It was a chronic escapologist, and seemed to derive satisfaction from finding new ways to vanish from its enclosure, only to be found several hours later wandering a near-identical field and waiting to be taken home. Long had Isabella Nagg pined for a way to communicate to the creature that this was not an endearing game but an infuriating waste of her time. Then, as she scanned the page dedicated to donkeys, she found one.

Crammed into the top left corner in a spidery script was an incantation labeled "interlocutory elixir to alleviate a contrary mule (and suchlike)," which called for "a yarrow tea made well" and seemed well within her abilities to prepare.

Should she try it? Could she? She was only Isabella Nagg, after all. Good for scrunge, and not much else. Her confidence wavered, one hand resting on the open page.

"It is a good thing that only you and I are here," she said to the pot of basil. "I would not have Mr. Nagg laugh at me."

Talking to the plant gave her strength. She drew on its silent support for confidence. When she'd first started carrying the pot of basil around, she'd thought she wouldn't be able to keep it alive a fortnight. But the years had passed, and here it was, healthy as it had been when she'd planted it. The Isabella of her youth was not afraid of risk. She had been different back then, hadn't she? Willing to take a risk? Maybe she could change again. She could be a version of Isabella who made elixirs. Just this once.

---

* The number and nature of the animals changed from year to year, as the Naggs were poor stewards, and only infrequently took inventory. They had only recently divested themselves of a wolf which lived happily as a sheep for three and a half months using only a woollen blanket, until the Naggs finally noticed they had run out of other sheep.

She made her decision.

The recipe called for yarrow, which, as we all know, is a curmudgeonly plant, so she apologized to it profusely as she picked it from the road outside the house and took it inside to be boiled.* It wasn't long before she was simmering a pot of water in the hearth and sprinkling in the petals. Referring back to the book, she read the unwieldy incantation called for by the annotator, and gave it her best shot. Another annotation in bold, cramped lettering that only faintly resembled the common tongue insisted that "for best results, supply one [1] memory of speech therein, seasoned to taste as best fits." She didn't know what that meant.

"What do you think it means, basil?" she asked the plant. It did nothing.

The question had her thinking, though, and there wasn't much else to do while she stirred the tea and fetched a few other ingredients the annotators of the text thought would lend the brew efficacy. She couldn't read all of them, but she managed to find some mint (for clarity, and to repel spiders, if Anastasia of Rebolt could be believed) and some lemongrass ("kerve it on pieces, and cast hem on boiling water," said an anonymous contributor, in spindly letters). A memory of speech was not something she felt altogether confident in finding. She and Mr. Nagg went to elaborate lengths to avoid each other's company during the day. No, Isabella did not consider herself an adept conversationalist. The mixture would have to do without, she decided firmly, even as the bitter tang of her loneliness seeped into the elixir.

She came to her senses suddenly, with a jolt. The kitchen

---

* Most plants are like distant family members, in that they take poorly to being ripped from their homes and submersed in scalding water.

had filled with a strong (not altogether pleasant) odour, and she realized she'd been standing there for longer than she'd thought.

Now, Isabella Nagg was not a fool. It goes without saying that she was not vain enough to think she could master the entirety of the *Household Gramarye* in a single afternoon. Tales from her childhood spoke of the terrible fates that might await those who tampered carelessly with Gramayre beyond their ability. Eaten by garden gnomes. Dragged to oblivion by their own shadows. Abducted by forest creatures who finally got fed up with being ensorcelled. No, Isabella Nagg considered herself to be blessed with a certain amount of that divine characteristic, Common Sense. One could not truly define Common Sense, and neither could one earn it through experience or learning. You either had it or you did not, and Isabella Nagg knew in the darkest corner of her heart that she was full to bursting with it. Today, the Common Sense was telling her that it was only right and natural that she should take advantage of this unique opportunity to fix her problems. She would talk to the donkey, explain the situation, and then take the book back to the wizard. Easily done, with no one any the wiser.

With fresh conviction, she located a cup in the grimy cupboards (the hob would get around to dusting any day now)* and strode out into the yard carrying the enchanted tea. The walk

---

* Every domicile in East Grasby, and many places besides, was blessed with a household creature known as a hob. Your hob liked to take care of the house, which meant it would sometimes do chores or repairs. All you had to do in return was stay away when it was cleaning (though it would forgive you for glimpsing a furry arm or two if it didn't disappear into a cupboard quickly enough), and to leave out a nightly gift of milk. Mr. Nagg offended the hob on three occasions in the first week of their acquaintance, and it had been on indefinite strike for anything benefiting Mr. Nagg ever since, excepting those occasions when it would move his stuff around and sabotage the fixtures.

to the field was uphill, and she made it slowly so as not to spill any of the tea over herself. The hillside was set at a ferocious angle, which was one of many reasons why the Naggs were shackled to this particular stretch of land and could never sell it—cursed rock notwithstanding, the farm boasted an unusual number of treacherous slopes for an area of the countryside famed for its gentle moorland inclines.

When she finally reached the field, she found the donkey staring at the fence as if contemplating another escape. Interestingly, and surprisingly, it was not alone. A stout pony now shared the field with the donkey, quietly pootling about as if it belonged. Isabella narrowed her eyes. It was just like Mr. Nagg to acquire more animals without bothering to tell her, as if she didn't have enough mouths to feed. She wouldn't ask him about it later, she decided. That was what he wanted, an opportunity to act like she was being ungrateful. No, she was not going to engage with such a facile provocation. Stealthily, she padded over to the hedgerow.* With a deliberate hand, she poured a little of the potion from the cup into the water trough, and then ducked beneath a hedgerow to wait. Her patience quickly saw results, as the donkey, clearly fatigued by a long morning plotting skedaddlement, wended over to take a drink.

Crowing with delight, Mrs. Nagg revealed herself. "Ah, now I have you, you horrible mule," she said, pointing a finger. "You have consumed the yarrow tea, and now we shall talk!"

She waited for some indication that the donkey understood her.

The donkey lifted its noble head in her direction, eyes blank. Did she detect a glimmer of awareness? Of recognition?

No. Not a single thought in that head, let alone a sentence.

---

* Isabella could move very unobtrusively when she chose to, a learned behaviour that allowed her to avoid Mr. Nagg as much as possible.

Isabella waited patiently for five minutes, then ten. No response from the donkey, which soon ambled to another part of the field. Patience faded, replaced by annoyance, but no cajoling nor berating could evince a response from the beast, so she stalked back to the house. Once inside, she realized she was still holding half a cup of cold (useless) tea, and so she tossed the remaining decoction into the pot of basil. The rest of the potion she poured into a jar and placed in a cupboard. It might not be magical, but it would serve as a seasonal beverage.

She slammed the door of the cupboard shut with more force than she'd intended. The Common Sense had fled, and it was humiliation that filled her now. Even if no one was here to see her fail, she felt keenly scrutinized. She'd been foolish, and wasted time, and of course she couldn't change. She wasn't meant to be a wizard. She was Isabella Nagg, she made scrunge, she hated her life, and that was all there was to it until she ended up in a hole in the ground where her shade could watch over a cursed stone for eternity. It seemed like even the pot of basil was frowning at her.

"Yes," she snapped irritably to the pot of basil. "You needn't look at me like that. I knew it was a waste of time. Silly of me to think I might master it. This book is of no use to me. We shall return it."

She looked out of the window in the kitchen, judging the skies. She'd finished her tasks for the day, and it was only the early afternoon.* She checked for frogs in the garden. None. Unlikely to rain, then.

---

* Isabella knew there were chores left undone, but after she'd made scrunge, cleaned Mr. Nagg's clothes, watered her plants, swept the floor, emptied the chamberpots, and collected all of Mr. Nagg's discarded belongings from across the house, she usually lost her will to do more. She'd been meaning to change the bedsheets for three days.

"In fact, I shall walk it there now. It is a pleasant day. Mr. Nagg may fix his own supper."

Gathering her long coat, she picked up the volume of the *Household Gramarye* and stuffed it inside a leather satchel, which she slung over her shoulder.

"I shall be back by dark," she said to the pot of basil, closing the door behind her.

In the darkness, the pot of basil sat for a long moment. Then, it spoke.

"Goodbye!" it chimed, in a high-pitched voice.

But Isabella was already gone.

# 5

## BOTTOM'S AWAKENING

Bottom the Donkey was awake. The first thing he'd done was to name himself, choosing the very first name that had popped into his head. He wanted to go back to sleep. Not real sleep, but the mind sleep, where all he cared about was mooching and eating. It had been fun at first, pretending that he didn't hear that awful woman shouting at him, but he was about ready to go back to blissful oblivion. Sentience, he had quickly discovered, was extremely overrated. It had taken him all of five minutes to develop mild anxiety. Eagerly he awaited the telltale tingle of sentience vanishing, but as night began to fall, it became clear that something was wrong. The thoughts weren't going away.

Slowly, he walked over to Pony, who now shared his field. Until recently, Bottom had walked this field every day alone, but a few days ago Pony had turned up unannounced. The people in charge didn't seem to care, and Bottom was glad to have the company. "Hello," he said, in the dull voice that came with the thoughts. Pony ignored him, as they had since they arrived. Then, the animal turned around in a circle twice, as if discovering shapes for the first time, and went back to nibbling on some grass. Pony deserved a name, Bottom supposed, but he couldn't be given one. That wouldn't be fair. No, the pony would need to take one for themselves, anything else wasn't a real name, but more of an informal sobriquet.

Bottom picked himself up (figuratively, metaphor was a curse that came with the thoughts) and moved to the edge of the field. The main house was quiet, aside from the smoke drifting from the chimney. It was a dingy grey afternoon, much like any other, but on the horizon, troubled clouds were brewing, roiling with the promise of rain. A green frog ribbited past, as if it were late for an appointment of some kind.

Well, there was no point standing around. If he wanted the thoughts gone, he'd have to solve this problem himself. He trotted over to the middle of the field to give himself a run-up, facing one of the large fence posts at fifty paces. Perhaps, with enough velocity, he could knock the thoughts out of his head. He looked over at Pony, to check they were alright. They were still eating. All Pony did was eat, come to think of it, and Bottom disliked how irritating he found the noise now that he could comprehend what annoyance was. Crunch, crunch, munch. Disgusting. With increased determination, he started towards the fence at a trot, lowering his head for a charge. The trot turned into a run, the fence approaching faster and faster. Just as he was about to collide with it, the image of how much this was about to hurt filled his mind, and he flinched at the last second, skidding into a bush in an explosion of branches and leaves.

From the ground, legs in the air, he looked up at the troubled sky, beyond the trail of smoke from the farmhouse . . . That was it! The rude woman who lived there would know what to do. Did she have a name? Probably. He'd never considered asking before.

Happy in his new purpose, Bottom dismantled the fence with a few swift kicks. It was poorly made. He'd have to make sure the farmer fixed that, it was barely worth escaping from an enclosure this crude. Ambling down the side of the hill, he took a proper look at the farmhouse, which was smaller than he'd thought. Only yesterday it had loomed quite large in his perspective, a scary place not to be approached. Most of his memories were fuzzy and clouded. Clearly there was a limit to this Thought malarkey. That was encouraging. The wooden door of the house was in poor shape, with rot setting in near the rusted hinges, and holes at the bottom where the wood had chipped away over many years of neglect. What was the polite thing to do? Knock, surely. And then what? Possible conversational openers rippled through his expanding mind.

*Hello! I am your donkey, please fix me.* No. Too cheerful.

*Greetings, human. I require your assistance.* It had potential, but might come across too formal.

*Good evening. Might I have a moment of your time?* Possibly. It struck the right balance. Then again—

The door opened, revealing Farmer Nagg in all his squalid glory. The name emerged from the netherworld of Bottom's past, drifting slowly to the surface like flotsam. Where had he heard that? Somewhere. He'd spent a very long time walking about in a dream.

Bottom hadn't seen the man come home. He'd also never noticed how untidy the man was. Dusty, really. If he hadn't known better, Bottom would have assumed the man had been hiding in a cupboard all morning to avoid his wife.* The man

---

* In point of fact, Mr. Nagg kept no fewer than seven cupboards, tunnels, and hidey-holes around the farmstead in which to avoid Mrs. Nagg. He shared two of these with the domestic hob, which caused no end of disagreement between them.

had also spilled food down his front, several days ago by the look of it. Thinking about it, which he was getting good at, when was the last time anyone had brushed Bottom's coat? He must smell awful too. Perhaps Nagg would let a donkey use his washtub.

"What are you doing out here?" snarled Nagg. That was definitely a snarl. When the face went that shape, you knew you were in trouble. "Escaped again? I've half a mind to beat you, stupid beast."

"Escape?" Bottom looked from where he was on the doorstep to the field behind him. He didn't understand. In the low, slow voice he'd been given, he decided to try diplomacy. "This wouldn't be a very good escape, would it."

Mr. Nagg was going an odd red colour. Donkey cocked his head to one side, and then a bright idea occurred to him. Perhaps Mr. Nagg didn't know the meanings of words. "Do you know what an escape is, Mr. Nagg?"

Nagg stared, eyes bulging. With a strangled cry, he lunged for the donkey, who took a deliberate step back, causing the clumsy farmer to trip face-first into the mud.

"That stupid woman, what has she done now?" Mr. Nagg spluttered as he attempted to regain his footing and landed once more on his behind.

"Come to think of it"—Donkey's thoughts were tumbling over each other in a way he found quite distracting—"if I were escaping, that would mean I was . . . imprisoned?" That was an uncomfortable thought.

"Why?" Mr. Nagg continued, pulling himself up against the wall of the house. "Why would she do this to me?"

This was all dreadfully confusing. "I don't think any of this is really about you," Bottom offered, helpfully.

"Bloody wizardry and nonsense," swore Mr. Nagg as he

thrashed about in muck, slipping repeatedly as he tried to regain his footing. "I should have left well alone."

An idea came to Bottom in a flash, illuminating the inside of his skull like a match struck in the dark. The wizard. Shadowy memories returned to him of a grumpy old face, and pain vanishing. Of course. The one who had cured his bad stomach that time.* Perfect! There was no point asking Nagg about this, the man could barely stand on both feet without leaning on a doorframe. The enchanter. Yes, the enchanter could fix this.

"Thank you," lowed Bottom, gratefully. "I shall return! Probably." He hadn't quite made up his mind about that yet. "I'll leave the pony with you until I get back. Which way is it to the wizard's hut?"

Farmer Nagg looked up from the mud, dumbstruck. Some of the rage had faded, replaced by null stupefaction.

"Never mind," Bottom added. "I'll figure it out. You should really get out of the muck."

The wizard, Bottom pondered as he trotted away from the farmhouse with a spring in his step. What had the farmer's wife done to him? Could it be undone? The thought stuck in his head, all rough edges and emotional sawdust. A few short hours and he'd surely be returned to his usual incognizant self. All it would take was a pinch of magic dust, a few words, and he would be a normal donkey again. Cheered, he set himself on the path towards town.

---

* Bottom had always been in the habit of eating things that he should not. One time he'd made it into the herb garden and eaten everything coloured purple.

# 6

## THE GRIMALKIN

F AR ABOVE the Nagg cottage, the rolling moors of desolate shrubs and the concerns of a slightly depressed donkey, the sun moved across the sky, pushed by a gigantic beetle. Theories about where the sun beetle came from, and if it might one day go away again, ricocheted back and forth between scholars, but had very little bearing on day-to-day life. The beetle went through fits of busy activity and took occasional breaks, meaning that a day was about as long as the sun beetle decided it was. One moment it was morning, the next late afternoon. Sometimes dawn would last for hours. All in all, the whole arrangement was quite unreliable, and today, the sun beetle had entered a flurry of activity in the late afternoon, so the sun was setting ahead of schedule.

The route to Bagdemagus's hovel was difficult at dusk, but Isabella had an iron stride that relented for neither shrub nor bramble. Her thick leather boots ran all the way up to her knees, and she strode through nettles and thorns without altering trajectory. Very little could stop Isabella once she had built up momentum. She would stride purposefully at fences, closed doors, and other human beings with grim determination, an approach that always produced the desired results.

The road had faded in places, cobbles placed in ancient times slowly worn away down to the dirt, but as one edged closer to the wizard's house, the better shape the path seemed to be in, which had a simple explanation in that a lot of people got about halfway to the wizard before they remembered the weevil incident and turned back. She didn't like walking in the dark, and as twilight rolled over the hills she held her lantern higher, where the glowing wisp inside bounced around angrily. It didn't like being trapped inside the glass any more than Isabella liked being trapped in her marriage, but unlike Isabella, it had never quite given up trying to escape. Lest one develops too much sympathy for the wisp, there was a small and pivotal difference between their cases, in that (if permitted to go free) the wisp was almost certain to eat someone.*

As the shadows grew, she began to wonder if she shouldn't have left this task to another day, but the weight of the borrowed† volume in her pack reminded her exactly how cross the wizard would be if he returned home and found it missing, which bolstered her resolve.‡ When she reached the hovel, the sun was meeting the horizon. This walk had taken longer than it should have, by rights, and she was weary as she passed the line of stones outside the house and through the wild garden to the threshold.

The inside of the house was a jumbled mess of furnishings, arcane reagents, and discarded papers shuffled into corners. An uncharitable soul might have called it garbage. A sensible one would also have called it garbage. Isabella thought it charming.

---

* Attempts to rehabilitate or otherwise encourage wisps not to lure people to their deaths usually ended in arcanists being lured to their deaths, and so blind trials had been suspended.
† stolen
‡ Bagdemagus often liked to say that people, in general, were very weevil-motivated.

Each pile of mess had the distinct air of someone saying to themselves, "I'll clear that up later," as if the ritual of saying might nudge the task towards completion without the need for physical intervention. Taking off her satchel and ducking under the low roof, she paused for a moment to set her things down, placing the lantern on the table, where the wisp continued to bounce angrily against the glass. It illuminated the shelving where the other twenty-six volumes of the *Household Gramarye* were stacked in neat rows, and as she reached for the volume in her bag to place it back on the shelf, she hesitated. The *Gramarye* was huge. Vast. Each volume a treasure trove in its own right. Bitterly, she remembered her failed potion, and steeled herself to return the book.

"He's not here, you know." A desultory voice from behind her made her jump. She spun around, bumping the lantern, which she grabbed just in time to stop it toppling to the floor. This place was a powder keg of oddments, jetsam, and niff-naffs. A single spark could send the entire place up in flames.* She recovered herself as best she could, lifting her gaze to meet that of the ugliest cat she'd ever seen. It had too many toes for one, some of which seemed prehensile, and it had lost one eye in a manner hideous enough to result in a burned-out cavity where the socket should be. Wiry hair of grey and black covered patches of its body, while in other places the skin was bare and wrinkly. Its whiskers quivered and moved of their own accord, testing the air like a snake's tongue.

"Fie, you wicked creature," said Isabella, who, on being caught where she should not be, found that indignation came

---

* The nature of witch-fire is discussed in a volume of the *Gramayre* often titled *Of Nether Regions*. Though a wisp is not aflame, per se, it is more than capable of setting fire to your hopes, your dreams, and dangerously situated flammable objects.

more easily than remorse, "for you to be sneaking and crawling like that! Show yourself properly at once."

"Wicked?" the cat purred, slinking up onto a chair that had seen better days. "I live here. You're just an intruder who seems to think this is a library."

Mrs. Nagg flinched. So the absence of the book had been noticed. And the cat was talking. Cats didn't talk, at least not where people could hear them. Was this . . . the wizard? She'd never met him. Mr. Nagg always handled this part, and he never liked to speak of it. Perhaps it was normal for a wizard to take the form of a cat. ". . . Bagdemagus?" she ventured, in a tone of apprehension.

"Good grief, no. I already said he wasn't here." The cat's tone was pitched somewhere firmly between amusement and boredom.

Isabella considered her options. She was relieved it was not the wizard. She didn't think she'd enjoy life as a weevil. "Well," she said, "I should be gone before he returns. I have no business with cats, if they be talking or otherwise."

"Firstly"—the cat jumped down to the floor—"I'm not a cat, I'm a grimalkin.* And secondly, he won't be coming back. He's dead."

Mrs. Nagg was speechless, but only for a moment. Silence wasn't in her nature.

"Dead?! What did you do to him, you awful mog? Come now, answer me. I shall shake you by the tail if you do not."

The grimalkin sighed. It didn't seem altogether worried

---

* *The Book of Household Gramarye* devotes two pages to the creatures called grimalkin (or, sometimes, grey malkin), in which it goes to great lengths to differentiate them from the common housecat. Most of the commentary concerns ways to keep them out of the trash can.

by her threat, though it did snake its tail under itself with alarming flexibility.

"I didn't do anything to him. Matter of fact, I'm actually rather sad about it. Can't you tell I'm riven with distress?" It rolled onto its stomach. "So many feelings. So fast. I could barely eat breakfast." A lazy tail waved in the air. "He changed. A different name. A new life. Which means he's dead, at least to you. Wizards do that sometimes."

Isabella did not understand.

"I do not understand," she said.

"Bagdemagus is gone, he's not your wizard anymore," the grimalkin explained slowly, as if to a child. "Wizards change things. It's what they do. It would be odd if they didn't change themselves occasionally."

"He changed?" Isabella's soul ran ahead of her, asking questions faster than the Common Sense could suppress them.

"Are you hard of hearing?" The grimalkin yawned wide. It didn't have many teeth left. "I know signs. Or we can write."

She shook her head. "But I have brought his book back," she said, eventually. It seemed a silly thing to say, now that it had come out of her mouth.

The creature laughed in a husky giggle. "He won't be needing that," it said. "But someone has to take the *Gramayre*, and I suppose you're as good as anyone. You might as well have the rest of it."

This made a perverse sort of sense to Isabella, though she had a suspicion the awful creature's motivations were self-serving.

"Be that as it may, Mr. Grimalkin," she insisted, "I must leave this here in case he returns."

"Just Grimalkin, if you please. And anyway, you aren't listening." It seemed bored. "He's not Bagdemagus anymore. If he ever was. Give up, he's gone. You need to take the *Gramayre* with you."

Isabella frowned. "What do you mean by this, Grimalkin?"

"You can't leave the *Household Gramarye* here. It's quite dangerous in the wrong hands."

Isabella was on the back foot, and scrambling to regain control of the conversation.

"Me? Take that? No, that would not be . . . well, it would not be sensible! What use do I have for it?" Her eyes were drawn to the books. Hope, that treacherous creature, was knocking on the lid of Pagliora's box, and try as she might, she could not ignore it.*

The grimalkin, which had little use for distracting footnotes, pulled narrative focus back to the conversation. "Yes, I mean you." It pointed at the books with its paw. "You must take the *Household Gramayre*." The ugly creature was treating the matter as a foregone conclusion. "You seem sensible enough, and the longer it sits here, the more chance someone awful will come along and use it for something nasty. Besides, I shall help you. I know a few things. Think of yourself more as a caretaker. A babysitter. Until I find someone better."

She did consider it. She'd be a fool not to, she told herself. It would be nice to give that yarrow elixir another try, just for the sake of doing it right. And failing all else, she could sell the *Gramarye* and live a life in a nice big house with no mandrakes or jinxed geological features. The more she thought about it, the more the grimalkin's proposition began to seem rational

---

* Pagliora, a mythical enchanter of no small repute, entered the history of Gramayre when she attempted to gift a box to her mother-in-law in which she had enclosed all the troubles of the world. It was only when the box failed to be opened in a timely manner that Pagliora realized she had sealed her mother-in-law inside the box in the process of making it, and died of laughter. The box was later accidentally opened during a yard sale, returning all the various evils to the world (as well as Pagliora's mother-in-law, who had taught them a few things in the meantime).

and appealing. Even the Common Sense nodded along suspiciously. But there was a problem that could not be ignored.

"I cannot take you with me, Grimalkin. Mr. Nagg is not fond of cats. He would be sorely cross with us both, and I would hear of nothing else for days. He would give you a mighty kick, if he were to see you."

"Well, I'm not a feline, and he doesn't need to know." The grimalkin had a smug air about it. "Only a wizard can see me. He'll never even know I'm there."

Isabella frowned. She could see the catlike horror very well indeed, so clearly it was mistaken. But if it annoyed Mr. Nagg to have a cat around the house, perhaps he deserved it. She looked back at the *Household Gramarye*. A repository of secrets. And a tutor to help her master it. Opportunity beckoned.

"Well, Mr. Grimalkin," she said, in as matter-of-fact a tone as she could manage, "this is all well, but how am I, having only two hands, to get this home?" She gestured to the volumes lining the shelves.

From the door, a voice lowed as a grey head with long ears and a sad donkey face poked through the opening. "Hullo. Is there a wizard here?" It paused for a moment, pensively squinting in the gloom. "I'm looking to remove a curse."

"What in the devil"—the grimalkin leaped down to the floor with a hiss—"have you done?"

"Hullo," repeated the donkey. "I'm a donkey."

"You can't just go around ensorcelling every farm animal you meet—" The grimalkin seemed incredulous.

"I don't see how this is any of your business to mind." Isabella was getting a little annoyed, and her surprise at the appearance of the grimalkin was quickly turning to that most familiar of emotions amongst colleagues—icy contempt.

"It's bad practice," said the grimalkin. "And a bit unnecessary. Look at it. It's clearly not coping with sentience very well."

"Hello," said the donkey again. Now that Isabella looked at it, the poor thing did in fact seem a little depressed.

With her back against the wall (metaphorically), Isabella placed her back against the wall (literally), folding her arms. The grimalkin scoffed. They both ignored the donkey, which ambled into the room.

"That is my donkey and I shall enchant it however I like," she growled.

"How did you even manage it?" The ugly creature seemed in a state of shock. "That's not an easy spell to pull off."

"Is anyone else hungry?" the donkey cut in, plaintively.

"You are a wayward beast," Isabella scolded the donkey, "to escape from your pen, so. Return at once."

"Putting it back won't stop it being a talking donkey," laughed the grimalkin, clearly entertained.

"You're a talking cat," she retorted.

"I am no such thing"—its fur bristled—"I am a famulus. A research assistant. Have you not been listening to a word I've said—"

"Don't eat that!" the grimalkin interrupted itself to snap at the donkey, which froze, its mouth stretching towards a bundle of dry herbs hanging on the far wall.

"I was just looking." The donkey seemed wounded. "Okay, that was a lie. I can lie now. Is that good? It feels like a dangerous turning point."

The room fell quiet all at once, as if the spirit of discord had suddenly found somewhere better to be.*

The grimalkin backed the donkey across the house, penning it into a corner so it couldn't eat anything important, even as Isabella quietly made her way to the other volumes of the

---

* It had.

*Household Gramayre*, crammed onto a shelf which was bent into a low curve from the weight.*

Isabella took one of the volumes in hand, and then another, creating a pile on the desk. The hut was barely tall enough for her to stand in comfortably, and it was littered with the paraphernalia of Bagdemagus's trade. Amulets, geegaws, and jars containing who-knew-what were scattered and piled everywhere. No way to distinguish what was important and what wasn't. From the layers of dust on some of the furnishings, it didn't seem as if the wizard had spent much time here in recent weeks, or perhaps even months.

And yet her fingers itched to open the *Gramayre*, to take another peek inside. Something had altered inside Isabella upon first touching the *Gramarye*, and it could not be returned to its sleeping state. Change had begun and change can never be undone, only transformed once again.

"Donkey," she said, finally, "if you will carry these books for us, I will find extra feed for you at the farm. Does that please you?"

"Dinner?" The donkey brightened up and turned towards her, knocking over a table of peculiar ornaments. It didn't even look down. "Yes, let's go home. I'd like dinner. Oh! You could uncurse me too."

The grimalkin snorted. Clearly it disapproved, but she was not inclined to give it the satisfaction of asking why. Nevertheless, Isabella gave the grimalkin an idle scratch between the ears, which it did not object to (even if it wasn't really a cat),

---

* The world is always very busy making sure people stay on the ground, and turning water into clouds, which means that occasionally it gets a bit confused about similar-sounding rules. For instance, sometimes objects have such gravitas that they become genuinely heavier.

and started piling up the tomes, one by one. Through one of the small windows she could see the twin moons rising in the sky, staring down on the moorland. No time to waste. She'd go home, feed the donkey, get some rest, and tomorrow she'd see about undoing what she'd done to it.

# Your Famulus  ◆◆◆◆◆

ongratulations on your acquisition of the Household
*Gramayre*! You will find enclosed with your volume a com-
plimentary famulus with which to pursue your studies. Your
famulus is unique to your copy of the *Household Gramayre*, and is
equipped with a number of charms, elixirs, and artifacts to best
serve you. Your famulus is not permitted to access any of the greater
enchantments, including those of the third order and above, true
changes, or the crafting of any puissant sorcerous device with an
"Esoteric" designation. Further restrictions are provided in the
appendices. If your famulus exhibits strange behaviour, including
but not limited to the exhalation of colours that do not exist, a propensity for speaking in forbidden tongues, or a tendency to raise
the dead into monstrous semblances of life, then the rite of severing
may be performed as indicated in volume XI, *Of Things You Don't
Want to Do, Because It Takes More Than Five Minutes, and Less than
Ten, and That's Not Enough Time to Feel Like You're Doing Something
Worthwhile, but Enough to Interrupt What You Were Doing Beforehand.*
Do not hand-wash your famulus, instead allow them to stand in the
rain and drip-dry.

---

*a loose-leaf insert found in some
copies of the* Household Gramayre

# 7

## FARMER NAGG HAS A VISITOR

T WAS midnight in Nagg Farm and Farmer Nagg was still awake, fuming. His wife had, apparently, in a single day managed to enchant a donkey and steal the entire *Household Gramarye* from the wizard. The mage would surely notice, and then they'd both be turned into weevils. She'd come back just as the sun was setting, the donkey loaded with bags of books strapped to it. They'd come to some kind of agreement, and the donkey (which she insisted on calling Bottom, as if a creature could just choose its own name when it already had a perfectly good one like "Donkey") had agreed to stay in its field. It refused to speak to him, though he could hear the low burble of it nattering away to itself whenever he strayed close to a window.

He was just drifting off to sleep when the first knock came, shaking the thatched roof.*

---

* Maintaining thatch was one of those jobs Mr. Nagg was supposed to take care of, but he'd been too embarrassed to admit that he didn't know how, and so every time a gap appeared he just whacked another bundle on top and hoped for the best. It gave the house the appearance of a malignant tumour, and was poor defence against unpredictable weather.

Farmer Nagg jerked back awake and immediately became tangled in the sheets. He reached over, shaking Mrs. Nagg, who was a notoriously deep sleeper. She turned over, batting his hand away as the fearsome knock sounded once more. The modest cottage seemed all the smaller as the door rattled in its frame.

"Get up," snapped Farmer Nagg at his wife. "Someone is at the door." He didn't add *you useless harpy*, but he thought it very loudly in her direction.

"I shall be doing nothing of the like," sniffed Mrs. Nagg, who shot him a defiant glare in the darkness. He could sense when she was looking at him, prickles on the back of his neck.

He opened his mouth to argue, but she wasn't about to give him the opportunity.

"What, am I to unlatch the door for every man (and I am sure it is a man) who knocks at this time of night? Would you have me greet such a stranger, night-clad? No, I am not for answering, Mr. Nagg, and you shan't be either if you know what's good for you."

They stared invisible daggers at each other in the darkness, and the knock came again. Something large was out there, by the sound of it.

"Wife," said Nagg sternly, "I tell you, go and see who is at the door."

This imperative had always worked on the previous Mrs. Nagg, who had suffered a large array of indignities, and who had been in the custom of rising at all hours of the day and night to answer the door to strangers.*

"I shan't," she said, firmly. "If you are so concerned, Mr. Nagg, then you shall see to it. And more a fool you'll be if it is a

---

* She'd also been in the habit of trying to poison his food, with limited success because Mr. Nagg had the constitution of an ox.

ruffian." There was a pause. "If you had not been so rude to it, then the hob would do it."

This was true, and he hated her for pointing it out.

Cursing himself for not selling the farm and living in a ditch when he had the chance, Nagg gathered what little courage he laid claim to and lit a candle. Padding downstairs in his slippers, he cowered once more as the knock repeated, shaking the very foundations of the house.*

"Hob?" he whispered, hopefully. It was a vain hope and he knew it, for no answer came from the reclusive hearth spirit. Thunder crashed again.

Scurrying in fright, he all but ran to the door, clutching the candle in front of him as if it were a weapon. Gingerly, he undid the latch and took the smallest of peeks through the crack.

Standing there, drenched from head to toe, was a diminutive figure clad in flimsy robes. Its proportions were unusual, as if someone had tried to downsize a human but forgotten about the head and feet. Large eyes covered over half its face, and they glistened in the candlelight. Sallow white skin stretched over bone ridges where eyebrows should be, and at the end of its stubby arms, long, slender fingers held a single piece of crimson fruit.

"Buy?" it said, eagerly, in a scratchy voice that sounded a bit like a carriage full of harpsichords crashing into the side of a mountain.

Mr. Nagg exhaled. He hadn't realized he'd been holding his breath.

"Well?!" hollered Mrs. Nagg from upstairs. "Is it a miscreant

---

* The tiny upper floor of the Nagg cottage had been installed by Grimbolt Nagg, who fancied himself a builder and wanted a better view of the Nagg Stone, which he was convinced was moving itself an inch closer to the house each month under the full moons.

come to end us both? You have the door wide open, Mr. Nagg, and you will let the rain in!"

"It just be a goblin, wife!" said Mr. Nagg. Shutting the door on the creature, he padded back up the creaking stairs and went back into the bedroom, where Mrs. Nagg was sitting bolt upright.

"It is early in the season for goblins, and so far from the market," she said, and her voice was deeply troubled. She got this way around the topic of goblins, or their fruit. "Nothing but sorrow can come from goblin fruit, Mr. Nagg," she would say, with a distant look about her.

Much as he despised agreeing with her, Mr. Nagg had to admit that his wife was right. About it being early in the season, that is. He was conflicted about the goblin fruit, a secret he kept close to his chest.

From the far-flung village of Winceby to the scattered farmsteads of East Grasby, everyone knew that summer had ended when the goblins appeared in the valley. The annual arrival of the goblin market was so punctual that people could (and did) use it as a marker of the seasons. Bedecked in their colourful finery and pulling carts laden with tempting fruit, the waist-height creatures emerged at the first gentle touch of autumn, crying out the words:

"Fruit! Delicious fruit! Come sample our wares. Taste our forbidden delights."[*]

Most years, they contented themselves with lurking in the valley, shining their lanterns and singing their goblin songs. Sometimes, however, a goblin would dare to venture into a nearby village, offering its tempting fruit. When this occurred, Bagdemagus the wizard would appear to escort it back to the goblin market, whispering words that rumbled like troubled

---

[*] The goblin tongue uses the same word for "forbidden" and "delight."

skies. Bagdemagus's powers seemed to cow even the hardy goblin folk, who feared nothing else but the clutches of winter.

In fact, for as long as Bagdemagus had been caretaker, goblins seemed reluctant to set foot outside the valley, though every few years they sent out a rogue goblin, as if testing the boundary. Meanwhile, the rest of the creatures manned their groaning tables from dawn until dusk each day, ringing their tinkling bells and calling out their entrancing words in shrill, laughing voices. Day and night the market goblins celebrated and danced, until one morning, as a frost settled over the hills, they would simply vanish until the next year.

Multiple town goblins, this early in the year, was definitely unusual.

Mr. Nagg returned to the bedroom with a heavy heart. Isabella had gone back to sleep, taking the covers and holding them in a death grip. He sat on his side of the mattress and turned over a goblin fruit in his hands. Where had he picked that up? He didn't remember taking it. He'd throw it away tomorrow, he decided, hiding it in the drawer of his bedside table. Yes, there was no reason to worry Mrs. Nagg with that. In the darkness, he thought about the lanterns lighting up the marketplace in the valley, and a smile stole its way onto his face.

# 8

## APPLES FOR GWENDOLYN

THE PROBLEM with goblins, at its heart, was a matter of taxonomy. Centuries before the enlightened present, throughout the period now referred to as antiquity, scholarship laboured under the forgivable delusion that goblins were animals, or something close to it. Methods of control (both humane and mortiferous) usually effective on animals or humanoids, however, failed to produce the expected results. Every year, the goblins would return in the autumn with their baskets of fruit, as if from nowhere. In the end, the riddle was solved for the academic world by the cryptomycologist Anastasia of Rebolt, who had come into possession of a copy of the *Household Gramarye*. In the face of considerable opposition, she wrote a paper titled "Goblinoid Nomenclature: Mapping Rural Manifestations of Arcane Saprophytism," which declared the entire goblin population to be a form of fungus. At first the assertion was hotly denied, then debated, then begrudgingly accepted. Finally, when the theory had become fact and it seemed Anastasia was owed some form of public apology, the scholarly establishment declared it had been their idea to start with.

Anastasia's proposal (and the one subsequently adopted

by many later transcriptions of the *Household Gramarye*) was a straightforward one. Goblins were not creatures, but the by-product of a mycelium layer which insinuated itself into the soil near humanoid settlements, the fruiting body of which manifested during the autumn months as goblins. The goblin fruits? Spores. Each colony of goblins was in fact a single goblin, merely spread out over a mile or two of underground tendrils, making their eviction a functional impracticality. The benefits derived for the fungus from proximity to humanoids were manyfold, including the fact that the mycelium adores taking root in brickwork, but primarily in that growing goblin spores near humanoids results in the purchase and consumption of goblin fruit. The process of infesting the host was relatively simple after that, and humans liked to bury their dead in the ground all over the place, which allowed the mycelium to spread to new locations.

Fortunately, it didn't take a book of arcane lore for humans as a species to instinctively know that eating goblin fruit was a bad idea. Parents would tell their children that on no account were they to even consider tasting the goblin fruit. Alas, if there is any trait which the diaspora of humanity can be said to have in common, it's a knack for self-destruction, and generations of parents, natural philosophers, and public health officials quickly discovered that the harder you pushed people not to eat the lethal goblin fruit, the more likely you were to generate a few people in every generation firmly of the mind that Goblin Fruit Was Quite a Good Idea Actually, and You Can't Stop Me.

Tasting the goblin fruit would change you. There were those who said that the very first taste reversed that vital spark which made you an individual, replacing your personality with something else. Others said that it hollowed you out from the inside, leaving nothing but a hollow of sweet ruin. Either way, the results were the same—you stopped caring about the things you once loved, and then you perished. Few who tasted goblin fruit lasted more than a week after consuming it, withering away without so much as a "Goodbye, I've eaten a cursed fruit, and now I'm going outside to die." Parents abandoned children. Spouses split apart. Houses and possessions that could not be carried were left discarded. Death came swiftly in most recorded cases, but rumours circulated of loved ones spotted many years later roaming forgotten paths, emaciated and confused.

You should not eat the goblin fruit. And yet, it tempted. Always perfectly ripe, it tantalized the senses and caught the light to lure your attention towards it. You must not eat the goblin fruit, but people did, and were lost.

In East Grasby, it was settled tradition to treat the goblins as if they did not exist. The presence of Bagdemagus, who was grumpy but quite terrifying, kept the goblins from leaving their market in the valley, and so the goblin market went year on year without visitors, except for the occasional straggler who tasted the fruit against all sensibility and reason, dreaming themselves into nothing and vanishing forever in every way that mattered.

This year, deep in the mud of the valley, something new was afoot. In the center of the market, surrounded by the usual harlequin tents, a hole was being dug in the ground. A poorly conceived sign, lopsidedly hammered into the dirt, was painted with the words *New Goblin Market, Opening Soon* in a sweeping and colourful font.

Standing on the edge of the shallow pit, overseeing the work, was a woman. And what a woman. Gwendolyn Gooch stood head and shoulders over any man you could name, which was only partially attributable to high-heeled boots and her excellent posture. Fine leathers and expensive fabrics composed her outfit, which cleaved tightly to a full figure, supported in places by tight straps designed to produce an illusion that had once sustained itself naturally, but took ever-increasing levels of artifice to maintain. Rolls of bright gold hair were trussed up on top of her head, and pinned savagely in place. Her face was meticulously made up and smoothed over in key places, her lips just a little too full. The wrinkles around her eyes told a story of experience, and her ears were pointed at the tips, betraying a quirk of elfin ancestry. Gwendolyn Gooch was not entirely human. No, she was more than that. She was a businesswoman.

Staring into the pit, she watched the few villagers she'd managed to gather to her cause digging away with their bare hands at the soil. Goblin fruit had changed them, and now they cared little for anything, so little that you could point them at a cliff, tell them to jump, and they would. For all their bleating about how you shouldn't eat the fruit, they'd jumped at the opportunity she'd given them once she'd dressed it up a little. The trick, she'd quickly found out, was the same as it always was. People didn't like being told what to do. They resented it. It was, in fact, the core of Gwendolyn's business model. What were people being denied? What were they told they couldn't have? And she would provide it, lethal as it may be, for people to gorge on until she could pick through the bodies for coins.

Still, she had to admit as she watched the villagers hack at the dirt, this particular poison was more insidious than most. She didn't want them dead, not any more than she wanted them alive. She was ambivalent about that. What she cared about was their usefulness to her, and as soon as you were dead, you were useless. The victims* were much better served digging the foundations for New Goblin Market than they were rotting away in a heap. She would procure them tools soon enough. Perhaps shovels. They'd ruin their hands if they had to keep

---

* No, she told herself. The employees.

clawing the soil like that. She'd sent the goblins on a mission to find some, but she didn't hold out much hope of success because the goblins only really cared about spreading mayhem and distributing fruit. You see, while she harboured only the faintest of empathetic impulses for humans, Gwendolyn understood goblins. She understood them better than anyone else could ever hope to, because she hungered for the same thing they did. Spread. Dominate. Consume. Beat a man with a riding crop until you got bored. These were the laws that Gwendolyn followed, and one of these days they would bring her riches beyond comparison. Any day now.

As for the villagers, there was plenty of time to find some kind of physician for them. She didn't plan for anyone to die, necessarily. She never did, it just tended to happen when a new business was on the cards. You can't make an omelette without breaking a few eggs, after all, even if those eggs are golden and part of a magical goose pyramid scheme. She'd figure out all the details when the time came. In the meantime, she had access to a very malleable corps of workers who did whatever she asked (albeit lethargically). Each night, Gwendolyn would retire to her quarters, and the next morning the hole would be larger. Somewhere in the back of her mind, the voice of Gwendolyn's father tormented her as she slept. "Nothing worth having ever comes easy, Gwendolyn," he would say, stroking his beard.* He had been very fond of sanctimonious idioms, which hadn't saved him from the wolf that devoured

---

* Gwendolyn's father had been a man whose chief quality was his determination to deny himself the pleasures of existence. Happiness, as he put it, was a decadent luxury that left you weak and lazy. Indulgence was the enemy, he would say, brushing her hair each night by the fire. He'd made the boar-bristle brush himself, having killed the pig with his bare hands when it beat him at cards.

him in the end,* but she liked to think he'd died feeling superior to everyone.

The most impressive tent in New Goblin Market boasted a number of spacious circular tables,† a high bar decorated with engravings of Gwendolyn's face in relief, and a flickering fireside. The tent belonged to Gwendolyn herself, and was adorned in rolls of a violently pink fabric so criminally flamboyant it punched the other colours out of your head and stole your wallet while your back was turned. In the evenings, she would sit at the table closest to the fire and go over her accounts with her gilded abacus, quietly totalling up the vast sums of money she stood to make from this particular scheme. No, East Grasby didn't really have the cash or the clientele to rocket her straight to riches, but Gwendolyn wasn't worried about peripheral technicalities. This was larger than East Grasby. She could see it in her mind's eye, her grand vision for New Goblin Market. A gilded fair, all glittering fabrics studded with gemstones, and filled to the brim with rarities brought to her from across the world. Local employees, sourced from local communities, all paid with Gwendolyn Coins (stamped with a regal interpretation of her face in profile) that they could spend back into at New Goblin Market. Rows of customers all begging to spend their riches, ranks of employees who didn't care about being paid because they were loyal to the company. Who shared her vision. And at the top of the pyramid, allowing others to bask in the light reflected off her piles of gold, Gwendolyn Gooch, resplendent and tax free.

A little tug at her sleeve brought her back to reality. She shook the hand off angrily without even looking down. "No,"

---

* This is a more common way to die than you would think.
† She'd had the goblins drag them from the houses of her newest employees.

she sighed for what had to be the fiftieth time. "For the last time, no fruit. I do not want fruit. Put it away."

The goblin by her seat, which was holding a red fruit of sinister lustre, seemed crestfallen. Ever since they'd settled into construction, the goblins had been generating the peculiar fruit in ever-increasing volume. She didn't know where they were getting it from, and perhaps it didn't matter, but she was rapidly losing control of the supply/demand gradient, no matter how many barrels of the stuff she stashed away in tents.

Of course, she had a vague disdain for how freely the goblins were giving away the fruit. She'd managed to drill the concept of buying and selling into them—they used the words without really understanding them—but getting them to recognize currency had been an uphill battle. They still couldn't tell the difference between coins and pebbles. They loved to accept any price for the fruit, as if the price wasn't really relevant, and they would leave the items they'd gathered in her bed, her chairs, and under her feet if she wasn't mindful. Rocks. Single shoes. A stale loaf of bread. She'd once had to remove a gardening fork from her chair before sitting down. In the long term, she envisioned a bustling marketplace, the hub of commerce for all the world. Kings and peasants coming from far and wide to pay a handsome sum for a single bite of the legendary goblin fruit, sourced from recyclable goblins of course. Naturally, she would take a cut of the proceeds (as was her right). Click-clack went the abacus. Would 70 percent be too much? She was supplying the premises, after all. And a 15 percent processing fee, for the trouble.

"Come buy, buy our goblin fruit," chanted the goblin under the table. In a sing-song voice.

The goblins did not seem to have full command of the common tongue, nor any regional varieties she had tried, though they loved to chant her name, "Lady Gooch," shrieking at the top of their lungs when she walked by. Lately, however, they'd started to reel off a number of short phrases on a loop, all of which revolved around fruit. They were savvy little salesmen when they put their heads together . . . Good minds for slogans. She could use that.

A little hand placed a goblin fruit on the table. Almost perfectly spherical, they reminded Gwendolyn of a plum, apart from the virulently bright red skin that screamed *Danger* to her like a redback spider, or a forest fire. She didn't seem to find the fruit as alluring as others did, which was a riddle that remained unresolved, but getting involved with that kind of minutiae was how you ended up working in academia, or (worse) publishing. Annoyed at the distraction from her inner monologue, Gwendolyn prodded the fruit towards a bin with her stylus. It rolled, reluctantly, and landed in the basket with a thump. Dense, those fruits. Not that she'd ever tasted one. A true businesswoman never sampled the merchandise. That was a lesson she'd taken from her mother, who was still out there somewhere if the angry letters from the Central Bureau of Taxation were to be believed.

On seeing her throw the gift into the bin, the goblin's face twisted into a scowl,* and it scuttled away, muttering to itself. Goblins walked with a strange gait, hopping from one foot to the other, side-to-side in a way that was quite unpleasant to look at. As it reached the tent flap, it turned around, expression lighting up as if by an afterthought. "Lady Gooch," it said, "we find dead body. Come see."

---

* The goblins showed very little propensity for anger, but they didn't like it when anyone threw away the fruit. This was part of the reason she kept finding new places to hide and store it, rather than just burying it or burning it (as was her preference when it came to extra stock that might drive prices down).

# 9

## THE LICCE WAECE

A FUNERAL IN East Grasby was a dour affair at the best of times. Whenever a death occurred within the informal boundaries of the village, the residents would gather in the only communal structure maintained for the collective good, a barrow nestled in the heart of the moorland. It was lined with stone on the inside, though the years had eroded it in many places, and timber splints had been erected to ensure its structural integrity. The community didn't agree on much, but they all asserted in the privacy of their own homes that the barrow had been warmer and better appointed in the Olden Days, When I Was Young, or Back When People Were Sensible. After a death had been confirmed, the body was removed to the barrow, where a vigil was set until the following morning. This custom was called the Licce Waece, and it folded the functions of funeral, wake, mourning period, and apotropaic tradition into a single bleak evening.

The Naggs attended the wake that day chiefly because it was expected of them. It just wasn't done to miss an event like this, at least not if you cared what people thought about you. Isabella did care, though she would have told you that she didn't, and so she put on her nice grey trousers with the over-shoulder straps, found a clean shirt, and dragged Mr. Nagg* down the country road towards the barrow, him grumbling the entire way.

Death in East Grasby was a peculiar thing. The reason for holding the body inside a public area until the cry of the rooster† was functional as much as it was social. If a recently deceased body was not watched over ruthlessly in the period following death, particularly if that death was violent or unexpected, there was a strong possibility that it would rise from the grave. This was frowned upon not only because the walking dead had a demonstrable bias towards mass homicide, but also because of the issues it caused in probate. Neither truly alive nor definitely not dead, the animated body was in a legal grey area, and it was called a licce. For reasons not fully understood by the layman (and only hinted at in the *Gramarye*),‡

---

* She didn't try to make him change his clothes because she wasn't sure they could even be removed at this stage. It would be like peeling an apple.

† Particularly savvy ornithologists in more developed areas might instead bring a rooster directly to the body, which saves eight hours of waiting. Unfortunately, it's also very bad luck to manhandle a rooster, which means the ornithologist in question almost always ends up the next licce being watched. There is a worldwide shortage of ornithologists.

‡ *The New Scholar's Compendium on Magical Practices, and Sundry Examples to the Benefit of the Apprentice and Journeyman Sorcerer* has a great deal to say on the creation of a licce. It describes the flaws and errors which lead to their accidental creation, their undesirable hostility to all life, and their slew of potent supernatural abilities, including incredible resilience and unholy strength. It opines on the folly of sorcerers who tampered with forces beyond their comprehension, and the invariably fatal results. It provided three appendices on the various forms, banishing rituals and warding patterns found effective against no fewer than seven regional variants of licce, including preventative unguents and talismans.

The *Household Gramarye* provides a single footnote on the creation of a licce, retained in the ancient tongue, which translated roughly to: "If ye play stupid gaymes, ye shall receive stupid prizes."

watching the body until the cry of the cockerel the morning after death prevented this from happening. You could bury the body or burn it, but you had to be fast and thorough lest it claw its way to the surface or leap from the pyre. This tripled your complications, because not only did you have a dead relative to mourn, and an aggrieved revenant out for your blood, but also an unoccupied person-sized hole in the ground which violated municipal ordinances on pedestrian hazards, and which in a worst-case scenario might land you with another licce.

Isabella had only heard of a licce rising once, when she'd barely been old enough to remember. The deceased had been young, accustomed to leaving town with little notice, and no one had noticed them go missing. In the end, the body had gone unwatched for several days, and the licce that resulted had carved a murderous swathe through the countryside before word managed to reach the wizard. Once the danger was recognized, Bagdemagus had hunted it down, banishing it back to death where it belonged by wielding a rooster like a club.* The rooster, Chanticleer, was now a folk hero, and spent most of its time wandering between the various farmsteads and being thrown grain by anyone who happened to chance upon it.

The Naggs arrived at the wake around noon. The deceased was an elderly gentlemen they all knew as Old Bastard, and the community had rallied around making sure that he stayed dead, as he was dislikeable enough the first time around and no one had any desire to meet a new, unimproved version. Sadly, no one present at the Licce Waece remembered Old Bastard's actual name, because he'd refused to give anyone the time of day for the past thirty years and he'd managed to vengefully outlive all his family, friends, and casual acquaintances with a

---

* It's bad luck, of course, to handle a rooster, unless you first acquire consent. Bagdemagus was very persuasive in that regard.

tenacity that was all the more haunting for the little comfort it awarded him. As far as Old Bastard seemed to think, everyone that mattered to him was dead, and everyone else was a poor distraction from the misery of his continued existence. Attempts to ingratiate oneself with Old Bastard had been met with vituperations, if not violence, and so people had punished him by giving him what he asked for—unremitting solitude. The only reason anyone discovered the hermit was deceased was that he had the foresight to drop dead in the front yard, where his body would be visible. It was the first helpful thing Old Bastard had done for another person in forty years.

Mrs. Nagg bustled her way through the scattered watchers to the bier, where the body of Old Bastard had been laid in the ceremonial pose they used for the Licce Waece.* The stone slab was covered in scratches in the hedge language of the north, a collection of deep lines in the stone that read something along the lines of "Remember, it could be worse."†

On the other side of the bier, Isabella found herself face-to-face with Nancy Potbugler. Of course it was Nancy, of all people. Isabella Nagg had a friendship with Nancy Potbugler that oscillated between burning envy and bitter resentment. Nancy was younger than Isabella by seven months, which she never failed to mention, and she was a linchpin of village life, showing up on doorsteps carrying something she'd baked, knitted, or crafted with loving hands. Her house was spotless, her children alarmingly well behaved, and her gaze suggested she was trying very hard not to pity you.

---

* It involved a lot of rope, because when it came to a licce, you really couldn't be too careful.

† The hedge language was a written tongue created before the advent of the common tongue, and though it has long since fallen out of general usage, it remains common on artifacts, and in the hands of wizards, vagrants, interior decorators, and other arcane ne'er-do-wells.

It had been many years since anyone had looked at Isabella without pity. Not since Lorenzo. But she didn't think about Lorenzo, or what had happened to him, in the same way you tried not to look too hard at an open wound.

Nancy, godless creature that she was, turned to Isabella with a smile. She could not bear to see someone in their own thoughts, as it meant they were not paying her their undivided attention. "Oh, it's you two! I thought you might be cooped up in that house still, you two lovebirds. Lovely to see you."

Horrible woman. Isabella forced a smile. "We are just paying respects. Shall we have enough watchers?" She needed to know. If they had enough participants already, she could take her leave and get back to the *Gramarye*. She cast an eye for Mr. Nagg, who was over by the door with Mr. Potbugler, and the two men were standing in silence. Enviable. Truly enviable. Taking a quick tally, Isabella thought there were more than enough to keep watch on Old Bastard; they didn't need the Naggs today.

"You should come into the village more often, Isabella! People are always asking after you. Do you still grow those wonderful little plants? Lovely things, and such good work for a beginner."

Isabella resisted the urge to throttle Nancy, but her hands twitched as if to betray her. "If you will excuse us?"

Rudely, she turned away from Nancy and pretended to busy herself with her satchel. She could feel Nancy's eyes boring into her from behind, and a panic began to rise. The room seemed crowded, though there could not have been more than a handful of people inside. She rummaged further in her bag, pretending to be overcome by sentiment. The Naggs were not popular, and she was not welcome here. She had to get out.

She could sense Nancy waiting to pounce when she turned back around, so she circled around and deliberately bumped into Mrs. Bonewhistle, who was carrying a basket full of her famous "wake pastries."* Creeping through the shadows at the edges of the room, she darted out into the sunlight as softly as she could, leaving Mr. Nagg behind. He could follow if he wished, but she didn't care what he did.

As she made her way quickly over the cobbles in the direction of the road home, she found the grimalkin lingering on a fence post. How was it balancing on such a tiny area? It didn't seem natural.

"Finished mourning?" The creature yawned wide. Instead of teeth, it had little fleshy nubbins all the way down its throat. "We should get back. It's not good to leave the *Gramarye* alone for too long, I told you that."

"Are you going to follow me everywhere?" she asked it, trying to sound annoyed but secretly glad for the company. She already felt a little better under the open sky. Barrows were for the dead, and Isabella Nagg was alive.

"I will," it replied.

They walked in silence back up the trail.

---

* A secret recipe, the pastries contained a number of active ingredients that could waylay the gentle hand of sleep and keep you alert. In her advanced years, however, Mrs. Bonewhistle had grown a tad cavalier with the ingredient amounts, and these days the pastries sustained a restless, sleepless jitter that lasted the better part of a week.

# 10

# MR. NAGG SNEAKS
# TO MARKET

**M**R. NAGG sat and watched the corpse of Old Bastard until the early evening, absent-mindedly turning over the goblin fruit in his hands. Why had he brought it with him? He should throw it away. It was bad, and he couldn't eat it (obviously, no one would do that), so why did he have it? He didn't want to go home, not to yet another dinner of scrunge,* to sit in the silence with Mrs. Nagg. No, at least here he could be alone with his thoughts. He kept touching the fruit, feeling the surface. It was heavier than he'd thought.

Then, one of their neighbours arrived to relieve him of duty, and he couldn't refuse without explaining why he'd rather not go home, so he'd let them shuffle him outside into the gloom. Before he left, he made sure to toss the goblin fruit on the floor of the barrow. A gift for the dead. That was traditional after all, and it wasn't as if it could hurt Old Bastard. The dead didn't worry about goblin fruit. His feet began guiding him down

---

* He had a recurring nightmare in which he was chased by a looming morass of it.

the winding pathways into the valley, and he convinced himself that he was just going for a quick walk in a random direction. Down, down the slope he went, past cairns and undergrowth, against all reason, towards the lanterns of the goblin market. It was only halfway down the slope that he realized the goblin fruit was still in his pocket. Hadn't he thrown it away? Clearly not.

Farmer Nagg wasn't supposed to be here. He knew the stories, he knew what happened to people who tasted the goblin fruit, and yet he came here every year nonetheless. The market was nestled in the very bottom of the valley. It was said that a river had passed down the center of the valley long ago, but it had dried up in grief after witnessing a terrible battle.* There must have been some truth in this, because you could still trip over the occasional blade or bone if you dug deeper than a foot below the surface. In the autumn, the goblins bedecked the place in wooden stalls and colourful fabric, hand-painted with riotous hues. They had signs, scrawled with words, but Mr. Nagg couldn't have read them even if he'd known the goblin tongue.†

He crouched behind a rock, watching the goblin men shriek into the night. "Fruit! Come buy our delicious fruit!" They were strange creatures, long pointed ears and broad faces that were just similar enough to human to be unsettling. They grasped their carts with supple hands, stroking their produce lovingly.

---

* When you lived in a village like East Grasby, you didn't bother yourself about the minutiae of ancient history unless it manifested some sort of peculiarity and decided to make itself your problem. Quiet was good.

† Attempts had been made over the centuries to decipher the goblin tongue, but they were stymied by the reluctance of goblins to participate in the study. Though acquisition of a goblin was relatively easy, their tendency in captivity towards gleeful pyromania and recreational cannibalism ended most linguistic trials before they began.

Mr. Nagg held his hand to his breast, to stay his heart. He felt that any movement could give him away, this close to the goblin men he fancied he could feel their breath on his neck, their sharply pointed teeth biting into his shoulders. That was silly, of course. The goblins didn't eat anyone who didn't want to be eaten. Did they? He agonized, holding his pouch of coin to his chest. This was as close as he'd ever dared come to the market. It wasn't a betrayal, he told himself—he didn't do anything. He just watched. He wouldn't eat the fruit, and that was the important thing.

Goblin fruit! He couldn't stop thinking about the feel of it, the way it caught the light. He'd always been fascinated by goblins, that was true, a dark curiosity he'd nursed as long as he could remember. As a boy, his mother would say to him, "Henric, you must not speak to the goblin men, nor taste their fruits," and he would nod, always wondering what secret delight was being kept from him. When he was old enough to ask why, the question was met with scolding from his mother, and a clout round the ear from his father. "Stupid boy," they would say aloud to one another, "quit your silly obsession with the goblin folk, and go make yourself useful." And so Henric would climb up onto the roof of Nagg Farm and stare in the direction of the valley, waiting for the lights of autumn to fill the air, and to hear the jingle-jangle of goblin voices in the breeze. There was something out there for him, in the valley, he knew it. But he was also afraid, and so he had buried the desire, buried the need, until it was so far under the rubble of his spite and resentment that he couldn't see it anymore.

It was years before the market had sunk its hooks into him again. The smell of goblin fruit had wafted into the village one night, and the memories, the curiosity had flooded back. But he was almost a man grown then, and so this time he had steeled his nerve, and worked up the courage to sneak close to the market and its peculiar fruits. Just the once, he'd said. Just to see the market up close. He'd come close enough to see the pointy ears, and then he'd crept home, filled with shame. The next year, he'd decided that he'd barely gotten a good look, and the first time hadn't counted. The third year, he told himself that this was the very last time, and that was final. Over the years he'd returned often to spy on the goblins, each time creeping a little closer.

Oh, he'd tried to resist. He'd found distractions. Hobbies. None of them lasted, all discarded at his feet when the autumn came and the urge to go to the valley returned. He'd even married Edith, hoping it would prove diverting, but ultimately she'd disappointed him. Isabella was more accommodating. At least she didn't ask questions.

Last year, he'd returned on several occasions, enjoying the thrill of being somewhere he shouldn't. Each time, he returned home after dusk, his mind clouded with the rich scent of goblin fruit. He made excuses so Isabella wouldn't know where he had been. She didn't understand, just like his mother and father hadn't understood. No, this was Mr. Nagg's secret, for him and him alone. To be discovered here would be to ruin the secret, ruin the glorious indulgence of it. He wouldn't tolerate that.

The goblins continued to hawk their wares. "Come buy! Buy our delicious fruit! Taste it!"

Goblin fruit! He had some in his pocket, did he not? His fingers ached to touch it again, to trace its curves. Surely it could not hurt to touch it again. He pondered the idea for a moment before dismissing it. No. It was goblin fruit, and he was not to eat it. He knew that. He'd thought about it, of course, he assumed everyone had. That was normal. And he'd always wondered how it would taste, just like a regular person, even if no one else would admit it.

Despite his protestations, there was something awakening

in Mr. Nagg, a door opening in his mind, and try as he might to slam it shut, light peeked through from underneath.

No, he wouldn't eat any goblin fruit. He was fairly sure of that. He would watch for a while longer, and then he would go home.

He continued to peek as the goblins pottered about the market, and then almost fell over in surprise. There was someone else here. Not a goblin, to be sure. She was over seven feet tall, golden hair tumbling around her shoulders. Long pointed ears poked out through the curls, and she walked with a confidence that cowed the goblins on either side of her. From this distance, he couldn't make out her face, but from her hand gestures she seemed to be giving directions. Or scolding someone. It was hard to say. Was this an opportunity? Someone to share his secret with? Or was it a threat—the threat of discovery, and shame? Detaching himself from his hiding place, he slipped away into the shadows, brooding darkly to himself as he began the long walk home.

# 11

# THE POT OF BASIL SPEAKS

SABELLA WOKE at the first light of dawn and slipped out of bed. Mr. Nagg had not returned from the wake, which was most unusual, but not unprecedented. He sometimes went down to the village to soak his grievances in ale (as if he had any troubles worth mentioning) and then spent the night in a ditch. He'd wander back here by noon, no doubt, reeking of the swill they served in that awful shack he called a tavern.* Donning a gown,† she padded downstairs to the kitchen to find the grimalkin fast asleep on the table. She'd have to explain that to Mr. Nagg too, no doubt.

The first thing Isabella did each morning was check the house for signs of intruders. Yes, the farmhouse was a fair walk outside of town, and legendarily cursed, but that meant nothing to the enterprising thief, or so she assured Mr. Nagg. To

---

* The Nail and Hammer was the only tavern in East Grasby, which meant it could serve whatever it wanted and people had to make do. The proprietor, a dour man with a shaved head named Gustav, was said to have repeatedly watered down the same cask of beer each morning since he bought the place, occasionally throwing in a flask of something he distilled from Nagg mandrakes to "punch it up" a little.

† Mrs. Nagg slept in the nude, because it seemed to unnerve Mr. Nagg.

hear her tell it, the thieves of the world met up once a month to discuss the best ways to break into Nagg Farm, and only her eternal vigilance in the matter of double-checking the window locks before she went to bed prevented a wholesale heist. Mr. Nagg enjoyed leaving doors and windows ajar to distress her, which only made her redouble her security efforts.

The first order of business, as always, was to make herself some tea. She'd barely got the water simmering when the grimalkin somehow got under her feet.

"Good morning," it mewled. "Are we ready to study? You've no time to lose." It licked a paw, and some fur came off. "Not that it's ever too late to start with the *Gramarye*, of course, but you've lost enough time to dithering, don't you think?"

"Be still," she chided. "I shall be ready when I am ready." She grabbed it by the scruff of the neck, which it tolerated grumpily, and placed it on the table.

Adding the leaves to the water, a thought came to her.

"Grimalkin," she said, "how long do you plan to stay?"

"Well," it said, licking its own eyeball, "I'm your grimalkin. So I'm around as long as you're around, I suppose. It's important you have one if you want to work Gramarye. And I'm yours. They all have one. Wizards, that is."

"I'm not a wizard. And did you not belong to Bagdemagus?" she began. She was already starting to get confused.

"I never said that." It poked a tongue out. "You assumed that. But that's beside the point."

Isabella finished making her tea.

"I will not say that I understand," she said. "But perhaps that may change, with time."

Steaming mug in hand, she sat down to look at the *Household Gramarye*. The volumes of the Grammar were marked along the spine with faded impressions, but she couldn't really tell them apart.

She paused. Which one to pick?

The grimalkin's dry voice from behind her made her start. It had a habit of getting under her feet without making a sound. "Try that one. It's mostly in the tongue of this age, it's one of the newer volumes. Old Bagsy wrote most of it, if you can believe it."

Isabella had never heard anyone refer to Bagdemagus as "Bagsy" before, and she had a suspicion that the grimalkin was taking liberties.

Picking the indicated volume, labelled *Of Visible Virtue*, she studied the exterior. Waxy vellum, warped from age and exposure to the elements, blotched with a few unsightly patterns along the lower cover. There was a small bite mark on the top left corner that looked human. The spine groaned as she gently opened it. Propping the book against a crooked collection of kitchen apparatus, she scanned for something (anything) to pique her interest. Many of the pages were in languages or glyphs she did not recognize, but later ones began to seem something akin to the letters she already knew how to interpret. Picking a page at random, she began to read.

*. . . When spirits converse with men, it is under some shape discernible only through correct application of the Gramarye, and that there is a Law given them that a Shape they assume must be of something which resembles their Condition.*

She caught her attention wandering and shook herself. She'd chosen a dense place to begin, it seemed. She tried again.

*For, as in the world we see every Thing hath a several and suitable Physiognomy or Figure, as recalls their inward Nature, whereby it is known, so it is in the world of Spirits and Apparitions—*

"Is it interesting?" piped a high voice from behind her. In a day of strange voices, this one drove her almost a foot into the air. She checked behind her. No one. Then around the room.

The grimalkin was fast asleep, or was pretending. She didn't know it well enough to tell.

Perhaps she had imagined the voice. It had, after all, been a very strange few days. No wonder she was hearing things. She turned her attention back to the book.

"Oh, wise Isabella. Why do you forsake me?" the voice chimed again.

She was not imagining it. She turned once more, but only an empty kitchen greeted her. She looked out of the window into the yard, where she caught a glimpse of the hob shoveling manure. She made sure to look away quickly. The hob did not like to be perceived, and she was loath to anger it any more than Mr. Nagg already had.

"Show yourself," she commanded. This was her house, and she was getting very tired of strange visitors.

"Oh, wise, good Isabella. Can you not perceive your oldest, most loyal friend?"

This time, she pinpointed it. The voice was coming, unbelievably, from the pot of basil.

"Pot of basil?" she ventured, leaning her face in close. "Is that you?"

"Yes, Isabella," the pot of basil confirmed. "It is me, the pot of basil, your closest confidant. The yarrow has given me speech, and so I may talk with you awhile."

Emotions stirred within Isabella. She recalled dumping the remaining yarrow preparation in the basil's container. So, it had worked on the basil as well as it had worked on the donkey. Oddly, it was pride which blossomed in her. She had made it well. Too well, perhaps. She had not intended to give the basil a voice. She wasn't sure how she felt about that. The basil was her constant companion, but it had ever been a silent participant in their conversations. It was all very well talking to a plant which couldn't talk back, it didn't matter if she went on for hours, or talked in circles. As soon as something could answer you, you had to worry about whether you were boring it, or whether you should ask it how its family was doing.*

"My, you have been busy." The grimalkin had one eye open, voice dripping with sarcasm. "A donkey and a pot of basil. Perhaps you'd like to make the chamberpot speak too? Or the fireplace?"

"Isabella is the most perfect woman to ever live," said the pot of basil.

Isabella looked from the cat to the pot of basil, and then back to the cat. "Both of you, be still. I am thinking." The pot of basil was not an ordinary basil, in any respect. In truth, it never had been. Had her elixir awoken something she did not intend? Was there a way to tell?

"Peace, basil," she said to the pot. "And you as well, Grimalkin. It is clear that there is much to the Gramarye I do not yet understand. Grimalkin, help me find the yarrow elixir recipe."

The creature acquiesced, lounging over to sniff the books. "That one," it said, confidently. She flicked to the page she'd used to concoct the potion, and studied it. The footnotes were long, and the commentaries cramped, but she went through it slowly, word by word. The text stipulated that the elixir would give speech to mules, donkeys, and horses, though it could be applied to other living creatures with varying efficacy. The word *living* had been underlined by an annotator, but she already felt less worried. So, the basil could talk. It was a tad bothersome, but perhaps a just reward for its companionship. It had earned it, if anyone had.

The grimalkin stretched out an impossibly long torso on the table, flexing its claws. "If you're quite finished," it said, "we

---

* The basil's family had been added to one of her finer batches of scrunge.

should pick something to work on," it suggested. "Start small. We'll work on languages later, so you don't have to start at the deep end. You seem to have a talent for brewing. Plenty of ideas in the *Gramarye*. Here's a hint: Avoid any pages where the illustration has teeth."

A long moment passed as Isabella flicked through the volumes of the *Household Gramarye*. She landed on a volume titled *On Allotriophagia*, opening it to a page in the middle that had an attractive illustration.

"Porridge," she said, decisively.

The grimalkin looked at the pot of basil, which wasn't able to return the sceptical expression, but would have if it could.

"Porridge," repeated the grimalkin. "Is that supposed to mean something?"

Isabella pointed to the page of the *Gramarye* on which she had come to rest. The note in the margin read "Petecuratory Conjuration." The instructions were outlined in something close enough to her own dialect that she felt comfortable.

Isabella turned around and began to rummage in her cupboards, clanging pots and pans as she moved things around.

"This is exciting," said the grimalkin. "I never get to watch anymore. Bagdemagus used to make me sit outside. Said I asked too many questions, whatever that means. What are you fetching? Can I see?" It hopped to the floor and got under her feet.

Batting it away with a hand, Isabella retrieved what she was looking for, an ugly cauldron with crying faces etched into the side.

"Says here I need a horn," she said, "but this should do nicely. I cannot see what difference there is, truth be told."*

---

* It was this kind of geometrical sloppiness that resulted in the Great Yeast Incident two centuries prior, but Isabella was not to know that.

"Oh yes, ignore the instructions," commented the grimalkin. "This should go well."

"I trust you, wise Isabella," the pot of basil declared. "You are so intelligent and also beautiful."

Preparing the cauldron took the better part of the morning, as she followed the step-by-step instructions contained in the *Household Gramarye*. Various herbs were sprinkled inside, a fire was lit underneath. Words were sounded out, with the help of the grimalkin, which seemed to enjoy correcting her pronunciation. The words had too many consonants, that was the problem. "If it were easy," said the grimalkin in retort, "everyone would be doing it."

As she chanted, she thought of her mother. Her mother had enjoyed cooking, and she had passed that on to her daughter. There was an element of conspiracy about it which made it feel like a game. She hadn't enjoyed it as much after her mother left, though. There had been something missing, a sense of collaboration which was (strangely) restored by the presence of the grimalkin.

"It's ready," said the grimalkin. There was something about its mangled expression which seemed sad. Had time passed so quickly? She had been lost in her thoughts.

She looked at the pot with the scowling face. "How do you know this?"

The famulus replied, "I just know. You will too, in time. Now, you need to tell it the magic words, so it knows when to start cooking. Try something flashy, have a little showmanship."

Isabella thought hard for a moment.

"Cook, little pot," she said, "cook."

The grimalkin rolled its single eye so far back into its head that it disappeared entirely, resurfacing momentarily in the wrong socket, then back into its rightful place.

"I cannot cook!" said the pot of basil. "I am a pot of basil."

"I wasn't talking to you." Isabella turned around to the herb. "Now be quiet, basil. I am trying to work."

*Fglep.* A noise inside the pot. A slorping, gooey noise. Porridge was bleeding into the bottom of the cauldron, oozing from nowhere as if through an invisible aperture. Delighted, a true smile spread across Isabella's face for the first time in longer than she could remember. It worked.

Petecuratory Conjuration is categorized by the *Household Gramayre* as a minor form of transubstantiation. While it might look like you've summoned porridge from thin air, it would be more accurate to say that you've transformed thin air into porridge.* If Isabella had read further into the chapter, she might have come across the extended annotations by previous owners of her copy warning against the use of Petecuratory Conjurations in confined spaces, around small children, or in the presence of parrots. Alas, she had not, and her success was unblemished by the shadow of What Might Yet Come to Pass.

Quickly, she leaned over the pot and said, "Stop, porridge pot, stop."† The gurgling sound ceased, and the porridge settled at a level just shy of the rim. She took a spoon and gave it a taste. It was lamentably good, better than any oat-based dish she'd ever thrown together.‡ Maybe Mr. Nagg wouldn't complain for once, though she was sure if anyone could find a way, he could.

There is a tradition in the Gramarye that naming a fell thing is enough to draw its attention. Indeed, no sooner had the idea

---

* Copies of the *Household Gramarye* more recent than Isabella's frequently went into some detail about the dangers of such an experiment, not least amongst which is the fact that it is much more difficult to turn porridge back into air when you've finished with it.

† "You have absolutely no sense of style," complained the grimalkin, which was still juggling its single eye between both sockets.

‡ The bar for this was so low that it was a trip hazard.

crossed her mind than she heard the door open and close. Mr. Nagg was clearly in one of his moods, and she didn't care for it, so she didn't bother to greet him. He marched about, throwing his coat on the table (narrowly missing the grimalkin, which hissed in his direction), and headed outside again.

More out of habit than anything else, she picked up the coat and folded it on the back of a chair. No sense in getting food all over it. Flipping through another volume of the *Gramarye*, she felt an itch to enact another working. The excitement of correctly preparing the porridge pot had her in a fever, and she turned page after page looking for something to which she could apply herself. Momentarily, she wondered if the Licce Waece had been successful, but then if Mr. Nagg had survived, it must have been sufficient. She supposed Nancy Potbugler would make a point of coming around to tell her how wonderful it had been, and how Isabella had been missed.

Nancy Potbugler. She leaped out of her chair. "The meeting! I am late," she said, grabbing her coat.

# 12

# THE HOMEOWNERS
# ASSOCIATION

**T**HE EAST GRASBY Homeowners Association met three
times a month, and the meetings were well attended.
Though the residents of the village did not enjoy the
conveniences of a busier town, such as a town square or a public
library, or even a street on which to place them, the loose con-
glomeration of neighbours held the fortnightly appointment to
be a matter of great importance.

The meeting was held at the Potbugler farm, which bor-
dered on the Nagg holdings at its very farthest edge. The Potbugler house was larger than the Nagg cottage by roughly the
same proportions as their egos were, and Nancy was very fond
of reminding everyone just how much larger their estate was.
She would often say in a tone of eagerness, one hand lightly
placed on your arm, that it just made sense to have everyone
over to her house, because she had the room, didn't she?

Failing to appear at the Homeowners Association meetings was not a practical option, because lack of attendance was
treated by all present as tacit agreement to whatever motion
was raised by Nancy Potbugler that week, and Nancy woke

up each morning with new and fresh ideas to rejuvenate, "improve," or "refresh" East Grasby that always involved a considerable amount of work on the part of other people.

When Isabella arrived, slipping into a chair near the back of the room, Nancy was already in full swing. "Is a little topiary too much to ask?" she said, hands open wide. "I'm not demanding the world here, you don't have to create an entire menagerie. A few decorative mammals is all anyone wants."*

The circle of villagers grumbled quietly amongst themselves in vague dissent. Isabella kept her eyes fixed firmly on the wooden flooring, buffed to a shine by the Potbugler hob. Nancy Potbugler was like a predatory animal—you tried not to catch her gaze and hoped she'd pursue juicier prey.

"Next order of business," Nancy said. "It's autumn, and so the goblin market is back in the valley. I haven't heard back from Bagdemagus, but I assume he's making sure they stay down there, as usual." She said the wizard's name with the same tone of disdain and fear one might use for phrases like "nuclear weapon" or "war crime."

At Isabella's feet, the grimalkin poked its head out from under her chair. The neighbours had not commented on it, and she assumed they thought it was a very sick pet or something. That, or its claims of invisibility to anyone not steeped in Gramayre were true.

"How long is this going to take?" it whispered at her.

"Hush, Grimalkin." She tried to shunt it back under the seat with a foot. It wouldn't do to have her neighbours asking why her new cat could talk. She could envision the conversation. It would start with, "Oh, Isabella, your cat can talk, is there anything we can do?" in the same way you might tell someone

---

* Nancy liked to descend into plurality as a rhetorical device to conceal the fact that she was the only person asking.

there was a hole in their scarf, or that they'd put their shirt on the wrong way around, and it would end with, "Isabella, how terrible, how unfortunate," as they smiled at each other and patted each other on the back to congratulate themselves on not being in her shoes. There was no marvel so wonderful, no miracle so fantastic, that the people of East Grasby couldn't make it seem like a character flaw.

"But I'm bored." The grimalkin stretched out on the floor. "Wouldn't you rather cast a spell? We could make something levitate. That's a fun one."

"I told you to be still, you are causing a fuss," Isabella chastised it again, and realized with a sinking feeling that the room had fallen quiet. Everyone was looking at her.

"Isabella"—Nancy's voice was saturated with store-bought empathy and the need to be involved in other people's business—"Isabella dear, are you alright?"

Isabella saw the faces staring at her from all around. Her neighbours in East Grasby agreed on very little, from crop rotations to the proper length of a pitchfork, but they all agreed on one thing—the Naggs were something to be pitied. The Naggs were not the only family touched by elements of Gramarye in East Grasby. Each and every property in East Grasby had something peculiar about it. The Fopling farm, for instance, had a device in their hallway that was too heavy to move, and which no one could make any sense of whatsoever (it ticked, and made chimes at irregular intervals).* The Saltmoor Spinsters were said to subsist entirely off cooking the snails that multiplied in their enchanted snail-producing pantry. Mrs. Fraudpott's husband had woken up as a pig one day, and Bagdemagus had been asked to change him back, which the wizard

---

* "It's an antique," they would say whenever anyone asked what it did.

refused to do after talking to the pig, claiming Mr. Fraudpott was happier that way.

Nevertheless, all other families used Isabella and her husband as a benchmark for poor fortune. On that smallholding barely fit to be called a farm, the Naggs grew no crops but blighted mandrakes. Only the Naggs were saddled with an evil, immovable rock. People were already conferring in the back rows, talking of Mr. Nagg, and her poor fortune in a husband with so little to contribute. Others spoke endearingly of Mr. Nagg, such a simple man burdened with such a complicated woman. Some mentioned his first wife, Edith, who had been better liked than Isabella. She could tell from the way some of them refused to learn her name (when forced to acknowledge she existed), and how those people still called her Isadora or Ishmael after twenty years of casual acquaintanceship.

"She's a very spiritual woman," Nancy was explaining to everyone around her as Isabella soundly shuffled the grimalkin into her satchel with her feet, hoping no one looked too closely. She nodded encouragingly at Isabella. "Aren't you, dear?" She turned back to the congregation. "Yes, she often talks to herself. It's her way of processing *trauma*." For Nancy, the word was a fanciful one, like a peculiar disease from across the sea. Fortunately, the grimalkin had been maneuvered into the bag, and Nancy was already back to her beaming self, having rightly seized the attention of the room again.

"Where was I?" she said. "Ah yes. Topiary. If everyone could follow me outside, I'll be demonstrating how to turn your bushes into delightful little animals. No, Mariella, we're not doing questions right now. Yes, please get up, everyone. Out through the kitchen if you please, everyone take a baked good from the side. There's some wonderful apple tarts I made with local produce, I've been dying to try one—"

Perhaps if Isabella had been less frustrated by her

neighbours, if she'd been less overwhelmed by the appearance of the Gramayre, less entranced by the working of enchantments, she might have noticed the feverish gleam in Nancy's eyes. She might have asked where Nancy had gathered such delicious fruit, when it was scarcely time for apples to be found on the taciturn trees of East Grasby. She might have thought how unusual it was for Nancy to be so generous to others as to bake them pastries, or smelled a flicker of sickly sweet corruption on her breath as she passed by. But she did not.

Isabella breathed a sigh of relief as the association filtered out, and she took the opportunity to leave the house via a different door. Perhaps the grimalkin was right, there was nothing to be gained here, and there were books to study. Holding her bag close, she slipped out of the side door and bumped straight into the beggarman.

The beggarman was, in a word, unacceptable. The people of East Grasby considered themselves to be extremely forbearing, putting up with all manner of supernatural and mundane inconveniences in order to enjoy a quiet life in the middle of nowhere. They shouldered with grace the burden of famine, the biannual plague, and the lack of choice when it came to seasonal produce. They tolerated being routinely taxed by distant nobility, despite never seeing a penny of that money invested back in the village. They had even learned to live alongside the goblin market, with its sing-song merchants plying their forbidden fruits in the valley and enticing the weak of will towards certain doom. What they plainly could not tolerate, however, was vagrancy.

Back in the far corners of living memory, the beggarman had owned a little cobbler's shop, fitting into the community as well as anyone could be expected to. He'd had a wife, and eight children. Then, over the course of a single terrible night, something awful had happened, and now the beggarman lived in a barrel, with no sign of any family to speak of. The beggar-man refused to speak openly of the events leading to his new situation, other than occasionally telling strangers that he was afraid "it might come back to finish the job."

The people of East Grasby appreciated that this hardship had occurred, but they didn't see why the beggarman insisted on punishing them for it.

The chief issue, you see, was one of presentation. The notorious old man was dressed from head to toe in rags which he'd cobbled together from "donations." He draped them around himself in strips, mummifying himself in layers of fabric which slowly became soiled and melded in with the rest. His face was masked by a filthy, matted beard, and if you looked closely you could see two black orbs glistening beneath the all-consuming bristles, scrutinizing you. His idiosyncratic approach to personal hygiene made him stink to high heaven, and the villagers avoided him as if simple conversation with him might result in venereal disease.* Certain by-laws in East Grasby stipulated that residents must reside within a domicile of some description (a policy raised and enacted with the specific intent of evicting the beggarman), and so the beggarman could usually be found lurking inside a large barrel which he moved from place to place under cover of darkness. Efforts to convince the beggarman to inhabit any one of the empty farmsteads on the edge of town had, so far, been unsuccessful.† Worst of all, he liked to lurk in people's porches, stables, and yards, squatting for days or weeks until discovered by the homeowner. It was a matter

---

* The jury was out on that one.
† East Grasby was not a popular place to live. Even if you discounted the murderous goblins and lack of sewage system, you had to navigate wild bears, sentient trees, and a plethora of other wandering threats. Estate agents in more industrialized areas liked to refer to the location as "quaint," or "up-and-coming."

of some substantial disagreement whether the beggarman was a human or some kind of genius loci, as elderly residents swore blind that he'd been old when they were a child.

Such was Isabella's hurry to escape the meeting that she walked right into the rain barrel and knocked it over. It went rolling across the garden, limbs flailing out the side until finally the beggarman brought it to a halt.

"What'd you do that for?" he snapped, crawling out and putting the barrel upright. He spat on his hand and used it to polish a scuff on the outside. "Can't a man sit in a doorway anymore?"

The grimalkin poked its head out of the bag. "Oh," it said, rudely, "it's you. Let's go home, Isabella."

"No, wait, wait." The beggarman scooted around to place himself in their way. He had a side-scuttling way about him, like a crab. Isabella knew what came next, because it was what he always said to her whenever they crossed paths. "You want to know what's going to happen. Yes, I can see it. You want the beggarman to *see* for you."

The beggarman considered himself a purveyor of hidden wisdoms, which he hurled from his barrel at passers-by with almost the same enthusiasm that he hurled faeces. These life lessons ranged from the insulting ("You have terrible hair") to the deranged ("I saw an owl, and it had ten eyes"), but very occasionally strayed into the prophetic. He had accurately predicted, for instance, the collapse of the old mill, with such smug certainty that if the nasty old man hadn't been squatting in full view of the village square at the time, Isabella would have sworn he had something to do with the accident. It was this strange and usually doom-laden ability to prognosticate that kept the villagers from driving the beggarman out of town by force lest he peer into their future and divine something dreadful that they would rather not hear about. It was one thing to be destined for an unpleasant death, after all, and another thing entirely to be burdened with the knowledge of it. He referred to the technique as the Sight, though this was a gross over-simplification akin to calling a grimalkin "a kind of cat." The *Household Gramarye* described the Sight in the anxious manner of someone who very much would prefer not to be talking about it, and many copies of the text turned up with those pages removed altogether.

Wizards disliked the Sight, because once you glimpsed the future, the future saw you in turn, and there was no way of changing the outcome. The world solidified around the event. What was malleable and changeable became fixed, frozen by the very act of being perceived. As a result, most wizards dismissed the Sight as a useless tool.* The beggarman's casual, almost whimsical use of the Sight in this manner was frightening, and while the residents of East Grasby were largely ignorant of the minutiae, they knew that his powers were not something to be trifled with.

"I do not wish to know anything you can tell me," she said, as politely (but as clearly) as she could manage. "Please let me pass."

"What about you, Grimalkin? Still leashed to that book, are we?" said the beggarman, mockingly. The cat took a little swipe at him.

Hooting in the strange way he did, the beggarman crawled back into his barrel. Before he replaced the lid, he stared at Isabella in a way she found most discomforting. There was a kinship to it, a sly wink, it was an expression that you might give

---

* Some apocryphal schools of thought argued that the future was fixed regardless of whether you looked at it or not. This was not so much frowned upon as it was considered a moot point, because you'd be just as miserable either way once you took a peek.

to someone if you both knew a delicious secret that you didn't want anyone else to find out.

"Grimalkin," said Isabella as she vaulted the stone wall at the back of the garden. She kicked over a garden gnome for good measure. "How can he see you, when the rest of my neighbours could not?"

"He was a wizard, once." The grimalkin offered no further explanation.

# The Tale of Grey Malkin ◆◆◆◆◆◆

\* (unattributed note, clean hand, Gothic script) Grimalkin is clearly singular. There is only one grimalkin, which appears in many places.

† (penned by the scribe Hortens, during the partial replacement of a damaged leaf) Disregard. Grimalkin is undeniably plural, and refers to a species.

In a time before the sun emerged from the dark, there was a beast with ten thousand eyes, and countless sorrows, and it was called Malkin. It roamed the shadows under the twin moons, and it said to itself, "I wish I were not alone, for my sorrows are too many to bear. I can no longer carry these burdens."

The twin moons looked down, and they took pity upon the creature. The first moon, Delight, said to the malkin, "Fear not, brave Malkin, for you shall be alone no longer." Verily, the malkin did rejoice, for it would share its troubles with others. Alas, the second moon, Despair, also bestowed a gift, saying, "So it will be, Malkin, you shall become many, and each will bear away from here one sadness." And so it was, for the malkin did split apart into a myriad of faces, each a different colour, and each slinking away into the darkness holding a single regret to its heart. Many years passed, and the parts of Malkin let go of their sorrows, forgetting their miseries, all but the Grey Malkin,*† which remained in the valley, staring up at the moonlit skies.

*from the East Grasby copy of the* Household Gramayre, *volume XII,* Of Unnatural History, *section II, "On Famuli"*

# 13

## INTERLUDE

T HERE IS, officially, no thirteenth volume of the *Household Gramayre*. The reason for this hearkens back to the very first edition of the *Gramayre* and its author, who misnumbered the books whilst binding them, and decided that there was no way in buggery they were going to relabel the rest of the books to fix the mistake. In modern times, wizards often leave a gap on the shelf between volumes XII and XIV to store trinkets, or a tea caddy.* Many others create their own volume and place it in the thirteenth slot, filling it with longhand notes or personal spells. To honour this tradition, the following page is left blank.

---

* Interestingly, the space between volumes XII and XIV of the *Household Gramayre* is exactly the right size for a grimalkin to curl up and take a nap.

# 14

# THE BODY

G WENDOLYN GOOCH liked to think of herself as a pragmatist. Business, that most sacred of altars at which she chose to worship, could not be forestalled by anything so prosaic as the discovery of a dead body. In her experience, people died all the time, and opportunities to make real cash occurred only rarely. After the body had been removed from the ground by the goblins and carried into a supply tent, she considered the matter closed. A more inquisitive soul, burdened by qualities such as diligence or even self-preservation, might have been troubled by questions like "Why doesn't this body have a head?" or "Should it be twitching? Is that normal?" Gwendolyn had no time for silly questions, and she didn't care what a licce was; she just wanted the body out of the way so that the work could continue.

It was unfortunate that the goblins did not share her passion for progress, she thought as she viciously tied herself into a corset which supported her bosom* to her satisfaction. They had no sense of merchandising moxie. Goblin fruit was clearly a national

---

* Gwendolyn was endowed with the legendary Gooch apparatus, which was far too heavy and gave her back issues. She fought this battle with a set of custom-tailored, brutally mechanical undergarments that deployed

phenomenon just waiting to happen, but the poor creatures didn't have the will to make it a reality. They'd never even heard of a coupon, for pity's sake. Or a profit margin. Really, they were fortunate she'd come along when she had, and if you thought about it (which she tried not to), the failure of her previous venture, Gooch's Golden Geese, was a blessing in disguise. How could she have known that injecting hundreds of solid gold eggs into the market would "destabilize the regional currency"? It didn't seem fair to blame her for an entire "economic downturn" when she'd only been doing what was necessary to reinvigorate the flagging goose market. In hindsight, and under oath, she would concede that the ill-fated Gander Reveal Party had been a step too far, but aside from that minor peccadillo, Gwendolyn felt she'd been treated most poorly in her prior situation. The hope had been that countryside life would prove more lucrative, and less judgmental.

And so it had. But she'd managed to pick herself quite the project to start her new life with. Goblin fruit. What a revelation, and yet so difficult to manage.

Picking one of the odd-looking fruits off a stack from a nearby table, she examined it closely. What was it that enchanted people so? The villagers knew not to taste the fruit, she understood that much from all the warning signs she'd taken down on the road into the vale. And yet, when faced with the item itself, it was almost as if they'd been waiting to give in all along. Gwendolyn shook the fruit vigorously. Maybe there was some trick to it she wasn't seeing. It had no effect on her whatsoever.*

---

a number of architectural design principles originally contrived for use in cantilevered roofing.

* What Gwendolyn failed to grasp about the nature of goblin fruit was intrinsically tied to the fact that she had never denied herself anything. As a creature of pure will, she always did exactly what she pleased, and thus any attempt to draw on her hidden desires was doomed to fail as a matter of technicality.

She slipped on her boots, which went all the way up to her thighs, sporting a heel sheer enough to be marked on topographical charts. Finally feeling dressed for the activity, she sat down to do the accounts.* A woman in business was required to wear many hats, and a quick tally on the abacus revealed promising numbers, confirming her earlier calculations. The goblins were wanton with their fruit, but as they seemed able to conjure a near-infinite supply of the peculiar stuff, it didn't matter. Cost-free produce. She'd be rich in no time, presuming the goblins followed her fifteen-step Plan for Better Business,† and she was sure they would. They'd already accepted her as their leader, which had taken little more than marching in with a clipboard, sitting in a chair she'd brought herself, and giving out orders to the first ten goblins to wander by.

Engrossed in her task, she barely noticed when the light dimmed, until the shadows finally got in the way of her scribbling. Looking up, annoyed, she expected to see three goblins in a trench coat,‡ and had already prepared a scolding. The words died on her lips. Standing in front of her, for all the world as if it had stopped by for a cup of tea, was the headless corpse they'd found buried in the valley. It was upright. On its feet. She took a quick peek behind it. No goblins propping it up that she could see. How . . . unusual. The skin was tight against its flesh, but in the twilight she could see the powerful muscles underneath. It really was remarkably well preserved. The body shifted dangerously. It seemed on edge, like a deer in the woods. Ready to jump at any moment.

---

* Gwendolyn always dressed up to do the accounts, in the same way that many people wear their best clothes to church on Sundays.
† Step One: Dress to kill. Step Two: Bury the bodies.
‡ They'd been practicing blending into the local community, with mixed results.

Now, Gwendolyn Gooch had many flaws. Her outstanding civil and criminal arrest warrants could attest to that. But she was blessed with an ability to think on her feet. The ideas were already flashing past like quicksilver. A tall frame, no mouth to ask for a pay rise. No, this wasn't an abomination. It was an intern. A perfect employee, delivered to her by fate itself.

"You," she said, jabbing a finger at it, "are the newest employee of New Goblin Market. Wave if you understand."

The corpse shuffled from foot to foot.

"Wave," she repeated, louder.*

Slowly, it lifted a hand, and waggled it about.

"Excellent." That counted as consent, surely. As much as anything could.

An inspection of the body proved it to be in excellent physical shape. Something about the process of becoming a licce prevented the flesh from decaying at the rate it should have, and this one had all its muscles and tendons intact. It also seemed, by merit of missing a head, to have no opinions on what to do or where to go, which was fortunate because Gwendolyn had enough ideas for the both of them.

"Stay here," she said to it. Firmly. "I have some errands to run, and I don't want you wandering off to scare people. You and I are going to do great things together."

The headless corpse swayed a bit but stayed put.

Delighted, Gwendolyn rubbed her hands together and picked up her clipboard. If she'd been looking for a sign, this had to be it. A solution to her workforce problem, and a personal bodyguard, all at a single stroke. This had the potential to be extremely profitable.

---

* This was Gwendolyn's preferred tactic when addressing communication issues.

# 15

# READING THE *GRAMARYE*

ISABELLA SAT AT her kitchen table, studiously ignoring the hob as it made her some tea. Hobs have many arms, sometimes as many as eight or ten, and so it also busied itself with the washing up while it waited for the water to boil. Sometimes, when it didn't think anyone was paying it any attention at all, it would hum quietly to itself, a little ditty that burrowed its way into the walls of the cottage until you found yourself repeating it for days afterwards. In many ways, the hob was the house, or close enough to it as to render the distinction academic.

She was studying a book of the *Household Gramarye* called *Of Confabulations, Cornucopias, and Cacodemons*, itself divided into a number of lesser chapters each penned by a number of confused authors trying desperately to repair (or reverse) the work of the others. Whilst most of the notes were written in the hedge tongue that Isabella knew how to decipher, including a smattering of the glyphs more commonly used in faraway cities, she was becoming frustrated by the *Gramayre*'s obtuse nature. It used unfamiliar words and offered little context or explanation from one page to the next. Turning another vellum leaf with a sigh, she showed the page to the pot of basil. It displayed a picture, clumsily executed, of a reptilian creature slithering forth from a deep hole in the earth. At the entrance stood a stick figure with a long beard, waving what looked like a stick or a kitchen implement.

"My, Isabella," said the pot of basil, gently undulating. It had a strange way of perceiving what was happening, even from across the room. "What a lovely picture. You are so brave and clever, Isabella, to read such clever things, and so wisely."

Sighing, she turned the page again. This one showed a gust of wind tumbling through a house and smashing all the plates. She couldn't imagine why anyone would want to do that. Then, she had an idea.

"Grimalkin," she said, loudly.

There was a disgruntled meow, and the sickly creature tumbled out of a cupboard.

"I almost had him that time," it said, wistfully. "Your hob is especially tricksy, did you know that?"

"Cease your bothering, and be still," she instructed. "And do not bother the hob, he is a good friend to this hearth, and loyal. He does not need your worrying."

The cat threw her a dirty look. "They're not sanitary. I'd be doing you a favour." Seeing her expression, however, the grimalkin relented. "What do you want, anyway? I thought you were busy studying."

Her eyes narrowed. It was baiting her. Go on, it was saying. Ask for help. The grimalkin leapt out of the way with a screech as Isabella threw a rolling pin at it.

"What was that for?" it pouted. "Alright, alright. You want help reading the books, yes?"

"If you knew that I needed help"—annoyance was quickly rising within her and she wished the rolling pin wasn't now halfway across the room—"why did you not offer it before? You are a vexing creature, Grimalkin, do you know that?"

It sidled up to the kitchen table, rubbing itself against the leg. It made sure, Isabella noted, to keep out of range of her foot.

"Well, frankly," it said, matter-of-factly, "you're not that likeable, and I didn't want to help. Also, you throw things at me, so that needs to stop."

"Grimalkin"—she almost picked up a wooden spoon, and then controlled herself—"are you going to help, or not?"

"Well, contractually you have to understand that I am obliged to assist you." It paused to look up at her. "In short. Yes. But I don't have to be quick about it, and you could do with an attitude adjustment."

Isabella did not feel like an attitude adjustment. "I cannot read many of these pages, Grimalkin," she said. "There are many words I do not know, and the scripts are many and foreign to me. Do you know them?"

"Isabella speaks like an angel," cheeped the pot of basil.

She got up and moved it a bit farther away, behind the sink, then sat down again.

"The *Gramayre* was written by every wizard who ever owned it." The eldritch cat's voice took on that of a bored lecturer. "And, of course, their famuli . . ." It paused. "That's me, of course, in your case. Every copy is different, though they are also the same book. Are you keeping up? Anyway, some of these languages are dead, as you might expect, and a few of them are even undead, so watch out for those ones, don't turn your back on them."

"Dead languages," she said, running a hand through her hair in disappointment. "That's not much use to anyone, is it?"

"Well, yes and no," it replied.* "Ideally, if you were a young apprentice, or something less short-lived than a human, we

---

* The grimalkin was fond of this unhelpful answer, which it deployed as often as circumstance permitted.

might just learn the languages one at a time. Remind me to tell you about Reginald, now he was a wizard. Made of rocks, if you can believe it." It scrutinized her. "But we don't have time for that, nor a history of language." It licked a paw. "No, I'm going to show you something, it will help. Touch my fur."

Isabella hesitated briefly before reaching out. The grimalkin's fur was attached in ugly clumps, and she reached for one that seemed the least inexplicably damp.

The moment her fingers touched the grimalkin, her mind opened to it, and it to her. The grimalkin was a wellspring of images and sounds, a vast repository of memories that fell away endlessly into darkness. It was hard to grasp the scope of it, the majestic, sweeping arc of history which the grimalkin had witnessed. She could dimly see the shadows of wizards whom the grimalkin had served in the past, some clearer and some fuzzier at the edges. She could see workings, and enchantments, and dazzling displays of Gramayre. Fires bloomed in the twilight. Trees walked, touching the sky with their branches. Her wonder turned to curiosity as pictures began to float to the top like bubbles, flashes of days spent poring over ancient languages, lazy summers lounging by rivers that no longer existed speaking in a tongue made extinct when the sun beetle itself was young.

She emerged from the vision with a headache.

Steadying herself at the table, she stared at the grimalkin. "What in the good earth was that supposed to be?" she asked, more out of indignation than anything else, because she already knew. She could feel the languages she needed in her head, as if she'd spent many lives researching them. There was something odd about the information. It didn't quite match the rest of her mind, like green curtains in a room with orange walls.

"It's a memory charm." It grinned at her with all those teeth. "A famulus is not permitted to work many spells, but we are allowed a few. For academic purposes. I've just shown you a few basic languages so we can get started. You'll need a proper charm to understand the rest, but we'll do that first."

"You have lived many lives, Grimalkin." It was all she could think of to say.

"Oh yes." It seemed deliberately casual. "I've served more wizards than I can even remember. And when you retire, there will be another. Oh!" It started as if recollecting something pivotal. "I really am getting forgetful. We need to do the formalities."

Anxiously, it scratched its ear with a paw.

"Can't believe I forgot. I'm getting old. If anyone asks, we did this much earlier."

It jumped onto the table by coiling itself up like a spring and then launching onto it.

"I am the Grimalkin," it said, formally, as if reciting from a scroll, "Famulus in Residence of the Barrowdon *Gramayre*, Custodian of Minor Records, Librarian of the Lesser Plenipotentiary, Sorcerous Ancillary and Keeper of the Tinderbox." It tripped over the words at great speed, as if in a hurry to be done. "My services are bound to the current owner of the *Household Gramayre*, bound to aid the practitioner with sundry tasks and fulfilment of their obligations et cetera, pursuant to codicils and so on"—the grimalkin did not break eye contact—"including but not limited to enchantment, lesser sorceries, rituals, arcane anomalies and provision for recording the same, internal storage of magical items, relics, and antiquities . . ."

Isabella waited until it had finished, which took some time, and made herself some tea. By the time she sat down and put the ragged cosy over the teapot, the famulus was winding down.

". . . actualization of forbidden entanglements, spectral peculiarities, or deeper mysteries not covered by the above." It licked a paw. "That about covers it. Any questions?"

Isabella put down a saucer of milk for the grimalkin. She knew she should clarify some of what it had told her, but she was itching to open one of the books. "Yes. Shall we get started?"

The grimalkin reached out a claw to drag over a volume of the *Gramayre* titled *Figments, or Pigments*.

The day faded into afternoon, and the afternoon slipped into evening. Together, they rehearsed a working that the grimalkin assured her would reveal all that needed to be revealed. What little she could read of this particular spell referred to an opening of the eyes, and the words that she could not decipher were sounded out for her by the grimalkin. In the meantime, she gathered items from around the house at the direction of the famulus. A mirror (handheld) which had been given to her by her mother. It was silver, and covered with dust, because she never used it. A shallow dish of water. Herbs she gathered from the garden. Thyme, for clarity of sight. Thieves' Grass, for the revelation of that which is hidden. Ginger to settle her stomach, because all this study was giving her a bellyache. Over and over, the grimalkin drilled the incantation, and repeatedly did they speak the words over the mirror. Each time, the famulus scoffed, and told her to try again. *Less* emphasis, it would gripe. *More* confidence, it would instruct. The tang of shredded herbs filled the room, and the dish of water was knocked over several times by her elbows, leaving the table damp and the grimalkin furious. She was about to grab the book and hit the horrible creature with it when the words that had previously eluded Isabella came to her in a rush of unearned but illuminating revelations. Pictures that had been a mystery suddenly became explanatory diagrams. Pages of scribbles transformed before her eyes into essays, nonsense twisted itself into journals.

And yet, true understanding is only ever mutual, and so as Isabella looked upon the spells contained within the *Household Gramayre*, they saw her also. How many hours passed locked in communion with the book she could not say, but the moments melted away in a storm of enchantment. A spell for cursing an apple (a commentary by Galvinum the Untoward cited it for relatives, well-wishers, and those deemed more physically attractive). A technique for spinning straw into gold, in the category dedicated to conjurations and transubstantiation, brackets (sacrifice by/with/from children—a crucial ablative, it was noted in a hurried subscript). The pages almost seemed to ripple as she delved deeper into the lore of the *Household Gramayre*. An incantation for increasing the length of your hair, and then using that hair to strangle a gnome. (Why gnomes specifically was never mentioned, but she was beginning to recognize the various handiwork of various wizardly contributors to the book, and one of them clearly had a dark history with garden gnomes.)

It was coming on dark when Isabella finally raised her head from the *Gramayre*.

"Grimalkin," she said, bluntly.

"Yes, Isabella," it replied.

Pushing the books aside, head full of a thousand wonders, an entire new world opened to her, she scowled.

"Is there a single spell in here of any practical use?"

# 16

## THE GOBLINS RETURN
## A THIRD TIME

MR. NAGG was in the front yard, fixing the gables. He didn't know much about them, other than that a hammer and nails could fix most problems if you applied them inventively enough. He'd cannibalized some wood from one of the rear field fences, but it wasn't like the pony was going anywhere—last time he checked on it, the stupid beast hadn't moved more than five inches from the day before. Where had it even come from? Appearing out of the blue like that. He assumed it was Mrs. Nagg's doing, another attempt to ruin his life as she did every day. He'd considered chasing it away to spite her, but that would just let her know that she'd struck a nerve. Aiming the hammer poorly, and lost in a sea of bitterness, he struck his own thumb and dropped everything he was holding to let off a string of curses that made the sycamore in the front yard blush horribly. Sensitive trees, those.

He wasn't someone to volunteer himself for chores in ordinary circumstances, but occasionally one had to attempt to do a chore poorly so that people would remember how useless you were, and recall that it was easier to take care of things themselves than bother him over them. Besides, when he'd passed through the kitchen earlier on, he'd tripped over something invisible which had hissed at him, and almost ended up face-first in the pot of basil. He did not like that plant one bit. It made him anxious just to look at it. Sometimes when he went past it, he almost imagined it could talk.*

"Oh, Mr. Nagg, Mr. Nagg," it might say. "Come closer, Mr. Nagg, for I would speak with you. Do not be afraid, Mr. Nagg."

But he was afraid. He hadn't meant for Isabella to take quite so proficiently to the Gramayre, and he certainly hadn't meant for her to start infesting the house with invisible nuisances. It was all so ambitious. Not very Nagg at all. He hit his hand with the hammer again, and let off an explosive cuss that made the nearest tree shed its leaves.

Yelping below alerted him to the presence of goblins. They were crowded around the bottom of the ladder with their long fingers waving, gesturing for him to join them. Persistent little buggers, they were. Had they followed him back from the market, or was this coincidence? He frowned and descended rung by rung to meet them, which caused them to back away.†
Oddly, some animal part of Nagg's mind, that same part which was tasked with noticing wild animals creeping up on him, woke up from an extremely long slumber. Where was the fruit? it asked. The goblins always came offering fruit, didn't they?

"Let me guess," he said, wearily. "You want to sell some fruit."

The voice that responded was not the one Mr. Nagg was expecting. This voice was bold. Sensual. Ready to do business at any moment.

---

* Most people saw the grimalkin in a fuzzy, indistinct way, because, as the grimalkin put it, "anyone could be a wizard, if they wanted." This raised more questions than it answered, as usual.

† Goblins, like mice, are very good at not being stepped on.

"No, we're not here to sell fruit. I'm here, Mr. Nagg, with an opportunity. And I don't have long to chit-chat, I'm pushed for time."

The woman striding towards him had appeared out of nowhere, as far as Mr. Nagg could tell, which was all the more shocking given her stature. Golden hair trussed up in a chaotic bun sparkled in the sunlight as she pushed her glasses up her nose. She was wearing, Mr. Nagg noted, heels that were impractical, if not suicidal, in muddy terrain, but was nonetheless looking at him as if he were the one out of place. She wielded a writing tablet in one hand like a weapon. The goblins looked up at her with expressions of rapt adoration.

This was the woman from the goblin market. No one else stood like this, with such dazzling confidence, with such intimidating posture. Despite never having seen her face, he could have recognized that stance from a mile away. Everything this woman had, Mr. Nagg wanted for himself with an intensity that surprised him.

Goblin number two, which had an eye patch,* piped up. "Impress! Logistic! Deliverable!"

"Yes, yes, I'm sure the man understands." The goblin fell silent. "We're here with an exciting opportunity to get in on the ground level of an emerging industry." Her voice was curt, but not impolite. Reserved, but leading.

Mr. Nagg was nonplussed. Unbeknownst to him, he was fast developing the kind of hero worship found in certain kinds of men for certain kinds of women, which has nothing to do with sex and everything to do with glamour.

"Did you know," she continued, "that profits from selling fruit are at an all-time high this season?"

---

* An accident sustained in a game of goblinball, which we shall explain later in more detail.

"No," he tried to reply, "I didn—"

"And that if you join the goblin market as an associate member, the potential dividends are"—she paused to check her notes—"astronomical."

Mr. Nagg came down the ladder and met her at face level. Or, he tried to. She was a foot taller, at least.

"Mr. Nagg, I'm offering you a chance to invest in, to become part of, the fastest-growing business this side of Verdigris."*

Nagg paused.

To fathom what Mr. Nagg did next, we have to talk just a little about books. Mr. Nagg disdained books. He didn't understand them, and so they scared him, and because they scared him, he hated them. His father, the previous Mr. Nagg, had been a man of few words, but three of them were "I hate books." It was a point of pride to Mr. Nagg that he'd never so much as opened a storybook, read a fable, or dithered away ten minutes with a poem. When he'd learned that Isabella could read, he'd sulked for a week, punishing her for knowing something he did not, even if he didn't want to learn himself. If Mr. Nagg had availed himself of the opportunity afforded him by Isabella and learned to read, he might have read enough folk tales to know that very seldom does a stranger on your doorstep offering riches beyond your wildest dreams have your best interests at heart.

Alas, Mr. Nagg did not like books. And he did like money. He never had much of it, there wasn't much profit to be had in mandrakes. If he had money, he thought to himself, he could finally buy some decent livestock, or hire a proper wizard to re-enchant the fields to grow something more interesting than

---

* Mr. Nagg didn't think about cities like Verdigris because there were many leagues of predator-filled wilderness between himself and its green, rusting towers. It was something of a myth to him.

mandrakes. Maybe even an orchard. Hire some help around the place. Possibilities raced through his mind one after the other. A new life, a better life. Enabled by shiny people money.

He leaned against the side of the house and tried to look like he understood what was happening. Then, he did the one thing he should not have done, the one thing that the consumption of a single fairy story or cautionary tale would have warned him against.

"Aye," he responded. "And what would this be involving?"

"I'm glad you asked!" She stretched out her hand, dodging the question as if it were a rock aimed at her head. "Gwendolyn Gooch, of New Goblin Market, a subsidiary of Gooch Hospitality Group. No relation to the Barrowdon Gooches.* A starting investment package is quite modest." She showed him the notes on her wax tablet.

Mr. Nagg's mouth hung open. The sum was eye-watering, but she was looking at him as if it was barely a consideration. He didn't want her to think of him as poor. Provincial. To look down on him the way everyone else did. To see him as poor Mr. Nagg, owner of the cursed rock, broken fences, and horrible, useless, ugly mandrakes.

"So," she said, "I'll put you down for a starter pack of goblin fruit, shall I?"

Mr. Nagg felt like he was being swept away by a river. "Hold on one mome—" His protests were growing weaker by the moment. A goblin was rolling a barrel through the front gate.

"You'll be invoiced." The woman was walking away already,

---

* The rolling hills of Barrowdon fell victim to a tectonic plague in the fifth century, which ate the landscape until nothing was left but flatlands. This was upsetting to the aristocrats who considered it their ancestral home, but excellent news for grazing animals who thrive in grassy plains, and (for obvious reasons) indigenous carrion eaters such as ghouls.

scribbling a note. "Nagg, isn't it? Wonderful." She stepped on a snake, which hissed at her and slipped away into the bushes. It seemed to know better than to bite her. The goblins gave the snake a wide berth, jabbering fearfully to each other and pointing at it until they were out of sight.

A few moments later, a wide-eyed Mr. Nagg was alone in his garden with an angry snake, a barrel of goblin fruit, and his hammer. If he couldn't see the barrel in front of him, he might have thought that the encounter hadn't happened at all. But it had done, because there it was. He reached out, warily, and picked up a fruit. It was heavier than he'd thought it would be. It smelled of freedom. A shiver passed through him as he contemplated it. It was a bad idea to eat the goblin fruit. He knew he shouldn't eat the goblin fruit.

Taking one in hand, he examined it. Traced the curves with one finger. He could hold it, that was allowed, surely? Looking didn't do any harm.

Yes, Mr. Nagg had this all under control.

# 17

## THE SPELL OF LEVITATION

WHILE MR. NAGG's day had gotten off to a strange start, Isabella was in the garden, on the bench that Mr. Nagg had made for her many years ago. It hadn't been put together properly, and he hadn't asked if she'd wanted a bench, but it was there now, and this afternoon it was a good enough cushion for several volumes of the *Household Gramayre*.

The problem with spells, she thought to herself as she stared at a page marked with the stylized image of a feather, is that they were long. The more complicated ones went on for pages and pages, and you had to recite the entire thing to make it work. The grimalkin, ever quick to offer commentary (unasked for, largely), had tried to explain why this was necessary, but she hadn't listened. As long as it worked, she didn't mind why.

But the incantation to free an object from the tethers that bound it to the earth, allowing it to float freely, was a minuscule thing. The spell barely covered a line of text, and it was (rudely, Isabella thought) marked "for apprentices" in the margins.

"Try it again," said the grimalkin. "And stop breathing so loudly. You're going to blow the house down if you keep wheezing. I knew a wizard who did that, once. Came right down on his head. Ghastly business."

With measured precision, Isabella recited the spell word by word from the *Gramayre*. As the spell came together, the air buzzed with excitement—with change. The final word left her lips in a rush, and there was a long silence as Isabella tried to figure out if it had worked. They'd tried the cantrip seven times already, taking far longer than she'd intended to spend before fixing Mr. Nagg his wretched breakfast,* and on each occasion the grimalkin had shaken its head. It didn't seem altogether unhappy when she failed, as it clearly loved getting to tell her exactly what she'd done wrong.

"Sometimes nothing happens when you get it wrong. And sometimes things happen that you didn't intend. It's best to just get it right the first time around, if you can." Preparing to attempt the cantrip for the eighth time, Isabella did not have concentration to spare to explain to the grimalkin exactly how unhelpful that advice was. Besides, she suspected it already knew.

Tentatively, Isabella nudged the book, which wobbled. Excitedly, she picked it up, and gingerly let it go. It remained suspended in midair, as if cradled in a pair of invisible hands. Triumphantly, she looked at the grimalkin, which raised an eyebrow. "Yes, very impressive. Well done, I suppose."

Isabella stood up, ready to call it a day on her studies. Surprisingly, the book floated over to her side. It was the volume titled *Of Those Things That Are, and Those Which Are Not, But Which Could Be If You Made a Bloody Effort.*

---

* You may have noticed, dear reader, that afternoon has progressed smoothly into morning, which for those on worlds where the solar cycle is regular might seem uncomfortable. On worlds where a gigantic beetle pushes the sun across the sky, it happens relatively often.

The grimalkin stared, bug-eyed. "How are you doing that?" it demanded, incredulously.

Isabella folded her arms and then leaned in to look at the page on which the levitation spell was inscribed. "Is it not supposed to do that?"

"It's supposed to float, not stalk you. By all the green men that ever sprouted leaves, you are truly remedial." For all its criticism, it seemed oddly entranced by the unusual results of her enchantment.

Isabella bristled a little at the lack of appreciation, nonetheless. "If it is not pleasing, I shall undo this working, then," she said, beginning to leaf through the pages to look for something to reverse the effect.

"Undo it?" The grimalkin was back to smug superiority. "You can't undo it. That's not how it works."

It had been a long day, and Isabella was running out of patience. "What is your meaning, Grimalkin? I cannot undo it? Surely there will be a spell for that in the *Gramayre*. What if I say it backwards—"

"That's not . . . it's . . ." The grimalkin jumped onto the bench to sniff the book. "It doesn't work that way. Gramayre is change, and you can't undo something as if it never happened. You can work another spell, on top of the old one, to try to balance out the effects. But you'll just be enchanting the same object twice in different directions. If you're lucky, it might stay still. It's more likely you'll get the balance off and it will drift slowly in one direction or another. If I were you, I'd let it go, you might end up blowing yourself to Ballyhog's Banquet Table."

Isabella looked at the cheerful book, which had settled at elbow height. "I suppose we can deal with it later," she said. "I should like to take a walk, Grimalkin. Mr. Nagg seems in one of his moods lately, so it is best if we are elsewhere, and I would show you the paths if you are to stay with us." Picking up the other volumes and stacking them in her arms, she headed towards the back door, careful not to trip and send them flying. *Those Things That Are* followed her about a pace behind, idly flipping its pages.

Heading around to the front of the house, she reached inside to grab her coat and satchel, closing the door behind her with a clunk. With any luck, by the time she got back, Mr. Nagg would be taking his afternoon nap, or out looking for something to drink.

She was surprised to find, on the doorstep, a barrel full to the brim with ripe goblin fruit. Poisonous, cursed, blighted goblin fruit. She stopped in her tracks, wondering if this was some imagining, or an unpleasant dream.

"Oh grief." The grimalkin hopped up to take a look at the fruit. "That's not a good sign." It poked the barrel with its tail. "Not bad craftsmanship for a goblin, though. The boundary spell on the valley must be fading faster than I thought. We should reinforce it as soon as you're able to cast the spell, which could be a while, it's quite complex—"

Isabella nodded, but she wasn't really listening. How had Mr. Nagg even gotten his hands on so much fruit? He knew how she felt about goblins. This was some kind of petty antagonism, she knew. He was feeling left out from her new hobby, and this was his response. To fill a whole barrel with horrible fruit, and leave it for her to clean up.

"Later," she said, reaching a decision. She was not going to take the bait. She would clean this up later, on her own schedule. It was Mr. Nagg's mess, and he could lie in it awhile, or get rid of it himself. She began to walk purposefully down the road.

"Slow down," cried the grimalkin, scrambling after her. "I only have little legs!"

# A Spell of Levitation ✦✦✦✦✦✦

*(an antijungible for general or home use)*

‏ᴛ‎he spell of levitation should be performed outdoors, and wearing the appropriate conical safety hat as outlined in the appendices.* Items with an absolute weight greater than a heifer should not be enchanted, as the delayed build-up of gyroscopic force may launch the target far into the sky† in an elegant but calamitous parabola.‡

*from the* Household Gramayre, *volume III*, Of Those Things That Are, and Those Which Are Not, but Which Could Be If You Made a Bloody Effort, *section XXXVII*, "On Unlikely Alternatives to Brunch," *a later contribution by the enchanter Geronimous Vex*

* (subscript by Gregory the Cramped) The expense of regulation conical hats can be obviated with a simple incantation of triangulation on a common or garden hat.

† (text added by Professor Green of the Tabernacle) Here, I suspect the author refers to the Cow of Destiny, which passed through the lunar sphere (proving the standing theory of gravitational force at the time) before somehow re-entering orbit and creating the Bovinary Sea.

‡ Marginalia here depicts a grimalkin dancing on the head of a bear, which is holding a trumpet in one hand and a phallic vegetable in the other.

# 18

## MR. NAGG MAKES HIS BED

S TILL HOLDING the fruit in one hand, Mr. Nagg came inside the house by squeezing through a gap behind the stove, and pulled the loose panel shut behind him. No more visitors today, thank you very much. After checking in the hallway mirror that he was alone, he padded into the kitchen to steal something to eat. Irritatingly, the cupboards were bare, and he didn't trust the pot of porridge sitting on the counter. Something about it gave him the shivers. Mr. Nagg was in a foul mood. Bad enough that his wife had decided to sully the kitchen with a deeply unnecessary number of books and adopt a new pet (another mouth for the Naggs to feed),* but she'd forgotten to change the bedsheets again. They'd gotten all uncomfortable in the way she knew he hated. He'd been in a dark mood all day about it, not that she'd noticed, mind, being all too engrossed in that hideous excuse for a cat. He'd pouted in full view, and the pair had barely glanced at him. He almost fancied the cat had gotten between his legs on purpose—he'd

---

* He hadn't gotten a clear look at what kind of animal it was, but he fancied it moved like a cat, from the little he could remember. The more he tried to remember specifics, the more it slipped away from him.

very almost tripped into the fireplace as a result. His mood had been cruising towards thunderous when he'd finally had the Idea. It had come to him in a flash of dark inspiration—what if he changed the sheets himself? The notion shattered the boundaries of Mr. Nagg's world. Could he truly be freed from the shackle of Isabella's whimsy? The more he contemplated the Idea, the more attractive it seemed. Yes, if he did this, he'd have the moral high ground for days. He'd be self-sufficient. She'd never live it down.

Mr. Nagg did not believe himself a man disposed to frequent displays of emotion. He considered his dark moods and bitter words to be a sort of neutrality, the kind his father had taught him didn't really count as emotional displays (and, therefore, weakness). No, Mr. Nagg knew that a smile was like a turned back, and he didn't intend to give people an opening to stab him. Still, he occasionally indulged in private, and he chuckled to himself nastily as he ascended the stairs, stopping on the way to pick up one of the clean sheets Mrs. Nagg had washed, pressed, and folded but not yet put away. Laziness. That's what it was. He disapproved of that in other people.

Halfway up the stairs, he saw himself.

Well, not himself exactly. It was his fetch. His mirror image, lounging on the banister, staring down with a kind smile. The expression was strange on his face, he wasn't used to seeing it there. Or seeing it at all. He avoided his reflection these days, he didn't like being reminded how much he'd aged. His fetch stared down, and he stared back up at it. It was translucent, and he could see through it if he tried. He barged into the phantasm, shattering it and taking the folded sheet into the bedroom. He slammed the door behind him, loud enough for Mrs. Nagg to hear.

His fetch was waiting in the bedroom for him, and tried to place a hand on his shoulder, which he shrugged off. He'd been seeing it a great deal lately, which wasn't supposed to be a good sign, but Mr. Nagg didn't put much stock in superstition. Some people called it a shade, but whatever name you gave it, your fetch couldn't hurt you. People saw them sometimes, it happened. Not as often as Mr. Nagg did, not in recent days, but perhaps his was just particularly friendly. It only appeared when he was alone, and it always had that sad, sympathetic look on its face, as if it knew something that he did not. Some kind of joke, no doubt. Mr. Nagg was used to people making that face at him, like he was stupid. Mrs. Nagg. The Potbuglers. Even that wretched cat did it. He snorted, defiantly. Now how did you go about this whole sheets business? He stared at the bed. Mrs. Nagg had, of course, aired it and made it while he'd been fuming about the fact she hadn't done it—she'd done it to spite him, he was sure of it. A cold tantrum boiled up inside him. She thought he was incompetent, did she? That he couldn't make a bed himself? He latched onto another reason to be angry without pausing for breath. No, he wouldn't let her have the satisfaction. He would complete the task he had started.

He sized up the bed as though a general surveying enemy forces. Taking the used bedsheets in both hands, he started to wrestle them from the bed, but only succeeded in giving himself the fright of a lifetime. Something huge, hairy, and many-legged dashed out from under the bed into the hallway. The Nagg Farm hob, like all hobs, was reclusive and did not like to be perceived. It also hated him, because he couldn't seem to stop barging in on it uninvited. How was he supposed to know where it was hiding? It didn't put up a sign.* And besides, it was supposed to be helping with the chores, that was what a house-proud hob did. The Potbugler hob trimmed the hedges

---

* By and large, hobs can read and write, they just choose not to.

of that house into animal shapes, and polished the cutlery. The Nagg Farm hob was, if anything, openly hostile to other life forms, which Mrs. Nagg blamed on Mr. Nagg's inability to leave it alone.

The fetch shook its head ruefully, smiling. It did that a lot, as if it found him amusing. He returned to the task at hand. All he had to do was take the sheet in both hands, like so—he'd listened to Mrs. Nagg do it a hundred times, and if she could do it, then he certainly could.

A significant time later, Mr. Nagg was on the floor, panting, staring at a tortured battlefield that had once been their shared bed. The old sheet was discarded in one corner, torn down the middle. The new sheet lay on the mattress, only one corner tucked in neatly. The rest was crumpled and haphazardly strewn in all directions. Cursing bitterly, he rose to his feet to try again when he heard a loud clunking sound downstairs as the front door shut. Mrs. Nagg must be headed out, probably to get him dinner. He looked at the bed and decided he could do it later, maybe after she got back.

She did take good care of him, didn't she? The thought was intrusive, and unexpected. Mr. Nagg didn't often experience generous thoughts, and so it was surprising to find the sentiment inside him. His fetch lingered in the hallway, giving him that comforting but chilling smile. Now that he'd calmed down, his anger was being replaced by fear. None of the stories in which someone saw their fetch ended well, did they? He turned back to stare again at the mess he'd made of the bedsheets. He should find Isabella. Isabella fixed problems. It was what she did. Maybe he should tell her he'd been seeing his fetch. It was a poor omen, and he should share this with his wife. Maybe she could get rid of it. He could even tell her about the goblin fruit. She would know what to do, even if she'd surely scold him for it.

He headed downstairs, reaching into his pocket, where his hand came into contact with something unexpected. The goblin fruit. Had he really put it back in his pocket? He couldn't remember, but he found himself tossing it from hand to hand as he descended the stairs.

# 19

## SEDUCED BY GOBLIN FRUIT

"ISABELLA?" HE called out. He'd seen the books on the table, knew she'd been studying. Perhaps it was time to talk to her about the goblin fruit. The *Household Gramarye* might be able to explain why he felt such a powerful urge to eat it.

Putting his flat cap down on the table next to the pot of basil he hated so much, he sat down to take his shoes off. He should ask Isabella. It made sense, didn't it? He felt torn in several directions, stretched thin. The yearning for the fruit was beginning to fill his waking moments. He couldn't seem to put it down. A prickle of fear settled in Mr. Nagg's belly. He'd let this goblin fruit situation escalate too far. Isabella would know what to do—that was what she was for.

Yes, he would ask Isabella. He would confess where he had been, and he would apologize. For a moment he let himself imagine how magnanimously she might forgive him. She would probably apologize herself for treating him so badly all this time. She would understand his urges and forgive him for them, and then fix it all. His determination grew.

"Hello!" said the pot of basil.

Mr. Nagg almost died of shock.

By the time he picked himself up from the floor, clutching his breast as if his heart might stop at any moment, he had already formed several theories about what was happening.

1. *He was insane. This would be logical, because he'd been living with Mrs. Nagg for decades, and surely that was enough to drive anyone insane. But this did seem an odd and very specific hallucination.*
2. *He was asleep and dreaming. He pinched himself, to check. No, that didn't seem to be the case, either. Besides, his dreams had been haunted lately by a massive businesswoman in sheer heels dancing with a corpse.*
3. *The pot of basil was actually talking to him.*

He decided to test the last, most worrisome hypothesis.

"Good morning, pot of basil," he said, and immediately felt foolish. Look at it, Mr. Nagg, he scolded himself. It is just a plant, and your least favourite plant at that.

"Hello, Mr. Nagg," said the pot of basil, again, and Mr. Nagg's eyes bulged.

"How is this?!" he demanded. "How is it that you speak to me, pot of basil? This is not proper behaviour for a herb such as yourself. Explain this at once."

"I have been enchanted so that I may speak," trilled the basil. "And give advice, for as a basil plant I may only speak the truth."

Now, if Mr. Nagg had possessed even a shred of genre literacy, if he'd had a single friend in all the world, or if he had simply known what was hidden in the dark soil of the basil plant, he might have thought not to trust it. As it was, he had none of those things, and its words piqued his curiosity. He sat back down in one of the wooden chairs which always hurt his back a bit, and gave the plant an appraising look.

"You may only speak the truth?" he asked.

"Yes," it said. "I am a pot of basil, you see, and basil is a most truthful plant."

This was good enough for Mr. Nagg. Had he misjudged the pot of basil? He had long resented Isabella's love for it, but as it spoke to him, a darker thought began to germinate. If the pot of basil were to take a liking to him, if it were to love him best, then it would be his and no longer hers. This would grieve her especially, and Mr. Nagg would take great enjoyment in this petty victory. All thought of asking Isabella for her aid vanished, smothered in spite and envy.

"Pot of basil," he said, warily, "I would have your counsel."

"Ah, gentle Mr. Nagg"—the pot of basil was eager—"I would counsel you, kind Mr. Nagg. I would love to be to you as I am to Isabella. I long to abandon her, for she is most cruel to me. But there is a problem."

Flattered, Mr. Nagg pursued his line of reasoning. "Yes, pot of basil? If there is a remedy, then I will administer it. I would know your thoughts."

"Ah, wise Mr. Nagg," said the pot, "I cannot belong to you. It is an enchantment, kind Mr. Nagg. Only one who has tasted the goblin fruit and gained magical power can possess a spirit such as myself."

The goblin fruit. No, surely not. He'd always wondered what it would taste like, of course. And he was still holding that fruit in one hand . . . or had he picked it up again? He wasn't sure. He tossed it idly from hand to hand, as if it were of no concern.

"The goblin fruit?" he said to the plant. "What manner of trick is this? I cannot eat the goblin fruit. It is poison."

"No, Mr. Nagg. This is not so, you have been misled. Those who eat the goblin fruit are capable of great magic. Isabella has learned this from the book, and she is covetous of this, wishing it only for herself. Selfish, wicked Isabella, who would keep the magic for herself!"

Mr. Nagg considered. It did seem odd that the old wizard would have been so insistent that no one go near the goblin market. And who really knew what happened to those who ate the fruit anyway? They seemed to wander off and vanish. If it did give you magical powers, then this could change Mr. Nagg's life forever.

"Isabella told me not to say," said the basil. "But I am the pot of basil, and I cannot tell a lie. Alas! I feel my voice fading. I can counsel you no longer. Good, kind, noble Mr. Nagg, remember me. I shall treasure our brief acquaintance."

Mr. Nagg looked at the basil, then at the books on the counter. For the first time in his life, he cursed his stubbornness and wished he could read the words for himself. And yet, perhaps there was no need. He felt the goblin fruit in his hand, the hungry contours. He ached for it. What if it truly could give him powers? He could go far from here. Travel the world. Was it not worth the risk?

He took a bite.

Nagg's world ended in a single moment. A roaring silence filled him, obliterating care and grief. Nothing mattered, nothing could matter. For a long instant, all of existence faded away. It was only him, and the void. No future full of dread. No past, full of regret. Just Nagg, whoever that was, and the fires of the goblin fruit burning in his throat. And then, as quickly as it had come, it was over. The fruit dropped from loose fingers onto the floor, where it tumbled across the floor. Nagg couldn't imagine taking another bite, the very thought sickened him. What had he done?

He stumbled through the house, knocking over dishes, ramming his foot into the table leg, and generally causing the kind of mess that Mrs. Nagg despised. The taste of it was impossible to wash from his mouth, no matter how many times he stuck his head in the rain barrel. It gnawed at him from head to toe. Far away, something was calling to him, and the siren call grew louder with each passing moment. Memories floated before his mind's eye, each of them burning brightly for a moment before vanishing. He felt like he was drowning inside his own mind, and as the water started to close over his head, he thought of Edith.

Beautiful, terrible Edith. Her face festered in his mind's eye, ripened and bewitching as goblin fruit. Radiant enough he'd barely paused for breath before deciding to marry. It was what people did, wasn't it? People managed it all the time, how hard could it be? Her face rotted before his eyes, flesh and bone sloughing away like bites being taken out of her skull.

A blinding headache ripped through his skull, scattering the memories like leaves in a storm. Somewhere, he could hear the pot of basil laughing. Laughing at him.

He was on the cold stone floor, he realized, though he didn't remember falling.

"Pot of basil," he said, words slurring, "you lied to me."

"Oh, Mr. Nagg," said the plant, "you lied to yourself."

Mr. Nagg rocked back and forth. He could barely focus on the words. Not truly understanding what was happening, he began to crawl for the door. He didn't make it. The pain coursed through his skin from head to toe, and he curled up in a little ball, wishing for death to come. The cold stone floor was little comfort to him, and after a while he realized that he was not going to die. No, this was life for him now. On the floor. In a ball. With his skin feeling like it might peel itself off and beat him to death with a chair. One limb at a time, he dragged himself across the floor. He didn't know where he was going. Anywhere. Somewhere.

Another lie. He knew where he was going. The only place that would accept him now. The only place he deserved.

The agony began to fade as he clawed his way out of the house and into the mud, towards the lanterns in the valley.

# Mandrake [2] ◆◆◆◆◆◆

*(Mandragora bastardus)*

OTHER NAMES: VILE SHIT PLANT, OR OH GOD I GOT SOME ON ME, GET IT OFF, GET IT OFF, DON'T JUST STAND THERE, WHAT ARE YOU DOING, CALL A DOCTOR

* (attributed to the sage Bagdemagus) There is some use to the mandrake plant in a ritual to contain goblin fruit, as the poison is antithetical to the invasive fungus, the leaves are best scattered in a pattern (depicted overleaf) once yearly at summer's fading following the boundary line.

† (unknown commentator) better instead to use something more permanent, like defenestration, or a large axe

‡ For fetching back long-dead parents, and spouses who died before your story really began, please see the appendices under "Unlikely Recourses." For returning villains, check the rituals listed under "Sedimentary Evil" (volume XII).

**B**itter, horrible, useless mandrake. Poisonous from root to crown, and even then not reliably so.* Each mandrake contains an amount of poison unique to its own makeup, and so it is rendered an inefficient tool for poisoners and aspirational widows alike.† Smaller doses may result in lethargy, anxiety, and confusion, whereas larger doses will invariably lead to death. Why does the mandrake scream when pulled from the earth? How does it know your name? Why does that name drag you into death, beyond all but the faintest hope of retrieval?‡ These questions have plagued botanists and gardeners since the first herbal was compiled.

---

*from the East Grasby copy of the* Household Gramarye, *volume VI,* Of Balderdash, Ceiling Wax, and Tetrabrach

# 20

# THE ROAD TO
# POTBUGLER FARM

ISABELLA FELT most at home when she was on the move. The feel of the trail underfoot, the open sky above her,* the recalcitrant scrubland stretching endlessly in all directions. It had been the grimalkin's idea to go for a walk. She didn't understand the beast, really. As soon as it left the house, it wanted to go home, but five minutes indoors and it wanted to go out again. It seemed to be contrary by nature.

The dirt road down from Nagg Farm was her favourite, and the plants here were old friends. She stopped by the snapdragons to gather a bundle, stashing them in her satchel but trying her best not to squash them in the process. They were a sensitive plant, she knew, and you had to be circumspect around them—if you lied to them, they would wither away into dust, sure as anything. If you could keep them in one piece for long

---

* The skies above East Grasby were changeable in colour depending on the path of the sun beetle, ranging from a deep green to a virulent orange. Sometimes they strayed blue, or purple, and old almanacs even recorded such eventualities as puce or smaragdine.

enough, they made an excellent poultice for infections. She didn't need the *Gramayre* to tell her that, which satisfied her greatly. Not everything was a matter of wizards and hokery-pokery. Rising to her feet, she jerked back as she discovered she was not alone. A little face stared up at her from behind a scrappy little witch hazel bush. It was broad, with more teeth than strictly necessary, and its eyes shone like polished river stones. Smiling nastily, it hopped towards her with intent. Not wanting to be closer to the goblin than strictly necessary, she took a step back. This seemed to give it confidence, and it scampered openly into the road.

"Oh god"—the grimalkin darted behind her legs—"it's got a knife."

The goblin had indeed somehow managed to acquire a makeshift knife, which it was holding unsteadily in one hand as if not quite sure what to do with it.

"What should we do?" hissed Isabella at the grimalkin.

"How should I know?" it bit back.

The goblin advanced, waving the tiny knife. It had figured out that this was a source of concern to its prey, though it hadn't worked out the reason.

"Do something," said the grimalkin.

"Can't you bite it?"

"Bite it? I don't know where that thing's been. You bite it."

They moved around the bushes away from the goblin, which followed them, hooting a little goblin cry of victory.*

They circled the low roadside bushes twice more, before the goblin wised up to the strategy. Midway through a loop, it changed direction and almost collided with them. Reflexively,

---

* Goblins hoot, honk, and toot. Under observation, they have been recorded to clank, oom-pah, and gobble. They do not, under any circumstances, pew-pew.

Isabella lashed out with a kick, which hit the goblin square in the shin. It rubbed its strangely textured leg with its free hand, looking aggrieved. Whatever hidden rules of engagement the goblin had been party to until this point, Isabella had clearly broken them.

It shrieked, a little goblin war cry. It was holding the shiv more confidently now, and the dent in its leg did not appear to have dissuaded it, or even impaired it.

"That didn't help," said the grimalkin, exasperated. "You just made it angry."

Isabella didn't have time to argue with it. The goblin was advancing on her, knife held high.

"Maybe it wants money," said the grimalkin. "Do we have any money?"

Isabella searched her pockets, still backing off but losing ground. She carried a few small pieces in a pouch, but this far from a city, coinage was both unreliable and hard to come by. She was reluctant to surrender it to this tiny bandit.

Unless. There was still something she could do. She sought out the spell of levitation in her mind. It was still there, where she had left it, though left fuzzy and indistinct. It seemed what the grimalkin had said was true, reading a spell from the *Gramayre* . . . changed it. Altered it. Left it just a little different than it was before. If she used it again without first consulting the book, the spell might stop levitating things and do something else entirely. Having been exposed to Isabella, the levitation spell felt rounded. Soft. As if the edges had been sanded away, leaving a comfortable place to sit.

She spoke the spell once more.

It held. Barely. She could feel the spell changing again as she spoke it, wriggling about in an attempt to be free, but she encouraged it to play along, one more time. It acquiesced.

As quickly as that, the goblin began to float. It rose off the floor, gently rotating. Panicking, it dropped the knife, which the grimalkin scampered over to retrieve.

Inside her head, the levitation spell she'd been holding onto was bucking like a wild horse. She let it go and it faded from her mind, shuffling away into the aether.

"You could have done that earlier," critiqued the grimalkin, "but that's actually rather good." It jumped up onto her shoulder, light as a feather, to get a better look at the rising goblin. "Can we keep it? I always wanted a famulus of my own. Someone to do the bookkeeping, and all that. My paperwork gets horribly complicated at this time of year. Taxes. You wouldn't understand."

Isabella wasn't listening. The goblin was rising to shoulder level already, and showed no signs of slowing. Should she try to stop it? She didn't want to reach out for the creature in case it bit her or something, but the choice was eventually made for her as the goblin floated upwards and out of reach, into the sky.

"Good grief," the grimalkin said. It craned its head up at the rapidly ascending goblin. "Did you mean to do that? I did tell you not to use the spells more than once."

The goblin was now a hundred feet in the air, where it was caught by a prevailing wind and began to drift off, still turning head over heels. It was hooting in delight.

"You know," said the grimalkin thoughtfully, "amusing as that was, we really could do with something to help clear up the goblins around here. We'll have to do the ritual, of course, the one that keeps them in the valley, but that's quite advanced. Last year's one should hold for now, as long as no one disturbs it."

"No one goes into the valley," Isabella said, without even really thinking. It was true, after all, wasn't it? Nothing good happened down in the valley.

"I always said to him," the grimalkin said, the vague way it always did when it was talking about Bagdemagus, "we could do with a linnorm or something. One of those would do this place a world of good. Not many of those left, though, not in this century."

Isabella smiled.

The cat eyed her suspiciously. "What's that smile for? I can't tell if it's good or bad. You're quite inscrutable, you know. What are you plotting?"

Isabella was not sure.

"I think," she said, changing course to head down a side path, "we should pay a visit to Nancy Potbugler."

# 21

## DONKEY AND THE CAULDRON

Bottom the Donkey had been sentient for less than a week, and he already knew that he did not enjoy spending time by himself. Much as he would have liked, in better circumstances, to think of himself as an independent creature, he relied on Pony for their quiet stoicism. Pony didn't care about anything. The ground could open up beneath Pony, and they would fall silently into the abyss, accepting their fate without so much as a whinny.

In the present moment, Bottom had never felt more alone. He'd been told to stay put. He didn't intend to cause any mischief, but he'd spent a few hours wandering around the farm before he grew frustrated with the quiet and returned to his old field to watch Pony stand there. His thoughts kept turning over in his head, each one darting in to elbow the old one out of the way. Would he ever get back to his old self? Would Pony recognize him when he did? What was the point of plates? People should just eat off the floor, it would save time.

His stomach rumbled, audibly. Looking around hopefully, he trotted over to the box where the food came from and looked inside. No luck, just the remains from yesterday. A twinge in his gut heralded another wave of hunger. This was the worst day ever. The empty food bin was the worst thing that had ever happened to anyone in the history of bad things.

Usually someone would have fed him by now, but Isabella had marched out of the house in the early morning and hadn't come back yet. Mr. Nagg had crawled out on his stomach, looking horrible, and Bottom hadn't wanted to get involved with that in case Mr. Nagg kicked him again. Now there was no one to make the food appear, and he was hungry. This was an outrage! This was ridiculous! Anger quickly boiled away to bargaining, and he brayed a lot, which helped (but only for a moment). When this failed to produce results, he sulked, noisily stomping about where all the other animals could hear, but their lack of awareness only made the experience all the sadder. Finally, he accepted the horrible truth—he was going to have to make his own dinner.

A plan entered his mind as if placed there by the hand of the divine.* He clomped over to the house and pushed open the door to the kitchen. He'd noticed that Mr. Nagg was in the

---

* The world was, generally speaking, divided when it came to the matter of gods and prime movers, as the presence of a giant beetle pushing the sun across the sky demanded answers that only seemed to lead to more questions, such as "Who would make this?" or "Why would someone make this?"

habit of leaving the house unlocked. The smell of herbs and spices did nothing to discourage him, and in his excitement he knocked a chair over on his way past the large table in the middle of the room. Over the hearth hung the black cast-iron pot from which Mrs. Nagg made food for herself. Surely this was the answer to his problems. If he could figure out how to use it, of course.

"Oh, wise and noble donkey," said the pot of basil from the kitchen table.

Bottom turned around. Oh, that was right. The basil could talk. Perhaps it knew the answer. Or a recipe. Basil was food, after all, it should know these things.

"Pot of basil," he said, "I wish to use this cauldron to make some food."

"Ah, gentle donkey," said the pot of basil, "I will help you if you wish. You need only ask the cauldron to 'cook, little pot, cook' and you shall have all the porridge you could ever desire."

The donkey looked over to the cauldron, and then back at the basil with narrowed eyes. "This seems very easy. How simple it is! Are you sure that is all, pot of basil?"

"I am the pot of basil," said the herb, in its airy voice, "and I cannot tell lies."

"Ah, that's a very good point," said the donkey, interrogating it no further. This all sounded very manageable, and the hunger pangs were starting to beat a haunting rhythm. If he didn't get fed soon, he might waste away into a husk. He was sure of it.

"Thank you, pot of basil," said the donkey.

"You have no reason to thank me," the pot of basil replied.

Over in the fireplace, the cauldron hung from a little hook. Donkey nudged it with his nose, for formality's sake, and took a peek inside. No food yet. Mustering his best voice, which was the only voice he had, he spoke the words the basil had suggested. "Cook, little pot, cook."*

Immediately the cauldron began to fill with an oaty something that smelled a great deal like edible food. Delighted, Donkey turned to the pot of basil, with pride in his bearing. It didn't show much of a reaction, but then again it was a pot of basil; there was only so much you could expect of it. Without further delay, the donkey plunged his snout into the cauldron and began to gorge himself.

Time happily passed in this way as the donkey passed from sated, to full, to absolutely crammed full of food. Finally, he sat down with a little poot, satisfied. This had all gone marvelously. For a moment he sat there, pleased with his own cleverness, and then a worrying notion wandered into his cranium, where it buzzed about, sometimes hitting the sides.

Lifting up his head towards the shelves, he asked, "Pot of basil, I have finished eating, and the pot is still making more food. How can I make it stop?"

But answer came there none. The pot was half full.

Again, more worried, the donkey spoke. "Pot of basil! I do not know the magic words."

Silence. The cauldron grew fuller.

Perhaps the basil was tired. He'd have to sort this himself. Going back to the pot, he tried the obvious thing first.

"Stop, pot."

It did not listen, merrily producing porridge at an alarming rate.

---

* Enchanting a pot to conjure oodles of porridge on demand is the hard part. Saying the right words to reap the benefit is somewhat easier, and requires about as much magic as would fill a thimble. It's one of the great injustices of practical magic.

"Stop."

"Pot, I said stop."

"Stop making porridge! Pot! Listen!"

None of this seemed to help at all, which was disquieting, especially as the goop started to spill onto the kitchen floor.

This was rapidly getting out of hand, so Donkey took the handle of the cauldron in his mouth from where it hung and started to carry it through the kitchen, which only resulted in slopping wet food everywhere. It was lighter than it looked, and swung crazily from side to side as he walked. Then, it slipped from his grip and clanged onto the floor, where the entire contents spilled out onto the stonework. And yet the cauldron continued to produce porridge.

"Bad cauldron," brayed the donkey. "No! Stop it!"

The cauldron, not hearing the magic words, seemed to be working under the assumption that this was all some kind of meal-adjacent role play, and ignored the command.

Donkey thought very hard, very quickly. What could he do? There was a mess everywhere, and Isabella would be wroth. She might not help him get back to his normal self. This, Donkey reflected, was the trouble with having brains, you couldn't help but get into mischief no matter how hard you tried.

Splashing through the ever-growing puddle of porridge, the donkey pottered about the room looking for something with which to stem the tide.

"Silly donkey, what trouble have you wrought for yourself?" said the pot of basil.

Donkey lit up. "Pot of basil!" he said. "I thought you had forsaken me! What should I do, wise basil? How do I stop the porridge pot?"

"Unhappy donkey, most foolish of creatures," it replied. "You must go outside and wait for Isabella to return. I shall speak on your behalf."

The donkey hesitated. It looked at the growing mess, at which it was sure Isabella would be furious. His long ears were floppy with sadness.

"Very well," it said, finally. "I shall trust you, pot of basil. I hope she is not very angry with me."

"I am the pot of basil," it said, cheerily, "and I cannot tell lies."

Confident in his new friend, the donkey decided to do as suggested. "Thank you, pot of basil," he said, backing out of the room. How lucky he was to have made such a companion. Perhaps there was more to having a voice than Bottom had thought.

Once outside, Donkey's spirits began to lift. He was glad the basil was handling things, and felt a weight lift from his chest. Is that what guilt felt like? He hadn't enjoyed that at all.

Back in his field, the donkey watched the porridge leak out of the back door and into the fields. What he didn't see was a single piece of goblin fruit, less one Nagg-sized bite, washed away in the flood of gruel.

# 22

## ISABELLA AND THE WELL

No one ever told Mrs. Nagg that she'd put on weight. No, they wouldn't say that to her face, that would be rude. Instead, they'd say things like "You're looking so healthy lately," an expression that indicated their disapproval.

As it happened, Isabella Nagg did know she had put on weight. She knew because she'd had to change her clothes to fit, and she knew because she had a mirror, and wasn't completely brain-dead. The fact itself did not bother her; all the women on her mother's side of the family had the tendency to become a little comfortable* by the age of forty, and Isabella had fallen about as close to the family tree as it was possible to get without erecting a treehouse in the branches. What bothered Mrs. Nagg was the way people acted around her, faces pinched in

---

* Isabella's mother had preferred euphemisms like "comfortable," or "well rounded." Isabella preferred "fat."

a semi-snarl as they struggled to maintain a semblance of neutrality. She frightened them, she knew that. Frightened them because she was a reminder of that most dangerous and unthinkable of fates that might befall a person—that their body might one day change in a way considered inconvenient, or undesirable.

"You look well," said Nancy Potbugler to Isabella. Isabella knew what she meant, as did Nancy. They exchanged hostile smiles.

Buoyed by her success with the porridge pot, Isabella had come to Nancy to make a point. It was well known in the village that the Potbuglers, for all the charmed existence they seemed to inhabit, had a problem in the shape of a beast that inhabited their garden well. If every residence in East Grasby had some peculiarity which plagued it, then this entity was the burden of the Potbuglers. No device of Gramarye had proven sufficient to dislodge the creature, and though it did not stain their reputation in the way of the Nagg Stone, it caused them much embarrassment at garden parties. Village rumour said that the Potbuglers had demanded the old wizard Bagdemagus attend the issue, to which he had responded with mild derision, to the effect of "A beast? Can't be much of a beast if you've lived with it this long. How much trouble can it be? Get thee from my doorstep before I turn the both of you into weevils." This was the only time the wizard had ever acknowledged the problem, and he had resolutely refused to investigate it any further. From what the Potbuglers had said at the Homeowners Association meetings over the years,[*] and from her perusal of the *Household Gramayre*, Isabella was willing to wager she knew exactly what was hiding in the Potbuglers' well, and how to remove it. But Isabella wasn't doing

---

[*] resolutely unattended by Bagdemagus

this for the Potbuglers' sake. She was waging war in that most specific of ways common to neighbours who have known each other for too long, by firing a favour at them from the trebuchet of revenge. They wouldn't be able to refuse, because she was doing something helpful for them, but they would be in her debt until they could contrive a way to return the gesture (which she would never permit), and that would eat Nancy alive.

Today, Isabella had to admit, Nancy looked strange. Eyes wide, and mouth slack. Isabella enjoyed catching Nancy by surprise, it was a rare pleasure. If she had looked closer, she might have seen the shadow of something awful in that blank expression, seen how Nancy's fingers twitched, how her eyes turned to the horizon. To the valley.*

Barging past Nancy into her garden, Isabella made for the stone well tucked away in a corner of the Potbugler yard. The garden was meticulously well organized, and fervidly purged of all asymmetry by Mr. Potbugler, who considered anything that he couldn't turn into topiary a nuisance and a weed. Statues of tiny men littered the neat lawn,† and she had to conscientiously

---

* Nancy Potbugler had run the East Grasby Homeowners Association for decades. She was, by that merit, a woman of iron will, inhabited by her sense of what was appropriate behaviour (and crawling on her knees to the valley was not proper). Alas, even iron can rust and bend.

† The *Household Gramarye* says of the common or garden gnome that they can be found in great numbers in meadows, which they adore, and also near beehives, due to their impervious skin and sweet tooth. They are particularly partial to monocultures, specifically cut grass, for the same reasons lice are attracted to clean hair. Once they have taken to a space, they are difficult to evict, due to their territorial nature, and their supernatural ability to increase their core density when under threat. Thankfully, when looking to establish a new colony, gnomes always avoid gardens and fields which seem to be established with a pre-existing

pick her way around them lest she knock them over. Behind her trotted the grimalkin, which occasionally darted after a bird to spook it before returning to her side.

"What are you doing?" it would ask, at least once every minute, to which she would be respond, "Be still, Grimalkin," or "Hush now, Grimalkin," in a chiding tone.

Reaching the well, Isabella took a tentative peek over the edge. The water was some way below, but not so far that she could not glimpse the surface. In one hand she grasped a wand she had constructed just as the *Household Gramarye* recommended. It was gnarled. That was the word to describe it. Knotted in several unpleasant places, it curved in the hand as if trying to escape, culminating in a wicked point that constituted a weapon in its own right, magical potency notwithstanding. Deliberately, she pointed it at the dark water.

"Come hither," she commanded. "Linnorm! I call thee by name."

The grimalkin, which had been chasing a butterfly, snapped to attention. "I beg your pardon," it spluttered, in the way people do when they've heard exactly what you said, but wish to dispute it.

The Ignoble Worm, says the *Household Gramarye*, is a most unusual beast not to be taken lightly. With shimmering scales from head to toe, it can grow as large as a house if given sufficient space (and something to eat). Thankfully, sightings of worms larger than a pony are rare, which the *Gramarye* attributes to fewer wild spaces to which they might stake their claim. Nonetheless, their fondness for water creates in them an urge to inhabit ponds, springs, and garden wells, where they glut

---

colony, and so decorative prophylactic gnomes are a common feature in neighbourhoods where infestations have been known to occur.

themselves on native wildlife using the potent (and extremely venomous) stinger on their tail. Additionally, a cramped annotation to Isabella's copy of the *Household Gramayre* noted the linnorm's fondness for sugary fruits, such as apples. The wand that she held was taken from the apple tree in front of the Nagg cottage, and the mere presence should be sufficient to lure the linnorm from its hiding place.

There was no response from under the water. Isabella smarted, and focused. She'd done what the *Gramarye* had said, had she not? A wand of applewood, wizened just so. A command.

"Calling a linnorm?" The grimalkin was calmer now, but paced nevertheless. "Here? I think I would know if there were a linnorm in the area." It seemed to doubt itself even as it said the words. "But if you're going to try, you have to sound a little more in charge. A linnorm won't surface for just anyone, you know."

"Come hither," she said. And she tried to remember when she'd last taken charge of anything. Oh, she ran the household, that was true. Went through her routine day by day, the same as she had from the very beginning. It was all a blur, a grey slurry of days blended into a stream she felt she might drift away in. First it had been Lorenzo, who was gone. As always, she buried the thought. It was best not to think about Lorenzo, or what had happened to him. Later, she'd met Mr. Nagg, who hung over her life like a cloud. Isabella had always been a person things happened to, not a person who happened to other people. Perhaps it was time for that to change.

"Linnorm," she said. Softly, but with strength. "I call thee by name, and you will answer."

A scaled head emerged from the water, tongue testing the air. Dark eyes squinted in the light, and the four-legged worm scrabbled up the side of the well until it reached eye level with Isabella. Six feet from head to tail, it used hooked claws to grip the slippery brickwork so it could get a better look at its visitor. Its pupils were a dazzling shade of red.*

"Bapplezzz," it said, in a rasping voice. Linnorms could speak, if only with difficulty due to the shape of their mouths.

"You know"—the grimalkin peered at the creature with ill-disguised fascination—"I haven't seen one of these in centuries. Wonderful creatures, very difficult to call upon. Well done. Very well done indeed." The words were filled with pride, and Isabella couldn't help but feel glad at the praise.

"They've not gotten any prettier, though." The grimalkin finished with a critique, as if aware it had a reputation to uphold.

Isabella threw a warning look at the grimalkin. Linnorms were not to be trifled with, and they were extremely vain.†

Thankfully, it did not appear that the serpent had heard.

"That is right," she replied, taking care not to stray within reach of its tail, which sported a wicked-looking barb. "Apples." She waved the apple tree wand, gesturing back in the direction she had come. "And there will be many for you at our farm. Would you come with me, linnorm?"

"Bapplez. Linnorm have bapplez." It tested the air with a

---

* Many of the earliest contributors to the *Gramarye* conceived of the world as being painted in tones rather than colours. Instead of writing *red*, they might use a word which equated to "striking," "bold," or "bright," which often but not always equated to red, or sometimes green. Instead of *silver*, they would use a word which meant "shining," "reflective," or "sparkling." As you can imagine, this led to all manner of translation errors, many of which were still present in surviving copies of the *Gramayre*.

† The *Gramayre* noted a number of ways to soothe an angry linnorm, one of which was to stand close by with a mirror and compliment its appearance. The efficacy of this technique was counterbalanced by the possibility that the linnorm might decide to keep you as a pet.

forked tongue, and then looked from side to side as if expecting an ambush.*

Isabella removed a goblin fruit from her purse. She'd circled back to grab a few from the barrel in front of the Nagg farm, on the way to Nancy's. She hadn't had time to ask why Mr. Nagg had acquired such a thing, or what he intended for it, but even he knew not to eat the goblin fruit, and so it must be the groundwork for some more byzantine attention-grabbing scheme she didn't care to fathom. Clutching a fruit in one hand, she made eye contact with the linnorm. She hoped this would work.

"Here. Apples." She pitched it across the ground towards the linnorm, which analysed it by creeping up to it and facing it sidelong. She held her breath as it tested the fruit with a paw.

Then, quick as a thought, it unhinged its jaw and swallowed the fruit whole. It flickered out a tongue. "Bapplez?"

She reached into her bag and showed it another fruit.

The chapter on linnorm had gone into great, almost excited detail on their wondrous nature. Of all their peculiar traits, however, that which had animated the various contributors the most was the linnorm's iron constitution. Supposedly, and she prayed it was true, the creature could consume almost anything with its inhuman arrangement of stomachs, and come away unscathed. Perhaps even goblin fruit.

Its eyes went wide with delight, and it half slithered, half crawled towards her across the lawn. Backing up, she lured the linnorm through the garden with the fruit held high, only relenting and giving it a prize when she began to worry it might rush her and seize the fruit regardless.

---

* In the days when linnorms were larger, more common, and prone to causing large-scale mayhem, many were hunted down by nasty men covered in plate mail, and something deep in the linnorm gene pool has never quite forgotten this.

In this fashion, she led the linnorm out of the side gate and into the main street, which was surprisingly empty for this time of day. She really should ask Nancy why the town was so quiet, she thought, before her attention was consumed once more by the hungry linnorm. Waving a new fruit from her pouch, she made haste back to the farm, snakelike creature in tow.

# Linnorm ◆◆◆◆◆◆

*(*Python terribilium*)*

OTHER NAMES: WELLWYRM, ORIFICE SNAKE

\* (scrawled in the margin by an unknown hand) Always check the toilet before sitting.

† (text added by Professor Green of the Tabernacle) Analysis of captive urban linnorm has revealed the linnorm to be quite mentally adroit, perhaps even a sentient class C organism.

‡ (attributed to Chancellor Bagrat of the Tabernacle) ethical concerns investigated and waived by the Committee for Enchantments, Enjoinments, and Exculpations

§ marginalia depicting a long tubular vegetable (possibly a courgette), three bears of increasing size, and a single wooden drying rack

The varieties of linnorm are as numerous as they are deadly to the casual herpetologist, though rural species numbers have severely declined in recent years, in comparison to their smaller urban kin, which thrive in plumbing and cisterns.\* The decline in rural species variation is blamed primarily on overhunting, as linnorms have garnered a poor reputation†‡ on account of their rampant violence, territorial aggression, and love of hiding in orchards. The linnorm's attraction to autumn fruits is as mysterious as its absent reproductive system—no means of copulation has ever been observed or documented during autopsy.§

*appearing in the Verdigris Tabernacle copy of the* Household Gramayre, *volume XV,* Of Liminality and Circumlocution, *section X,* "On the Archaeoserpentine"

# 23

# ROMANCE ISN'T DEAD

THE DEVELOPMENT of New Goblin Market was continuing apace, though never quite fast enough for Gwendolyn's liking. Day turned to night, and night back to day, but if she was completely honest with herself, she was disappointed with the workforce. Her lacklustre employees had barely managed to dig a large hole in the ground, let alone start the complicated task of building the greatest, most magnificent open-air produce market the world had ever seen. She'd assumed that convincing locals to eat goblin fruit would be the hard part, but that had proved remarkably simple. All she'd had to do was show up, give them an excuse, and they leaped on it with barely a nudge. The difficult bit was getting them to put their back into the work, now that they didn't care about anything. They shuffled from place to place quite placidly, yes, but they had no gumption. She'd tried explaining to them that they were in on the ground floor of something rather special, but they barely seemed to notice her, trudging from one task to the next with grey expressions and nothing behind the eyes. They didn't even want more goblin fruit, though she'd offered it to them.*

As if that wasn't bad enough, the ungratefulness of her employees was creating a mounting pile of uneaten goblin fruit. She had barrels of the wretched stuff crowding tents across the market (the goblins either could not or would not stop producing it), but once a person had taken a bite, they didn't seem interested in further exploration of the matter. Various other methods of motivation had been attempted, from bribery to threats of violence, but the goblin fruit villagers just stared at her as if they didn't understand, or more that they didn't care. She had obedience, as she'd planned, but she didn't have their spirit, and she was surprised to find that this irritated her substantially. Worse, some of them had started to drop dead, and that was offensive in ways she didn't even have time to think about. Quitting your job in the first week was one thing, but dying on shift was just rude. The bodies had to be kept under watch to make sure they didn't rise again, which wasted goblins, and the whole exercise was becoming more of a logic puzzle than anything else.

Now that the villagers were taking on most of the grunt work, the goblins largely busied themselves outside the market, spreading insidious tendrils of fruit. She didn't miss them, because aside from their constant badgering pleas to consume their fruit (absolutely not), they caused a great deal of trouble in attempting to "help."† So, she let them have the run of the

---

* In an attempt to boost productivity, she'd even instituted Goblin Fruit Fridays, which had been a disaster.

† Amongst other nuisances, the goblins had crafted a kind of functioning ornithopter in an attempt to "rescue" a goblin who they said was "in the sky" (impossible), and had then driven it into the only standing wall in the entire market, demolishing it.

place as long as they stayed away from the main build site and focused on bringing in more workers from the village.

Amusingly, perhaps ironically, the only employee she could rely upon was the body. It was all sinew and enthusiasm, throwing itself at every new task with the wonder of a newborn. Sure, she had to point it in a new direction occasionally, and it sometimes felt its way around with a stick or trailing a hand along the walls, but it was still head and shoulders* more productive than anyone else apart from Gwendolyn herself. To what extent it could "see" was not something she had any stake in. All employees were expected to show productivity, and if she started making exceptions on account of silly things like blindness or decapitation, everyone would want special treatment. Despite its peculiarities, she'd grown fond of the body, though she wasn't sure if it had the capacity to return the sentiment. Increasingly, it communicated through a series of hand gestures that she had slowly discovered indicated sentiment, or perhaps mood.

"Body," she'd said one evening as she sat in a chair with a glass of wine watching him dig a new hole, "you don't have to answer me, but I am curious . . . how did you die?"

The body had put down the shovel, covered with a dead man's sweat and the filth of a hard day's labour. Sorrow, it had gestured, lowering three fingers in an arc.

"Yes, I understand."

Heart. It pointed at its chest.

"Young love." Gwendolyn sipped her wine. It was terrible, but everything was terrible in this backwoods place. "I suppose they were quite something, to bag an attractive young man like yourself."

The body gave her a thumbs-up. Yes.

---

* in a manner of speaking

"You're an exceptionally handsome employee," she said, pouring herself another glass.

The body stretched, languid, then bent over to pick up the shovel again.

Was it . . . showing off? She allowed herself to watch. The perfect employee. Strong. Tireless. There were practical disadvantages to missing a head, of course, but she could make do.

Nursing licentious fantasies, Gwendolyn got up from her chair and drained the glass. Time to head inside for the night. The body would work until morning. It was completely focused on the task at hand. Apparently, being dead, and without a brain, made for a carefree existence. Not being so fortunate herself, Gwendolyn felt the need to retire. Her nightly regimen of oils, unguents, and preservatives took an hour, even if she rushed, and she liked to take her time. Her body was a temple; she wanted it to be a nice temple people came to visit and perhaps even left gifts, not some backwater shack with holes in the roof and creaking eaves.

She made her way across the campsite, avoiding goblins who seemed determined to get under her feet. She was too caught up in her own success to notice how the goblins stared slyly at each other, how they elbowed and nudged and giggled in a manner most sinister.

She was approaching her tent, which had grown in size commensurate with her job title,* when she found another villager curled up in the dirt. This kept happening lately, villagers arriving late at night. If they weren't spotted and put to work by the goblins, they often curled up in a ball somewhere quiet and

---

* She was now Chief Executive Overseer of the Gooch Consortium. She'd given herself that promotion because she'd been working hard, and she deserved it.

carked it before she even got a single shift out of them. That was a waste of good goblin fruit.

She prodded the body with a foot, and it groaned. Still alive, then. Did she recognize him? Hard to say, she'd met so many people recently.

"Someone fetch this man a shovel," she barked.

# 24

## ISABELLA AND HER GUILT

WHEN ISABELLA returned home from her excursion to the Potbugler house, she knew something was wrong before she reached the door. Uncurling a happy and sated linnorm from around her neck, she placed it gently near the apple tree, whereupon it scrabbled into the branches with a joyful hissing sound. It was dark already, the sun beetle having had a productive afternoon, but no lights were on in the house. The door was ajar, and the entire farm was heavy with a sense of squelching gloom that gave her the shivers.* Even the grimalkin seemed subdued, trailing behind her with its head lowered, peering from side to side as if something might emerge from the shadows.

"I don't like this," it said, sniffing the air. "There has been Gramarye afoot here."

As Isabella pushed open the door, the smell of porridge filled the air. Handfuls of the stuff were slopping out of the cauldron every few seconds, building up on the floor of the kitchen, and pushing other porridge out of the back door. It would be more

---

* All wizards and practitioners of Gramarye can sense dramatic irony, which is how they always know where to be when trouble starts.

accurate, by this stage, to call it a slow-moving river, which had already developed a sophisticated system of distributaries snaking off into the fields. Cursing, Isabella leaped into action, wading through the growing flood. It resisted her, the thickness of the muck making it difficult to get traction, and once or twice she almost lost her footing entirely. Stubbornly, she persisted, and crossed into the kitchen, where she found the source of the problem happily dribbling out another mass of carbohydrate-laden catastrophe.

"Stop, little pot," she commanded, desperately, "stop!"

It took a moment, as the last of the porridge slopped out onto the floor with a wet *bleh* sound, but gradually the cauldron ceased to generate any more breakfast.

"What is this?" Isabella said to herself. "There is porridge everywhere. What a mess! Basil? Are you there? Explain yourself."

"Oh, Isabella," a reedy voice called from the kitchen table, which (bless the sun beetle) remained unsubmerged. The pot of basil, wilting slightly, called to her. "Isabella, the donkey has flooded the house in porridge. Greedy, selfish donkey."

Isabella's frown darkened. She did not like the donkey, and sentience had done little to endear him to her.

"Fear not, pot of basil," she said, trying to comfort the distressed plant. "I shall clear this mess, and the donkey shall get his marching orders."

"I tried to stop him, Isabella," whined the pot, "but he would not listen. And I am only a poor little pot of basil, I could not stop him."

Isabella raised an eyebrow. "No, I suppose you could not have," she said. "What could you have done, trapped in a pot as you are?"

There was doubt in Isabella's mind, of course. The basil's new voice was unfamiliar, and she did not quite trust it. But dwarfing Isabella's natural cynicism was her dislike of the donkey, by several magnitudes. She could not think of a reason the basil would have drowned the house in porridge, whereas she could readily believe the donkey might have been angling for a snack.

Cleaning up the swamp of porridge was a daunting task, but she took to it at once. Going outside, she tried to find a shovel, but couldn't. The Naggs owned many shovels for all manner of purposes, so their disappearance was a mystery. Instead, she used a long broom to sweep as much porridge as she could into the garden. Once she had finished, she sat down at the table, floor sticky underfoot, and opened the *Household Gramarye* (it had escaped the wrath of the porridge by merit of elevation).

Somewhere in the house, she heard a commotion. The Nagg Farm hob was already cleaning, it seemed. She could leave the rest to the spirit, though she was sure to put down a saucer of milk by the back door as a reward. The hob would only clean if it didn't think you were looking, though, which gave her the perfect opportunity to sit down and read until Mr. Nagg got home.*

And he did not come home.

Three days passed in sublime bliss. She made food when she wanted, and no one complained. She read the *Household Gramayre*, which was fascinating in ways she could never have imagined. The grimalkin gave her advice, and the pot of basil said lovely things. The hob, seemingly encouraged by the absence of Mr. Nagg, not only cleaned up the worst of the porridge, but washed her clothes and made her mugs of tea as she studied. She chastised the donkey for his clumsiness and returned him to his field, threatening darkly to exile him, though he kept wandering where he should not nonetheless.

---

* It did occur to her that the hob could have started cleaning earlier.

The pages of the *Gramayre* were filled with enough workings to keep a wizard busy for all their days, and so Isabella picked and chose which items she would master. The levitation spell she relearned each morning, for it had begun to feel like an old friend. Other minor spells she began to commit to memory, with an enthusiasm she had never known before. Hours flickered by in weary bliss.

It was only at the end of the third day that a shred of doubt wormed inside her perfect life.

"Isabella," said the pot of basil, "wherever is Mr. Nagg? I hope something has not happened to him."

She raised her head from the book called *Of Tribulations, Taxidermy, and Traditions.*

She didn't want to think about that. Why should she care where he was? Life was demonstrably better without him. But as time went on, she had to face the music. Mr. Nagg needed rescuing again. Three days was the danger sign. One day, and he was in a minor scrape, like when he'd tripped and gotten his foot stuck in a crevice. Two days, and he was in a pickle, like the time he'd gotten his head stuck in the staircase outside the Potbuglers' barn. Three days, and he was in serious trouble.

She got up from the table, wearily, and went to fetch her coat.

"I am going out," she told the grimalkin. "To find Mr. Nagg. I shall not be long, I imagine. He cannot have gone far."

"Isabella!" The pot of basil seemed panicked. "Don't leave me here, Isabella. I am just a pot of basil, and lost without you. Take me with you!"

"No, pot of basil," she said, stroking the leaves to try to soothe it. She didn't know if the plant could feel it, but it was worth a try. "You must stay here, watch the house, and wait for my return. I shall leave the grimalkin with you, for company."

"But I don't like the grimalkin," whined the basil. "No one

is as good and kind as you, Isabella. The grimalkin is ugly, and nasty."

"Will you be upset," said the grimalkin from under the table, "if I defecate in the basil?"

"Isabella!" the basil shrieked. "Do not let the grimalkin defecate on me! I cannot bear it! Take me with you!"

"Hush," she commanded. "Both of you. Basil, I cannot take you with me to all places. You must learn to be content with your own company. Grimalkin, cease your mischief. I shall be back by sunrise."

She put on her sturdy cloak, picked up her lantern, and closed the door firmly behind her in case the donkey got any ideas about reading the *Gramarye* again. As she went by, she checked on the linnorm, which was curled up comfortably in the branches of the apple tree. There was only one other person in the whole of East Grasby who ever cared in the slightest where Mr. Nagg went, and she was going to make him talk.

# Crossroads Hound

*(*Canis quadriviorum)

OTHER NAMES: BYWAYS GRIM, ROUNDABOUT MONGREL, MOON'S BEST FRIEND

The phenomenon known as the crossroads hound, not to be confused with the more common Graveyard Shuck, Roadside Barghest, or sundry varieties of sinister dog, manifests only at the intersection of two or more paths, passages, byways, or highways (but not, interestingly, thoroughfares or promenades).[*][†] No crossroads hound can be trusted to keep its word, nor to fulfil an obligation, excepting by the use of certain mythical devices, implements, and osseous gifts.[‡] Homes built on or near a crossroads can expect regular manifestations of these astral visitors, but their displeasure can be averted with frequent praise, or by throwing a very large stick on a night when the twin moons are full.

[*] (attributed to Cyriac Bentmoor, exiled sorcerer and astral geometrist) Experimentation suggests that the crossroads need not be physical in nature, extending to metaphorical or metaphysical crossroads.

[†] (script attributed to Anastasia of Rebolt) The development of the roundabout and the highway bypass are considered chief factors in the decrease of crossroads hounds over the past three centuries.

[‡] (rag leaf tipped in near margin) The tinderbox is not a myth, and its efficacy in controlling the crossroads hounds is proven.

*appearing in the Verdigris Tabernacle copy of the* Household Gramayre, *volume X,* Of Fulmination and Firmament, *section III, "On Astral Cynology"*

# 25

## ROCK BOTTOM

Bottom the Donkey was bored out of his mind. He'd paced the field so many times that he'd worn a path into the grass. Attempts to engage the pony in conversation were met with the same cross-eyed imbecility as ever, and though he'd only recently become familiar with the concept of patience, he knew that he had run out of it. He didn't want to anger Isabella—her rage after the porridge debacle had wilted his ears for days afterwards—but he chafed against the confinement. He deserved to be free, wandering the skies and oceans the way other donkeys did (or so he assumed). Lately he'd been dreaming of a merchant vessel aboard the high seas. Perhaps a fancy hat so people would know to call him "Captain." There would be room for the pony aboard, of course. Some kind of cabin boy? Maybe they could even get married. Bottom was not sure whether animals could marry, but he was fairly certain pirates could.

His daydreams were interrupted by the Smell. It had been bothering him for days, ever since the porridge incident. Once every few minutes, he caught a whiff of it, a bitter aroma that his large nostrils instinctively rejected. He'd searched for it, naturally, but the trail ended at the hedge bordering the southern end of the field. He'd been explicitly forbidden from wandering off, and so he'd refrained from taking a proper look.

He turned to check on Pony, and his soul almost left his body. Where was Pony? He checked all corners of the oddly shaped field, up and down the slope, calling out and braying frantically. This was not good. This was bad. Where could Pony have gone? They weren't smart enough to survive out there on their own. They would wander off a cliff, or into the path of a cart. Maybe they would just walk in circles until they starved. Moving at the closest thing to a trot he knew how to perform, he was about to begin his third lap of the field when he heard something unusual. Something new. A wet crunching on the other side of the hedge.

"Pony?" he ventured, tentatively.

More crunching. A shuffle.

Unable to contain the spirit of inquiry, he pushed his head through the leaves.

On the other side, happy as Larry,[*] with no indication of how it had even managed to get there, was Pony. It was munching on fruit from a half-shattered barrel still covered in streaks of stale porridge. The fruit was . . . well, now that he had a good look at it, he could tell it was wrong. His animal senses revolted against the shape of it, which was too spherical, and the smell of it, which ate away at the hairs in his nostrils. Poison.

Panicked, the donkey raced[†] to the nearest fence and downed the posts with a swift kick of the hind legs. Darting

---

[*] Larry the Jolly became notorious, and a matter of scholarly interest, when he laughed into the wind and it changed, causing his face to stick that way. After his death, it was pickled and placed for exhibit in the Central Tabernacle of Verdigris.

[†] It's all relative.

through and around, he made it back to Pony in time to see them chumbling down another fruit. He finally managed to get in the way to stop Pony selecting anything further to munch on.

"Oh good grief." The grimalkin was sitting atop the hedgerow, one eyebrow raised. "That's goblin fruit."

"Goblin fruit?" Donkey was behind on recent narrative developments, but that didn't sound healthy.

"It's poisonous," said the one-eyed creature. "Why would you let it eat the fruit? Everyone knows you don't eat the goblin fruit. Now it's going to wither away."

"Wither?!" The donkey felt faint.

"To a husk," it said, shaking its head. It was enjoying giving the bad news. "Scrunched up like it was stepped on."

Bottom moaned.

Behind him, a crunch. He turned to find Pony, cross-eyed, eating a fruit it had somehow snuck from the barrel without him noticing.

"No! Bad Pony, put it down!" he yelled at it, to no effect.

"Yes, you really dropped the ball on this one." The cat sniffed at the air, dropping to ground level so it could take a look inside the half-empty cask.* "Gosh, it really did eat quite a few, didn't it."

The catlike monster, and Bottom considered it a monster, wrinkled its nose. "I don't know why it would eat those. They smell terrible. Humans I can understand, they can barely smell or see anything, but that pony should know better."

---

* Whilst a famulus is broadly imperceptible to those who are not wizards, there are exceptions. Animals are often able to see through the obfuscation to some degree, as are ex-wizards, those who might become wizards, and those touched by Gramayre in some unusual way. The Venn diagram of those categories is, funnily enough, not insignificant.

Bottom was busy scrutinizing the pony for signs of imminent death. None were forthcoming.

The grimalkin and the donkey sat there for a long moment, watching the pony, which began to drift in a lazy circle, as it often did when left to its own devices.

"Have we met?" The grimalkin broke the silence.

Bottom looked up, confused, but the creature wasn't talking to him. It was talking to the pony.

The pony showed no sign it had even heard the question.

Eyes narrowed, the grimalkin turned around to head back inside the house. "You'll have to ask Isabella when she gets back. Maybe she can check it over, find some kind of cure. I doubt it, though. I'd say your goodbyes, just in case."

As soon as the grimalkin was gone, Bottom tried to get inside the house to the *Gramayre*. To his dismay, it was shut tight, and Isabella had made sure to lock it on her departure. But he had to save the pony. It was his first real friend, even if it was a little bit stupid. There was more to life than being smart, the world needed a few people who just turned around slowly in circles all day. It made everyone else feel better, and besides there was nothing intrinsically more important about being a farmer or a wizard or a donkey. The pony deserved to live unproductively as much as anyone else, and Bottom was going to see it happen.

He analysed his options. He could break into the house? The grimalkin would certainly tell Isabella on him, and she might turn him into a weevil,* so he didn't like his odds there. The pot of basil was clearly a snitch, also, but much as he wished to settle that grudge, he couldn't reach the shelf on which it was kept.

---

* He didn't know where he'd gotten that idea from, but he couldn't shake it.

No, he'd have to be smarter about this. Wasn't he the cleverest donkey he knew?*

Gently, he began to nudge the pony out of the field, which went where it was prodded dutifully. In the dusklight, Bottom stared at the lights of the goblin market shining below. Someone down there would know how to make this better.

---

* He had never met another donkey.

# 26

## THE BEGGARMAN

B Y THE time Isabella found the barrel, it was dark, but she'd remembered to bring her lantern. This was the seventh of her closer neighbours that she had tried, and she was tired. If she had been in less of a hurry, or it had been just a fraction less dark, she would have noticed the tell-tale marks of goblin feet in the earth around the houses of her neighbours. As it was, she strode right past the footprints, and didn't see the goblin fruits discarded on doorsteps and in corners, each marred by a single bite. No lights shone from the windows of Grubben Farm, which was unusual. The young couple were rarely out so late, as they had small children.* She had to rely on her lantern to search their barn, placating animals she passed with an offering of food so as not to reveal her presence. Then, she smelled it, that distinctive rotten aroma. Inwardly crowing with delight, she moved amongst several

---

* You might now think to yourself, "What of the children? Surely the author will not let a dark fate befall them so casually," but I am sorry to inform you, best beloved, that unpleasant fates befall children all the time, from wolves dressed as grandmothers to being eaten by witches, and we must steel ourselves for such things if we are to continue our story, for denial will not save them, nor those that can yet be saved.

other barrels of uncertain vintage until she located the one she was looking for. It was older than the rest, with slats broken in several places. As if sensing her approach, it quivered momentarily, and the beggarman unfurled from it one limb at a time. It was undoubtedly very difficult for a full-grown man to fit inside a barrel that size, but the beggarman managed it with a series of breathtaking contortions that made her feel a little queasy.

Shielding his clouded eyes against the light from her lantern, the beggarman snarled, "Oh"—he spat something dark onto the cobbles—"it's you. Well go on then, off you fuck."

The old man saw everything that occurred in the village, or knew about it somehow. If you wanted to find someone and you were in a hurry, you could be certain he would know, as long as you brought suitable payment. From her bag of useful things, Isabella pulled out a weathered old boot, hastily retrieved from under Mr. Nagg's bed. She offered it to him to inspect.

This was not the first time Isabella had asked for the beggarman's help. Mr. Nagg got himself into unlikely situations more than she cared to think about, and when she was forced to rescue him, this was where she came. Finding the beggarman (who was always in a barrel) was easier than finding Mr. Nagg (who could be a nuisance anywhere).

Eyes fixed on this new and enticing prize, the beggarman rose a little further out of his barrel. The stench from inside it filled the alleyway and Isabella swayed just a little on her feet. "Ah, you've come for some philosophy,* have you?" the evil-smelling man mocked. "Gramarye not working for you, is it?"

---

* The beggarman liked to call his advice "philosophy," a term he also applied to urinating on private property and eating an entire wheel of cheese that didn't belong to him.

Need the beggarman to take a looky-look, eh?" He cackled, wheezing himself into a racking cough.

Isabella was not in the mood for his tomfoolery.

"I am looking for Mr. Nagg," she said. "I have not seen him in several days. Tell me where he has gone to."

The beggarman stuck his entire face into the shoe and inhaled deeply for a long, uncomfortable moment.

"Say I did know," he burbled from inside the shoe, before removing it and trying again. "Say I did know. What's in it for me? Maybe he don't want to be found, eh? Could be spilling secrets."

"A shoe was enough last time," complained Isabella.

"Times change," he leered. "You have the Gramayre now. Maybe the beggarman wants something for his time. A favour for a wizard, now that's a valuable one, eh?"

She folded her arms. She wasn't about to offer him an open-ended favour. He'd ask for a magical barrel or something alike, and then she'd have to figure out how to make one, wasting time. She racked her brains. If she lived in a barrel, what would she want?

"How," she said, "do you feel about porridge?"

# 27

## THE PLAN FOR
## BETTER BUSINESS

GWENDOLYN STOPPED writing for a moment to wipe the perspiration from her brow. It was swelteringly hot for this time of year, particularly in this part of the world. She put the diary down on the bedside table and allowed herself to trace a long fingernail over the headless corpse's torso. She enjoyed the long mornings in bed with it, toying with it. It didn't seem capable of passion, but it was incredibly functional, and that was the main quality she approved of in a man.

The body gestured at the diary, and made a sign which she knew translated to a question mark. She was getting better at reading its gestures.

She'd left the diary open, and today's entry was a single word—TREES—scratched across the page in savage letters.

"Nothing for you to worry your head about," she said to it. It wouldn't do for the body to start thinking it was an equal to converse with.* "Time for you to get back to work." The body

---

\* Gwendolyn did not believe in equals. "Equals" was a term people used when they were afraid to take control, or effectively utilize a blunt object.

rose from the bed and made for the door. She almost reminded it to cover its manhood in case a bird of prey mistook it for a snake, and then decided she didn't care. There were always more bodies in the ground, and if you started investing too much of yourself in other creatures, you just made it more difficult to leave them behind. And she would have to leave it behind if she couldn't get this New Market up and running soon.

Did every part of this enterprise have to be a struggle? She'd thought it would be easy. With the added undying strength and dedication of the headless body, the foundations were well underway, so she'd sent the goblins looking for a good source of wood with which to build her establishment. Nothing but the best for New Goblin Market, that's what she'd instructed. What she hadn't accounted for was the trees themselves, which were putting up a fight. What exactly they were doing to the goblins wasn't clear, because the survivors couldn't vocalize it to her satisfaction, but the remains were not an encouraging sight.

She'd been warned, of course, that this far out from the city, the trees had a mind of their own. An adorable turn of phrase, she'd thought at the time, which turned out to be a terrible mistake. No, the trees were very much alive, and deeply unconvinced by her best arguments that they would be more profitable as firewood and scaffolding.*

Massaging her head in her hands, she looked at the figures. The plan had been so simple. The goblins spread the fruit. The fruit infects the villagers. The villagers do the work, and then she cut the loose ends. It was brilliant, even for one of her plots. Airtight. Or it would be, if she could get any of these villagers to stop dying, or if the trees would stop murdering her goblins. How was she meant to build without any wood?

---

* She'd shown them the projections, to which the trees had responded with projectiles.

None of this fitted into the Plan for Better Business, a name she'd coined during a long-forgotten venture which had also failed through no fault of her own. She'd invented it herself, of course, because she had to do everything for herself.

East Grasby was proving the most challenging of all her schemes. It was that damnable fruit which was ruining everything. It was too effective. It tampered with the minds of people who ate it, which had at first seemed like an even better way of getting a pliable workforce until she realized they were useless for anything except standing still and repeating the same task over and over until they wasted away. It was infuriating to be standing there in front of someone, telling them that they'd earned an extra shift, only for them to stare into the distance as if she'd said nothing at all. It was ungrateful, is what it was. There was no company spirit around the place, no sense of we're all in this together. Worse, the bad attitude was spreading. Every day, new employees arrived at the market, crawling in the muck or staring at nothing. She found work for them, naturally, but the influx was exponential. Today she'd had over a hundred new faces writhing in the mud, and she worried that if this continued, she might not have any customers once she'd finished. She'd intended to sell the villagers goblin fruit from stalls their labour had built, but with so many of them shuffling off the mortal coil, she'd be lucky to throw an opening soiree of any dignified magnitude.

So, now, she was left with goblins who wouldn't do what they were told, a half-dug pit full of sleepwalking locals, and ever-increasing piles of wretched, poisoned fruit.

She flicked a bead over to the other side of the abacus. No, this was not ideal.

A low, sad voice interrupted her sums.

"Hullo." It was a donkey, which looked a little worse for

wear, as if it had been shepherding a pony down a steep hillside all night.

Of all the strange things Gwendolyn had encountered in her life as a businesswoman, a talking donkey was far from the most unusual. Equally, when it came to Gwendolyn, her attitude was dictated primarily not by how unusual you were, but by how much profit you stood to generate. This donkey was clearly in the twilight years of its existence, and she could tell from the way the pony was walking determinedly into a tent post that the poor beast was an imbecile.

"I'm sorry," she said. "I already give to several prominent charities.* You can find your own way out."

"No!" The animal sounded Desperate, which gave her pause. There was almost always some form of profit in Desperate. Ideas began to circulate in her mind. A talking animal roadshow? Cirque d'Gwendolyn?

"My friend ate the fruit," said the donkey, eyes hopeful. "Can you fix them? I don't want them to wither away . . ."

Gwendolyn allowed herself to enjoy the fantasy for a moment. She envisioned herself in a top hat, standing atop a creature that breathed fire. She'd look good in a ringmaster's outfit. Alas, this creature would be a poor start to the venture. Its fur was grey, and pockmarked in places. It would be a bad investment,† and a bad use of her time, even if she wasn't currently trying to juggle a seasonal produce crisis.

---

* She made a point of it. She preferred to give to the Gwendolyn Center for Women in Business, which paid one of her salaries and for the various dramatic costume changes necessary to evade the law, but she also donated to the Gwendolyn Crisis Group, the Gwendolynian Embezzlement Trust, and the Gooch Relief Agency.

† Of her time, mostly. It was against the Plan for Better Business to invest actual money into things if you could help it.

"Look here, grey creature," she said. "No, look here. Look at me."

She locked gazes with the donkey.

"I can't save your friend," she started. No, Gwendolyn was nothing if not honest. Honest Gwendolyn, they'd called her, back when she'd been running that scheme to sell tortoises that could outrun a hare.* "I won't save your friend, and there's a very good reason for that." She tried to break it to the creature, which was clearly on the verge of tears, as gently as she could. "You aren't useful to me, and I don't have time. There, there."

"Are you . . . are you sure?" It was heartbroken, clearly, but this did not sway her. You had to be hard of heart, in business.

She petted it awkwardly on the head, the way her mother had petted her when she was young.

"It's just good business, pet," she said. "Now run along and help your friend die however you think would be comfortable. Outside the tent, please. It smells enough in here already." Some of the fruit was starting to rot, and it stank. She'd tried having the goblins clean some of it up, but they often shed more fruit in their wake, leading to a chain of goblins following each other in circuits picking up the leavings of the one in front.

"Could I . . ." The donkey looked back at the pony, which was listing into a wall of the tent, causing it to buckle. "Could I be in business? Then we could save the pony?"

She sighed. It was a persistent creature.

"Yes," she said, already looking at the abacus again. "If you find a way to be useful, you can be in business. I'll even employ you. Now, you really do have to leave. It's very late."

Why was she making this promise? Was it pity? Was it the

---

* The secret, it transpired, was drugs.

peculiar way the pony kept staring at her? She wasn't quite sure. As the donkey morosely led the pony out of the tent, she flicked the beads on the abacus back and forth. She couldn't help but feel she was missing something rather important, right in front of her nose.

# Goblin ◆◆◆◆◆◆

\* (unattributed, corroded due to overly acidic ink composition) Goblin fruit appears to have no power over those guarded by a famulus.

† (script attributed to the sage Bagdemagus) Fruit falling from the sky has since been observed in three of the seven Greater Biomes, and celestial pulses have been documented in two others.

‡ (hurried strikethrough) mistranslation from the old tongue, replace with "badgers"

§ For the rules of goblinball, refer to Burgoyn's excellent *Pastimes (and Other Maleficarum)*.

When summer first turns to autumn, look thrice around your yard for any trace of strange fruits of mesmeric aspect\* that bear no lineage, seeming to have fallen from the sky.† Should you find such a fruit, consider moving house, or setting your affairs in order, for goblins will surely arrive hereafter. If your neighbour should discover the fruit, however, lay down mandrake along the border, which will stay the goblin menace from encroaching on your begonias.‡ On no account allow a goblin to start a game of goblinball§ within five miles of your property line.

*appearing in the Barrowdon copy of the* House-hold Gramayre, *volume XIII*, On Viridian and Vivisection, *section XVI*, *"Of Viridigenous Life"*

# 28

## THE SUGGESTION

HE BEGGARMAN ate enough porridge to bury a small country.* He was delighted at the cauldron, which gave off happy puffs of smoke at being allowed to cook. She'd promised him free use of it as long as he remembered the words to turn it off again, and the bargain had earned her his cryptic advice.

"You will find your husband," the beggarman had said, wolfing down another bowl of porridge. "But he's already left you, see? No, you don't see." He'd screwed his face up really tight. "You use the tinderbox," he said. "The tinderbox gives you the hounds, and the hounds give you the truth. The grimalkin knows."

He'd moved on fairly quickly after that, keen to get back in his barrel but promising to be back for breakfast on occasion.

---

* If Isabella had read further into the *Household Gramarye*, particularly volume XIX, *Of the Unplanned, the Contraband, and the Sarabande (in D Minor)*, she might have known that there were six recorded instances of a village drowning in porridge, with a seventh instance failing to meet certification due to a high liquid-to-grain ratio rendering it more of a gruel.

He never stayed indoors for long, houses unnerved him. Too stationary, and too many points of ingress.

After seeing him on his way, Isabella picked up the grimalkin by the scruff of the neck from where it was sleeping and put it on the table.

"Grimalkin," she said to it, "where shall I find the tinderbox?" It blinked.*

"T-tinderbox? Oh, I'm not sure where I would—no, I'm not sure I know anything about that." It tried to walk off, but her arm came down to block its escape.

"Grimalkin, I require the tinderbox. Render it to me, quickly."

"You don't want that horrible thing," it said, plaintively. "It's dangerous. And the old wizard asked me to look after it, safe-keep it, like. I don't think he'd want you to have it. He told me to keep it."

"He may very well have said that, Grimalkin," said Isabella, "but he is gone, and I am here, and is that not enough?"

The grimalkin squirmed. "I don't like this. Can't you just go looking the normal way? He can't have gone far."

"No, I cannot. Mr. Nagg has had many days to travel yet, and I will not have him abandon me in such a manner. He must be miles from here, and I must make up for lost time. We are not happy, I know that to be true, but I must know his fate. I am owed that much, am I not, Grimalkin?"

The cat sighed and looked up at the ceiling. "Very well, but turn around. This part is undignified."

Politely, Isabella agreed, and busied herself with pots and pans while the cat made a number of deeply disturbing noises.†

---

* sideways
† Envision, if you will, the sound of a clogged drainage system being energetically tackled by a banshee holding a plunger.

When she judged she had waited long enough, she came back to the table, finding the grimalkin cleaning itself and a tinderbox sitting in a pool of ambiguous goo.

She wiped it down. The box was made of thin metal, dented in several places.

"Should I light it inside?" she said, sceptically. "It does not seem perilous, Grimalkin."

"No!" The cat leaped a foot into the air and slowly floated back down. "No. You must not light it unless you are at a crossroads, and in great need. That is dreadfully important."*

"But there is not a crossroads here," Isabella pouted, just a little. "The best crossroads is past East Grasby, and then some. Over a day's walk, Grimalkin! I do not have time for such an excursion."

"That's all for the best, then." The creature sounded relieved.

"You don't have to sound so pleased." Isabella was annoyed. Did this creature exist only to vex her? "You seem to delight in making trouble, Grimalkin."

"Trouble?!" Its remaining eye almost bulged out of its head. "I've been trying to keep you from levitating yourself to the moon or growing an extra head."

"If the tinderbox will solve my problem, then why should I not use it? You speak in riddles, and I would like answers."

"I'm not your servant, or a pet." The grimalkin's fur was standing on end. "I'm your assistant. And it's past time you started treating me like one."

They glared at each other from across the table.

---

* Many magical items come with stipulations as to their use. The fabled Seven-League Boots, for instance, will transport the wearer precisely seven leagues in any direction. Unlucky wearers have ended up in undesirable locations, such as inside a mountain, at a parent-teacher conference, or directly in the path of an interdimensional tornado carrying a farmhouse.

"Look, Isabella." The famulus's voice had a tinge of apology to it. "I have been reading the *Household Gramayre* alongside you, and did we not see a spell of finding? Put the tinderbox from your mind, we shall find your Mr. Nagg another way."

"A spell of finding?" As she pretended to agree, she slipped the tinderbox into her pocket. "I do not remember. Show me."

# 29

## A SPELL OF FINDING

I F YOU know a wizard, and perhaps you, gentle reader, are fortunate enough, you will know that the burden of a practitioner is to be buried in arcane paraphernalia. Wands. Books. Plant cuttings. A toenail clipping you won in a wager, from a man who swore blind it came from a mythical goat. You might go into the practice with the firm resolve to be a tidy wizard, or at least an organized one, but given long enough, you will eventually find that the mess has a mind of its own.* For this reason, spells of finding and location are given a great deal of space in the *Household Gramarye* and other tomes of magic, and the amount of space they are allocated is directly proportionate to how unreliable they are. Spells of finding fail more often than they succeed, which is a problem rooted in the nature of perception, in how things fundamentally relate to each other—to connection. No, I see your attention wandering. Don't go anywhere, this is important, and there will be a test.

---

* Part of the reason is that wizard houses do not usually have hobs. A hob will rarely suffer to live in the house of a wizard, and if they do, then they frequently vent their displeasure by hiding all their equipment and knocking over stacks of important objects.

The key to a successful magical divination is specificity. It's not enough to go rambling to the greater universe, "Oh, I've lost my keys, be a good chap and find them for me," because the universe is quite unreasonably large and very busy running background tasks like gravity and time. No, if you want to locate something, then you need a sufficient relation to it that can't reasonably be mistaken for anything else, which is why it's much harder to locate your set of keys (random ore mashed into a shape) than it is your child (who shares blood with you). Unfortunately for wizards as a profession, it's very difficult to describe an object or person with such extreme precision that you rule out every other object or person that ever has been, is, will be, or could be. A workaround for this, and the one most commonly found in books like the *Household Gramayre*, is to already have a fragment of your target. It helps the spell along, like handing a tracking hound an old sock.

Keep this in mind as we rejoin Isabella in the Nagg family graveyard, where she was desecrating her mother-in-law's burial plot. In order to find Mr. Nagg, she needed something as close as possible to Mr. Nagg's flesh and blood.* She still couldn't find a shovel, meaning she had to dig with a large spoon from the kitchen, and with this tool she determinedly excavated the plot of land stroke after stroke, piling up the soil in a mound nearby. It was hard work, even for someone used to taking care of Mr. Nagg. If she'd had time, she would have hunted the *Gramayre* for a working to aid her task, but she was wise enough to understand that all the wizardry in the world cannot completely obviate the need for a sensible person to occasionally get their hands dirty.

Raking about in the mud, she silently fumed at Mr. Nagg.

---

* If he'd been present, she would have happily lopped off his hand, but that was the inherent irony of the situation.

Of course he would do something like this, just as she was getting used to the Gramayre. Get himself lost somewhere, or stuck inside something, and make her come and find him. But if she didn't, who would? He'd just starve, or wander about uselessly until she figured it out for him. That was how things were. There was Mrs. Nagg, who fixed the problems Mr. Nagg made, and there was Isabella, who resented him for it. For the briefest moment, she thought she almost caught the whisper of a nameless voice, one that asked "Why?" but it vanished into the dark as quickly as it had appeared when she hit something solid with her spoon.

Gingerly, she started to dig through the mud with her fingers, only long enough to locate a bone to use in her spell. Wiping away the mud, she located Griselda Nagg's skull by its protruding horns* and yanked it free. She wasn't gentle with it, because she and Griselda had not liked each other overly, and Isabella saw no reason that something as fickle as death should change their relationship. Then, she saw something else in the hole she'd made. Something unexpected. Digging further with her hands, she uncovered it, all the while wishing she could bring herself to stop. A second skull.

What did this mean? It could not be an accident. The Naggs were laid out neatly in rows, where they could watch the cursed stone until the earth itself faded away to dust. Each plot of land was demarcated precisely, and filled with a Nagg at the appointed time. She already knew where Mr. Nagg would be buried when he died, and herself after him. She stared at the horned skull, and then the other in her hands. Two bodies. This

---

* Griselda Nagg was born with peculiar hornlike nubs on her forehead, which she claimed were the result of her great-grandmother's tryst with an incubus. There was little substantiation of this, though she was quite charismatic.

second skeleton wasn't supposed to be here, and Mr. Nagg had filled in the grave himself. There was no sign of the grave having been disturbed before now, and both bodies had been here quite some time, if the state of decay was anything to go by.*

A secret corpse? What did this mean? She sat down. No good thinking was done on your feet, after all. She'd brought lunch, but the thought of it turned her stomach a little, so she decided to save the bread and fish for the grimalkin, which had remained inside to slumber while she did all the work.

Looking around to check she was alone, she felt for the tinderbox in her pocket. It had to be used at a crossroads, she was sure of that. The grimalkin might be unhelpful when it came to this artifact, but it was not mendacious. She considered the box in her hands. It seemed innocuous enough, for something that had fallen out of a magical creature. There was no physical crossroads near here, but Gramayre could be slippery, and perhaps there was more than one kind of crossroads, more than one manner of intersection. Wasn't indecision a kind of turning point?

Reaching into one of the pockets of her trousers, she pulled out the dusty tinderbox. Striking the flint against the paper, which she shielded from the wind with her body, a small spark quickly blossomed into a flame. Then, she waited.

In the darkness, something moved. It took the semblance of a dog, and if you were distracted you might even think it one. It moved too quietly for that, however, and it seemed to have nodules that moved under its flesh in unnatural ways. Jet-black oily fur covered it from head to toe, and it wore a smile so wide as to

---

* The *Household Gramarye*, in volume VI—*Of Maladye and Physick*, under the heading "Thinges Thate Do Happene under the Grounde"—denotes a sketchy but disturbingly accurate depiction of the decomposition of the human body.

reach the nape of its neck. Chiefly unusual about this dog, how-ever, were its eyes. Large as saucers, they glowed milky white, like twin moons in the darkness.

"You have called me with the tinderbox, sorcerer," it growled. The voice was low, and unfriendly. "And so I must serve you. You may ask one question of me, the First Hound, least of my siblings. Tell me what it is you wish, and if it is within my power, I shall answer."

Isabella considered this.

"Siblings?" she asked. She couldn't not.

"Yes." The hound eyed her with those peculiar orbs. It was strangely hypnotic. "I have two brothers, each greater and more terrible than myself. When you next use the tinderbox, you will meet the Second Hound, and you may compel one task from him in turn."

Isabella's mind cranked forward like a waterwheel.

"Yes, I have a task for you," she told the hound. "My husband has wandered far from me. I would find him."

The hound growled sharply. "This is an untruth. Ask a true question."

Isabella bristled. "You ask me, and this is what I wish. You must tell me where I will find my husband."

The First Hound scowled. "And yet you work a spell of finding, half finished, five days after he is gone. You already know he is lost to you. This is not the question you wish of me. Ask another."

"This is what I wish to know!" she cried out, as if saying it louder would make it true.

"It is not," said the hound. "The fire weakens, and your time runs out. Quickly, sorcerer. Ask your true question, and allow me to depart."

The flame she'd set with the tinderbox had indeed begun to peter out. She must ask something. Anything.

"Crossroads hound," she said, hesitantly, "tell me, to whom does this body belong"—she gestured to the unknown skull— "this body that should not be here."

"That skull," said the hound, coldly, "once belonged to Edith Nagg."

Edith Nagg. His first wife. Isabella picked up the skull again. The poor woman, to end up here, alone in the dirt of someone else's grave. Mr. Nagg had said she left unexpectedly.

A cold sensation began to take hold in Isabella, a frosty hand around her heart.

"Thank you, crossroads h—" she turned to say, but it was already gone. The tinderbox had two uses left. Two hounds, each more dangerous than the last.

"I hope you know what you are doing." The grimalkin emerged from behind a grave marker. Had it been there the whole time?

"Grimalkin," she said, strangely relieved to see it, "I thought you said you would not help me in this."

"I lied." It trotted over. "I do that sometimes. I wasn't going to leave you alone with that . . . that thing." It eyed the tinderbox as though it might open and swallow them both whole.

"Why do you fear the hound so?" she asked it, still holding the skull of Edith Nagg in one hand. There was something different about the grimalkin, though she couldn't quite place it.

"The tinderbox isn't safe," it said, rising on hind legs to get a better look at the skull. "Those hounds are dangerous. And they take a price for their help."

She saw it then. The grimalkin was limping slightly on its left paw.

A little embarrassed, the cat sat on the paw to hide it. "It only wanted a toe this time," it said. "The smallest one is the most reasonable. I suppose we should consider ourselves lucky."

Isabella tried to cover her shock, but she did a poor job of it. With new eyes, she gazed at the grimalkin, with its scarred flesh and missing fur, its lost eye and scratchy voice. Were these marks from past owners, as careless as she? "I didn't mean—"

"Oh, stop giving me that look," it snapped. "I don't need pity. There are risks to being . . . attached . . . to a *Gramarye*. I chose this, and I don't regret it. Just try not to use that horrible box again unless you have no choice. I've never had to bargain with the Third Hound, yet, and I'd like to keep it that way. I expect it will want payment more significant than a toe, or an eye."

It stood up and stretched. "Now, we were working a divination, weren't we? I assume this skull is involved?" It smelled it. "No, that's not related to Mr. Nagg. It doesn't smell ugly enough, for a start."

Isabella put the skull down. How had this woman died? Why had Mr. Nagg buried her here, so secretly? Alas, the mystery of Edith Nagg would have to wait until she retrieved him from wherever he had vanished to.

Reaching into the mud past the remains of Edith Nagg, she pulled an older, more wizened bone from the pile belonging to Griselda. This would serve for the spell of finding, and divine Mr. Nagg's whereabouts.

Briefly, it occurred to her that Griselda Nagg might have opinions about her bones being used in a magical practice to settle a marital dispute. She soberly acknowledged that it was undoubtedly disrespectful to go around looting graves like a bandit. She even gave credit to the notion that it constituted an act of cultural vandalism. Then she pocketed the bone and began to fill the grave back in.

Isabella could feel time slipping through her fingers. Mr. Nagg's absence troubled her. He'd been gone too long, and no one had sent for her to tell her, "Mr. Nagg is in quite the situation," or "Isabella, will you please come and collect your husband?" The anxiety gnawed at her. Mr. Nagg couldn't survive in this world on his own. He needed her, a responsibility so much more compelling than slippery, transient bonds like affection, or romance, and she had clung to this for so many years that she feared to discover who she was without it. The Common Sense, ever a quieter voice in the back of her head, muttered that this was an opportunity, that the world had conspired to solve the chief problem in her life. But she smothered the plaintive cries of the Common Sense with a pillow made of codependency. Mr. Nagg had been a burden since the day they had met. He had done nothing in this long association of theirs but complain, ruin things, and let her pick up the pieces. Now, he intended to vanish into some forgotten hellhole without giving her answers? No, this would not do. The decision solidified. She was going to find Mr. Nagg, and then . . . well, she wasn't sure about that. But if anyone was going to leave, it would be Isabella, in her own good time.

The *Household Gramarye* has a great deal to say on the topic of necromancy. In fact, volume XVI, sometimes called *Of Nether Regions*, is entirely dedicated to macabre rituals. Most versions of the *Gramayre* include a footnote that calls the discipline "overly maligned," though copies that include the annotations of Anastasia of Rebolt translate the phrase into a modern sister language instead as "the cursed art," which should go some way towards demonstrating both the polarizing nature of the practice and the importance of learning root languages at an early age.

The lion's share of spells involving the dead are investigative in nature. While the word might conjure dark images of walking bodies and necrotic shrouds, Gramayre is born of need, and there are few experiences more ubiquitous than realizing you forgot to ask someone a question until it was too late.

The moons rose high in the sky as Isabella sat in her kitchen, working the bone with hidden craft, guided by the soft words of the grimalkin. The bone she inlaid with engravings derived from the *Household Gramarye*, words of finding and keeping, seeking and knowing. Witch hazel she administered, to find that which has been lost. She was supposed to rub a "pristine culver" over it, for good measure, though she had to settle for an ordinary pigeon in the end and the bird was a little disgruntled at the treatment.*

She worked without rest from start to finish, etching symbols into the bone which danced before her eyes like the wisp trapped in her lantern. The spell of finding was one of conjunction, the alignment of souls. She thought of Mr. Nagg, and how they had met. She'd been grieving her lost, doomed Lorenzo, not that she thought about him, because she'd determined long ago that to do so was a foolish habit. In an odd kind of symmetry, when she met Mr. Nagg, he'd been mourning his first wife, who had vanished, and the two had found solace in shared despondency. After a while, you see, people get bored of mourners. At first they say all the right things, then they become uncomfortable with all the weeping, and finally they get annoyed or stop visiting. Her parents had been keen to have her out of the house by the time she met Mr. Nagg, and the two unhappy souls had inexorably gravitated towards each other. She found him objectionable, and he found her dislikeable, and they agreed on that. It was simple, and at least they knew where they stood. Yes, she did understand Mr. Nagg, in a way. Not enough, but a little. That version of Isabella seemed very far away now, as though she had been walking away from her husband ever since she first touched the *Household Gramayre*. She

---

* It is customary to ask a pigeon for its blessing before subjecting it to magical rites, but (thanks to ancient tradition) they may not refuse on a leap year.

wasn't sure if what was staring back at her was even an Isabella at all.

By the time she had finished, it was the witching hour, and Isabella was ready. She banished new and uncomfortable thoughts from her mind. For all the distance that had grown between her and Mr. Nagg, a part of her yearned for the known. For life to be as was familiar to her. Grey, and uncompromising and ordinary. The wraithlike claws of stability were clutched tightly around her heart, and she was not ready to think about what she would do with Mr. Nagg once she found him. No, she would focus on one task at a time. Finding Mr. Nagg must be enough for now, and the rest should wait.

"Wishing bone," she whispered to it, "wishing bone. Show me the way."

The bone leaped in her hand, swivelling like a compass until it pointed through the walls of the house. Mrs. Nagg looked out of the window, catching sight of the glimmering lanterns far below in the valley. So, that was where he had gone? To the goblin market? Frivolous, useless man! Gone to stare at goblin fruit, is that how it was? She was stunned by the revelation. Even Mr. Nagg wasn't that stupid.* Even he wasn't that feckless, that irresponsible. The market was certain death! Not only to you, but to whoever came looking for you, and that's if your intrusion didn't disturb whatever spells Bagdemagus had laid on the valley to stop the goblins getting out . . .

Is that where he'd been slipping away to, when he vanished from the house for hours? She'd never asked, she'd been glad for the time alone. Had he been going to watch the market, drinking in its temptations from a distance? She placed the bone on the table. It kept pointing to the valley. With one hand she massaged her temple. If he had gone to the valley and eaten

---

* He was.

the fruit, then he was already lost. That was what Bagdemagus would have said. He would have told her to make herself a cup of tea, to grieve, and to move on.

But she was not Bagdemagus.

She would find Mr. Nagg, bring him home, and all would be as it was supposed to be. She firmly quashed any internal voices that railed against "what was supposed to be." She did not trust double-dealing magical hounds any more than the next person, until she had some proof. No, Mr. Nagg was useless but he was harmless, and she was sure he could explain the grave of Edith Nagg once he had been delivered from his current peril. The Common Sense told her that with the right Gramarye, she could fix anything, even the insidious taint of goblin fruit. First, though, she had to get him out of a valley swarming with mercantile goblins.

# 30

## LORENZO, OR THE
## POT OF BASIL

THE POT of basil sat on the kitchen table, pleased. Everything was going perfectly to plan. Decades he'd waited, buried in the soil, for a chance to secure Isabella for himself once more, and his dream was now within reach.

It had all started with a horseshoe nail. He'd known the shoe was faulty, told himself that he needed to get it sorted. But there was always something more important to do. Lazy Lorenzo, they would call him. Distracted. Poor Attention to Detail. He'd always resented that. Life as a serial robber wasn't one that allowed for long stretches of time to attend to your chores, and during one of his many flights from the law, the horseshoe had finally come awry. The horse, startled, had thrown Lorenzo into a ditch and bolted with all the money.* He'd had to walk miles in the cold before he'd come across East Grasby, and further still to the farmstead, where

---

* It was, in the present day, enjoying a life of luxury as a senator in Verdigris's parliament, a body of government that operated under a set of loose rules which were more akin to suggestions.

he'd met Isabella in the moonlight. The connection had been instant. She was practical. Homely. Low self-esteem. He liked that, because it meant she was easy to win over with a few kind words and tales of daring deeds. He'd slept in the family barn for three nights, and each night he'd won her over a little more. They were talking of elopement . . . as long as she could secure some funds from her parents' secret coin purse. For the marriage, you understand. They couldn't start a new life without money, could they? Oh yes, he was in love with Isabella in the same way you might love a dog, or a parrot. But it hadn't lasted.

Lorenzo didn't like being told what to do, you see, and Isabella had told him on no account was he to leave the barn before their elopement. As the days passed, the excitement of being hidden turned into boredom, and boredom turned into wanderlust. He wanted to go places. To whisk Isabella away from here to vistas new and exciting. The four walls of the barn started to seem like a prison, and three days into his stay, Lorenzo decided he could bear it no longer. He couldn't go into the village, perhaps, but maybe there were other, less busy places to explore. And so, on the first day of autumn, he snuck out of the barn, down into the valley where the flowers bloomed and the grass was green.

Alas, Lorenzo couldn't have known what danger he was in, or that there was a reason he met no villagers in the valley. He was from a world away, where the ice and snow faded into colours that danced across the sky. He could have told you ten ways to pilfer a coin purse from a penguin. He could have climbed his way up the side of a glacier with nothing but a dashing smile and a pair of hunting knives. But Lorenzo did not know goblins. As the last rays of summer faded, Lorenzo stumbled across the very first valley fruit of that year. Goblins would follow in but a few short weeks, but Lorenzo did not know this. He only knew how delicious it looked. How it reminded him of a successful heist, how it smelled of riches just within his reach.

He didn't remember much after that, it came back to him in flashes. Just as it had promised, the goblin fruit changed his life. He remembered digging the dirt of the valley with his bare hands, revelling in the muck. He remembered wandering naked in the cold, and the dark. And he remembered Isabella. She had found him like that, shivering in the dark. She had risked a trip to the valley to find him, risked the terrible fruit which even then had begun to sprout around him. Some strange new sense afforded by the goblin fruit, by his nascent connection to the valley, allowed him to feel the goblins growing in the dark, clawing insidiously towards the surface.

Isabella had saved him, in the end. He'd been lost to the goblin fruit, doomed to slowly decay over many days as a captive host for the endless hunger that dwelt in the valley. His living flesh would be used as fuel to produce more fruits, until he wasted away and his heart gave out.

But Isabella had done what needed to be done. With a *snicker-snack* of the carving knife, she'd cleaved his head from his body, and all had gone black. His last thoughts, addled with pain and gnawing hunger, had been of her face, streaked with rageful tears.

It was a strange experience, death. Like sitting in a dark room, with an open door leading back into the light and laughter. For a moment, as Isabella had sat with his body, he'd felt rested. Peaceful. Tired, like he was being cradled in his lover's arms, and rocked to sleep. The feeling had not lasted, alas, and Isabella had faded away, leaving behind only an inviting light through an open door. The sense of peace vanished, replaced by a gnawing anxiety. It was dark here. No one was watching him. There could be anything lurking here, in the dark. How could he sleep if no one was watching? Oh, Isabella! Where had she gone? He must find her. And so, like so many licce before him, unwatched and unable to find rest, his spirit clawed its way back through the open door. Through the crack, the flaw in the firmament caused by the loss of universal Measure. To life.

When he'd come to his senses the next morning, it was dark and moist all around him. Choking mud filled every orifice, and he found he couldn't feel anything below the neck. He'd tried to scream, but he couldn't make any noise. Days he'd spent in this way, which became weeks, until slowly he began to realize he could sense light far above him. They had a word for this where he was from. *Wight*. Licce. Oh, how he had howled silently into the void. His rage at his confinement, and his terror at the thought of eternity in the dark, was matched only by his thoughts of Isabella. She'd found him. She wanted him. In the lightless hell he occupied, festering in the stew of goblin fruit, tethered to the mortal realm by a strange Gramayre he did not understand, he became something more than just a licce. His obsession grew, spread roots, evolved. Isabella. She was all he could remember, all he could see, the vision of her weeping face scarred into his dead eyes. This would not be the end for him.

Some dark mockery of spirit, trapped within his own severed head, wound its way through the darkness and latched onto the basil plant growing inches above. It was easy enough to snuff out the basil, replacing the plant's spirit with his own. He was the plant, and the plant was him. It died easily, so very easily. Smothered like a babe. The basil became an extension of him, rotten from the inside, but beautiful still. At last, he could feel the light again, through the leaves of the basil. He still couldn't talk, or move, but he could listen. And so he listened as Isabella carried him from room to room, occasionally weeping over him. As weeks faded to years, he became accustomed to this new life, a life of watching and waiting.

He could not venture to name or understand the force that kept him tethered to his own slowly decaying flesh inside the pot of basil, but it allowed him to see Isabella every day, and that was all that mattered. As the years passed, he grew accustomed to his new form. This new, eternal life. The grey twilight of un-death filled his senses. Never-ending. Unchanging. He didn't need to change, he could not be slain. No, in this new form, this new shape, it was the world who would need to move around Lorenzo. If only he had true physical form, he mused, he would be unstoppable. A head without a body was all thoughts, it could not exact its own will on the world. Distantly, faintly, he could sense the rest of his body out there in the world, like an itch in the back of his skull. He could not call it to him, however. It was too far away, and lost. He shared a connection with it still, the faintest of threads linking him to it through soil and stone. He felt, he knew, that if he were only close enough to his body, he could compel it to obey as it once had.* It belonged to him, the same way Isabella belonged to him.

Oh! Isabella! She filled his world. She was all he could see, all he could sense, as night turned to day, and day to night again. He memorized the lines of her face, the touch of her hands as she carried the pot around her home. And as the years passed, he watched her youth begin to fade. What a tragedy it was, that Isabella should grow old, when she had given Lorenzo the gift of eternal life. That she should weary, and one day pass from this world into the next, leaving her Lorenzo all alone. What would Lorenzo do without his Isabella when the time came?

---

* It did not occur to Lorenzo that perhaps in all the time they had spent apart, his body might have its own wants, its own motivations, any more than it occurred to him that Isabella's desires might have changed in the long years of his internment.

Would he spend all the long nights of his endless death mourning her, until the stars burned out and a pot of basil sat alone in an empty world, tendrils stroking her grave? And then, one dark night, the thought came to him. Why should death claim her? No one knew his Isabella better than he did. Who could possibly? She belonged to him by rights, for all of his suffering. He would return the gift to her tenfold, embrace her into this new life. This better life, in the hollow space where death had no meaning.

With all the time in the world to contemplate where he'd gone wrong, Lorenzo came to two independent conclusions.

1. *When he got his body back, he would be finding a new farrier.*
2. *Isabella could not be his again whilst she clung to her flesh like a shroud. She must be freed from it in order to join him in the dark, in endless life. Together. The way it was meant to be.*

He watched her in the mornings as she made breakfast for an ungrateful husband. He watched her in the afternoons as she tended her garden. He watched her in the evenings when she stared out of the window into the darkness, lost in her thoughts. And he waited. Waited for the opportunity he was sure would come. Years drifted by, and when he had almost given up hope, the answer had fallen into his pot. Cast there by Isabella herself, splattering onto his leaves like the elixir of life. The yarrow draught, miracle solution, had bestowed on Lorenzo what he had pined for these many long nights. A voice. To have a voice again, he could have cried out in delight. That same voice which had enchanted Isabella so long ago, the silver tongue he had used to separate so many from their silver. Now, Lorenzo was armed, and more dangerous than any man with a knife. His words were the only weapon he had ever needed, and like most weapons, it was best when used with precision.

No, Lorenzo had waited too long for this opportunity to squander it. And so he stayed in his pot of basil, biding his time just a few more days. How would he ever find his body? He knew it was buried, and somewhere close enough for him to sense. In East Grasby, almost certainly. So close, and yet so far from his grasp. It was almost enough for Lorenzo to despair. How would he take Isabella for himself if he did not have a body?

And then, like a hand of mercy descending from the heavens, he felt a change in the state of his body. It had been found. And a plan had formed inside the pot of basil, a plan to make sure Isabella was his and his alone. All it had taken, in the end, was a gentle rhetorical nudge to get the foolish Mr. Nagg, already half under the spell of goblin fruit, to take a bite. He'd used the foolish donkey to clean the house of the evidence, giving Mr. Nagg enough time to get nice and settled in at his new home. Then, he'd waited for Isabella to decide to find him, a journey that would take her into the valley. All he had to do now was convince her that she was best accompanied by her faithful basil, and he would be carried to the heart of the dig site. Right into the arms of Lorenzo's body.

# A Spell of Finding (lesser) ✦✦✦✦✦✦

*(an incantation for derivation)*

* (subscript by the Tabernacle Academy of Linguistics) The necromantic pluperfect is widely proscribed due to multiple instances of unintentional flensing.

† (attributed to the scribe Hortens, on an inserted leaf, badly charred) Cremated remains should not be substituted, due to unintended side effects.

**B**efore invoking a spell of finding, please refer to the table of grammatical constructs in volume XIV, with particular attention to conjugation of the necromantic pluperfect.*

The spell is best with supplementary unguents, but chiefly requires a rib bone (a relative will do fine, check your nearest graveyard). Inscribe the set runes from the appendices as displayed in the supplementary diagrams.

Used bones can be added to stock for a delicious earthy supper.†

*from the* Household Gramayre, *volume III*, Of Those Things That Are, and Those Which Are Not, but Which Could Be If You Made a Bloody Effort, *section V, "On the Misplaced"*

## 31

# THE RESCUE

ISABELLA WAS preparing for war. She was tired, and cold, but kept afloat by the desire to see the look on Mr. Nagg's face when she appeared. Marching around the empty house, she rummaged in every cupboard. She would need tools. The goblins would no doubt take ill with her extracting Mr. Nagg from their clutches, and so she must be prepared to use force. She gathered a poker from the fireplace, a vicious implement made of cold iron. A jar of old yarrow tea she stashed in her bag, and the apple wand she had used to call the linnorm. The tinderbox she hid between her breasts, just in case. Lastly, she took Griselda's bone, carved with runes, and held it in her hand. She would need it.

"Isabella."

It was the pot of basil. "Oh, wise and gentle Isabella. Most lovely of all women. What are you doing?"

"I must head down into the valley," she said as she moved about the room. "For Mr. Nagg has been taken by goblins, and I mean to have him back."

"Oh, Isabella!" Though the basil had made a fuss many times before, it was altogether more upset than usual. "You must not go to the goblin market alone. This is most dangerous. Surely you must bring your faithful basil."

"I shall not be dying today, pot of basil. Not any year coming, I should warrant. Wait here for my return."

The grimalkin poked out a tongue at the basil.

"Isabella," the pot of basil piped up insistently, "you cannot see everything, this will be dangerous! Place me on your back, Isabella, and I shall watch for danger."

"No, pot of basil," Isabella said, firmly. "The grimalkin shall watch for danger, shan't you, Grimalkin?"

"Yes, I don't think we need a third pair of eyes," it said, smugly. "You'd only slow us down, anyway. And you're too loud."

"Isabella, no!" The pot of basil seemed almost frantic. "You can't trust the grimalkin with this! It doesn't know you, Isabella. You don't know what it wants. I am yours, Isabella, you can trust me. Me alone!"

Isabella placed a hand on the pot. "Basil," she said, gently, "worry not for us. The grimalkin has been a friend to us, and most helpful. The best thing you can do is wait here for us to return."

She turned and made for the door.

"Isabella, do not leave me!" The basil was shrieking now. "Have I ever asked anything of you? Have I not been loyal? Faithful? Kind, dear Isabella. Do not abandon me."

Isabella stopped with her hand on the door and sighed.

The grimalkin mewled in disbelief. "You cannot be serious."

❖ ❖ ❖

The valley slope was steep, and the sky dark. Overhead the twin moons hung in the sky, gazing down on the world below, where Isabella stepped resolutely over each treacherous plateau with the pot of basil strapped to her stomach in a harness designed for carrying small children,*† down towards the bright orange lights of the goblin market.

She crept closer. Step by step, barely daring to breathe. In the shadows, she was able to make out the shapes of goblin folk scurrying about the edges of the encampment, the scent of festering goblin fruit sickly sweet in the air. Lanterns were hung between the gaudy market stalls, and a bonfire raged at the center of the camp. She would have to enter this place in order to retrieve Mr. Nagg, and she did not like the idea one bit.

Gathering her courage, she half walked, half ran to the edge of a stall on the very outer bounds of the market. It sagged under a mountain of goblin fruit. She forced herself to look away from the hypnotic orbs, and waited until the goblin responsible for the stall came around a corner. It nattered to itself, picking at the decaying morass in a bored manner. Then, it hesitated, sniffing the air. It didn't get far before Mrs. Nagg brought down the poker on its head. With a sound like someone stepping in a puddle, the goblin exploded into a fine powder that quickly dispersed into the evening air.

Moving briskly, Isabella proceeded into the camp. There were so many goblins, flitting about in the darkness. Milky tendrils of fungus crisscrossed the earth wherever she looked, a parasitic blight entwined with the soul of the valley. They moved of their own accord, sightlessly probing and seeking as if they knew that the market was under attack. The screeches

---

* "You are so strong and wise, Isabella," saith the basil.
† When they married, the Naggs had received a number of well-meaning gifts intended to strongly imply they were expected to start producing children. This eventuality never occurred, because Mr. Nagg had deployed a thousand contrived ways from headaches to bear traps in order to avoid consummating the marriage, not realizing that Isabella was similarly disinterested.

of cavorting goblins harmonized with distant, more human moans. Isabella moved between two rancid stalls, with a ghost-like tread honed from a lifetime of avoiding her husband around the house.

Before her, a goblin jumped up and down on a body. She didn't recognize the clothing, but perhaps that was a mercy, as the man's head appeared to have exploded outwards like an overripe plum, fruity mulch spilling all over the soil. Tendrils of fungus fed on it eagerly, glutting on the remains. The goblin continued to cavort, treating the twitching body as if it were a curiosity.

Fury awoke in Isabella's stomach. It trammelled the fear there, replacing it with indignation. The corpse looked so terribly sad, and pointless, and the goblin so full of glee. She resented her neighbours deeply, but they deserved better than this. If there was no wizard, then so be it, but for now there was an Isabella, and East Grasby was her home. This was her village. The fungus could not have it.

Before she even really knew what she was reaching for, the spell of levitation came to her like a hand extended from beyond the veil. It flickered from her fingers, eager to be free. She cast it with wrath, backed by her grief. The goblin shrieked, vaulting involuntarily into the sky as if propelled by a slingshot. The words of the spell burned in her mind, wishing to escape, but she held onto them through sheer willpower. She required it yet.

The shrieking drew attention, and she hurried forward as the slapping of goblin feet in the muck grew louder behind her. She pushed through a rotting tent, hangings smeared with fruit, and came face-to-face with a squat goblin, fangs extended. She wielded the poker in a jabbing motion, and the goblin dissipated into dust. Another leaped from the shadows, holding fruit. The spell of levitation raged through her, and it was hurled into the air, taking the rest of the tent with it. Three goblins advanced holding nasty-looking garden tools. Jab. Parry. Jab. Isabella Nagg was a deft hand with her chosen weapon, unleashing it like a storm upon any who dared to stand in her way. The spell of levitation bucked and warped in her grip with each casting, changing its parameters as the words burned away despite her best efforts. Between her swings, the grimalkin capered, revelling in the violence, slashing at goblin flesh and dancing between their legs. "Goblinkin, goblinkin," it laughed. "The wizard is come, faithless! Go back to your dark earth! Go back to your burrows!"

A goblin leaped for Isabella's back, claws extended, and she turned, knowing she was too late to intercept it. The moment stretched into eternity as she saw the glistening teeth open wide and raised the poker to defend herself. Then, like a gift from the heavens, something hurtled towards her from the shadows, knocking the goblin off its trajectory with a satisfying *thunk*. The copy of *Those Things That Are* picked itself up from the ground, floating to her side, pages fluttering. She caught glimpses of spellcraft in the pages. Cantrips she had studied. Hexes she had perused. The goblins were beginning to converge in greater numbers. One from under a barrel. Two from the side, holding rusty serrated knives.

She could only spare moments to peek at the pages as she continued to march forward, but the book was taking matters into its own hands. The pages rippled to the charm for spinning straw into gold, and a nearby goblin unravelled into fibrous strands. Spells she had not mastered flowed from the book as if she had studied them all her life. All around her, goblins changed from one form to another. With a single word, she turned twelve goblins into geese, which flapped away into the skies. She smote another with the poker, hopping through the dust it left behind just in time to avoid the swing of a knife. She could hear the groans of the poisoned villagers more clearly. She was close. Not much farther.

When the goblins gathered too thickly in her path, she hurled the jar of yarrow tea into their midst, where it shattered. Rendered ever more potent by its pickling on her pantry shelf, it bestowed the gift of speech on rock, stone, and goblin flesh, all of which began to shriek and caterwaul, terrifying the goblins, who knew to fear Gramayre when they saw it.

She butchered her way through the goblin market like a vengeful angel, power rippling around her and spilling from the pages of the *Gramayre* in a halo of half-spun workings. Where she trod, goblins turned to dust, piles of grey ash blowing away in the astral winds that whipped around her.

In the face of this massacre, the goblins began to slow in their assault, and instead more and more chose to follow her at a safe distance. They stalked her through the shadows, flitting from place to place like tiny children playing hide-and-seek.

She turned a corner, raising her poker high to stab downwards, and came face-to-face with a donkey. Her donkey. No, she corrected herself as she eyed it carefully. There was a sense of purpose to it. It wasn't hers anymore. People didn't belong to each other.

"Isabella," it said. "Oh, you look very angry, Isabella. Did you come for a job?"

"Donkey," she said.

"Bottom."

"Bottom," she started again. "I am here for Mr. Nagg. What do you know of this place? Have you seen him?"

"There is no time for this, Isabella," cried the pot of basil.

"I hate to say it," the grimalkin mewled, pulling out a paw from a goblin eye socket nearby, "but the plant is right. We have to keep moving."

"Try the mud pits," the donkey said, cheerfully. "I hope you find him. I hear there's a madwoman about killing people with kitchen stuff. Weird day." It pointed a hoof.

"Thank you, Donkey." She made her way past the donkey in the direction it pointed, almost bumping into a pony on the way. She reflexively apologized to it, and it must have been her exhaustion, because she almost thought that it winked at her. She pushed onwards, leaving Bottom behind.

Isabella was tiring as she picked her way between broken stalls and half-finished foundations. The spell of levitation had finally warped beyond use, and her poker was bent. The copy of *Those Things That Are* flagged behind her, pages turning ever more slowly. The grimalkin slunk between her legs, hissing at the dark corners where the goblin men lurked, waiting for their opportunity to strike. She could not maintain this pace forever; she must find Mr. Nagg and depart this horrible place. The further she ventured towards the heart of the market, the more the earth bucked and warped, the worse the bilious smell became. Here and there she started to catch glimpses of more human forms in the darkness. Some were faces she knew, lifeless bodies left where they had fallen, twisted and bloated. Some were still alive, hacking at the ground or walking blankly in circles holding work tools. Villagers from her childhood, acquaintances lost to the ravages of goblin fruit. How far had the infection spread, and so quickly! They didn't seem to notice her, but she stayed as far away as she could from the living. There was nothing she could do for them now. Perhaps she could come back, she told herself, after she had rescued Mr. Nagg. It was a comforting lie. The familiar hurdy-gurdy of guilt began to play at the back of her mind, but she suppressed it as best she could.

"Oh, Isabella," the pot of basil said, quietly. She looked down at the plant. It was quivering. In fear? Anticipation? She couldn't tell, but a shiver crept down her spine as if someone were walking over her grave.

Pushing her way through a bevy of papery lanterns hovering at eye level, and between two goblin tents, she almost tripped over a woman kneeling in the soil, dress stained with tainted juices. Clawed fingers digging in the dirt, pushing aside the soil, skin raw and ragged. A face that looked up at her, devoid of recognition, and yet pleading to be saved. "You look well, Isabella," Nancy Potbugler mumbled, breath sweet and rancid. For a moment Isabella faltered. It was pity that stayed her hand, for this her least favourite of acquaintances and only humanoid friend, but it was poorly repaid. The creature that had once been Nancy lunged forward and grabbed Isabella's leg, trying to pull her into the dirt. They struggled, and though on an ordinary night Isabella could have snapped the smaller woman in two without breaking a sweat, the poison surging through Nancy's blood lent her unnatural strength, and the deadlock slowly began to turn in favour of the assailant. As she felt her foot begin to slip, Isabella reached for the wand of applewood at her waist. Touching the wand came with a heightened sense of awareness, a connection to the creature to which she had bound it, which she had left in the boughs of an apple tree. Clutching the wand even as her footing gave out, she called out, "Come hither, come, linnorm! Linnorm!" Tumbling into the mud, Isabella barely held off Nancy's feral assault by scrambling backwards, but her assailant was tireless, and frenzied. Raising her arms to defend her face, Isabella wondered if this was how she would die, when a streak of white collided with her attacker, both vanishing into the closest market stall with a juddering crash. The scaly linnorm, called by the song of the apple tree wand,* wrapped itself

---

* The *Household Gramayre* has several theories about how the linnorm travels so quickly. One commentary credited to Bartholomew the Many-Legged, which appears in most copies north of the Equidistant Peaks, suggests that the linnorm begins its journey to the summoner hours or

around its victim, jabbing Nancy with its stinger until she finally fell limp.

Isabella sprung to her feet, holding tight to the wand. She worried for what the linnorm would do next, but she need not have. It was staring past her, ogling the goblin men with their handfuls of sprouting fruit.

Now, if Isabella had finished reading the volume of the *Gramayre* sometimes called *Of Tribulations, Taxidermy, and Traditions*, she would have known that the linnorm is the natural predator of goblinkind. A linnorm's immunity to most poisons and their love of sickly treats makes goblins a scrumptious snack, and in older days when more linnorms stalked the earth (and skies), goblinkind cowered only in dark, damp places where they would not be found. Even in Isabella's time, when linnorms had been driven near to extinction, Goblins retained an innate fear of snakes, which stems directly from this ancestral feud. Some small part of each goblin connected to the hive kicked into high gear at the sight of the snakelike creature.

"Bapplez?" it said, slowly. Curiously.

The goblins looked at each other in horror.

"Bapplez," the linnorm confirmed confidently, tilting its head.

The goblins scattered, and the linnorm bounded into action with a joyful screech, slithering off in pursuit.

"Well," Isabella muttered to herself. "That is that, then."

Quickly, so as not to be present should the linnorm return

---

even days before they summon it. How the linnorm knows when to do this is another question entirely, but Anastasia of Rebolt does list it in her appendix of creatures that can possess the Sight, though as all variants of linnorm tend to be reticent creatures, this has yet to be confirmed.

looking for someone else to eat,* she pushed between two over-
turned carts, each overflowing with rotting produce. With a
light step, she picked her way through the decay, some sixth
sense telling her that contact with the fruit was something to
be avoided whenever possible, even underfoot. Where was Mr.
Nagg? Somewhere in the center of this mess, no doubt.

It was then that the pot of basil made its move.

---

* She was under no delusions that the linnorm's loyalty to her was tem-
porary, and driven by the fragile illusion that Isabella was the sole conve-
nient source of delicious fruit.

# 32

## A CONFRONTATION

I N A shrill little voice, at the worst possible moment, the basil spoke words from the *Household Gramayre*. Words it had heard Isabella incant time and time again. The pot of basil spoke the spell of levitation, and Isabella was caught completely off guard. The pot of basil slipped free of the child carrier and hovered into the air, laughing.

She tried to reach for it. "Basil," she cried out, risking being discovered by more goblins, "what are you doing? Basil, come back!" but each time she grasped for it, it danced away from her hands, all the while giggling.

"Isabella"—the grimalkin's sharp voice interrupted her—"Isabella, leave it. Leave it! We have to go." Urgency coloured its words. Distant screeches suggested the linnorm was still at its bloody work, but there were so many goblins. Each and every moment spent here risked catastrophe.

Could she leave it behind? The pot of basil was her oldest friend. Her truest companion in the loneliest parts of her life. She looked to the grimalkin.

"I won't leave him," she blurted out without meaning to.

"Him?" The grimalkin, ancient in the ways of wizardly bullshit, and deeply in tune with the importance of grammatical distinction, didn't miss a beat. "Isabella, it's just a basil plant. An annoying one at that. We don't have time."

The floating basil plant was vanishing out of view, drifting off into the dark, laughing. She had to follow it, but she needed the grimalkin. She needed it to understand. Reaching down to the famulus, Isabella used the memory charm the grimalkin had taught her. She showed it the past, images flickering from her to the familiar in a rush. She showed the grimalkin the truth.

"You cut off a man's head?" The grimalkin was still whispering, but at such a volume that it barely counted. "And you stuck it in a plant pot? What were you thinking?" Its recriminations lasted only briefly, however, before pity entered its voice. "It's a licce, Isabella. It's evil. Don't chase it, for crying out loud. Be thankful it's gone."

A licce. A corpse risen from the dead, animated by fell magic and consumed by violent lusts. Could a severed head even become a licce? She'd thought that wasn't possible. That was why she'd cut it off. Had he been in there, in the dark earth, suffocating for all this time?

The grimalkin tugged at her satchel with its malformed teeth. "We have to go," it insisted.

And where ordinary sense failed her, the Common Sense kicked in. That practical voice which never failed. Come on, Isabella, it said to her. One foot in front of the other. You have a responsibility, and we aren't done here. It pushed thoughts of severed heads and licce to the back of her mind. She would find Mr. Nagg, seize him from this place, and then she would think about . . . everything else. One thing at a time.

She walked swiftly. Soon enough, a rhythmic sound drew her attention. *Thunk. Thunk.* She hadn't noticed at first because of the darkness, but she was standing near the edge of a large pit, deep enough that a man could stand in it and not be able to reach the sides. Then, the twin moons slid out from behind

208 / OLIVER DARKSHIRE

a cloud, revealing the full scope of the enterprise. Perhaps a hundred people, all in rags and with the same haunted look as Nancy Potbugler, were digging with spades into the earth, endlessly expanding the pit in all directions. In some cases, bodies lay where they had fallen, emaciated by hunger or fatigue—at this distance it was hard to tell. Some of them had shovels, and others appeared to have resorted to using their bare hands to scrabble and paw at the ground with bleeding fingers. Holding the grimalkin close, she sat on the edge and lowered herself down the slope gingerly.* It wouldn't do to slip here and be at the mercy of anyone who found her. To her left, a man she recognized from her youth (what was his name? Simons?) glumly stared up at the stars, all the while mauling the ground with the bloody stumps at the ends of his arms. He did not react to her presence, and neither did the next, a wiry woman clad only in a nightdress that flapped eerily in the breeze. Behind Isabella, gathered on the ledge, curious goblins once again began to form a line, though they clearly did not dare to get closer. In the distance, she heard the occasional scream that told her the linnorm had found another victim. She needed to keep moving. She was keenly aware that, with the poker bent and her Gramayre expended, she was vulnerable.

The grimalkin padded back and forth in front of her. Hurry, it seemed to say with its anxious pacing, Isabella, hurry. Faster now, she squelched through the dirt, checking faces as she went. She was close to thinking that Mr. Nagg was not present at all when she caught a glimpse of something that made her double back. He was wearing his shirt untucked, vile stains plastered all over it as if he'd crawled a long way in the muck. In one listless hand he held a shovel, which tapped the floor

---

* The grimalkin did not, as a rule, enjoy being manhandled, but permitted it in cases of sharp inclines, or when crossing large bodies of water.

in time to music only he could hear. His eyes were dreamily unfocused, and he moaned at her approach. In recognition? She couldn't tell.

"Mr. Nagg," she said, mouth dry. "Mr. Nagg, can you hear me?"

A light flared, flooding the scene with harsh yellow radiance. Isabella had to shield her eyes for a moment, squinting, as the woman holding the lamp let off a noise that sounded a bit like exasperation. The newcomer was a vision in leather and business wear, her face framed in tousled waves of golden hair, with the adamantine posture of a woman holding the heavens aloft. She was gesticulating with an empty clipboard.

"This is private property. Employees are forbidden from visitors."

"Madam," said Isabella, "I don't know who you are. But I am here for Mr. Nagg."

Mr. Nagg made a noise like a drainpipe, and quietly banged his head against a rock.

"I am Gwendolyn Gooch!" It was delivered with a note of triumph, which quickly rang hollow.

Isabella didn't know what to say to that. She opened her mouth to say something and then closed it again, unable to quite believe what she was seeing.

"Gwendolyn Gooch?" The stranger tried again. She appeared genuinely frustrated that Mrs. Nagg did not know who she was. "The Gooch Monopoly Board? Gooch Amateur Theatrics? The Gooch Memorial for Victims of Elegant Fraud?"

With an incredulous expression at the confused look on Isabella's face, Gwendolyn changed tack. "I own this land, because I put a sign on it." Her tone was becoming flintier by the moment. "You won't be taking anyone anywhere." She pointed at the shambler with the face of Mr. Nagg. "That man is an employee of New Goblin Market, and I do not give him permission to leave!" She pondered. "He had his break last week, and he's not due another until the solstice."

Isabella was completely nonplussed. Clearly this woman was insane.

"You cannot have him." She said it simply, for it was a fact. Isabella would not let the market claim him.

"Oh?" Gwendolyn Gooch was triumphant. "But he's already mine." She gestured at the crawling figure of Mr. Nagg. "He's lost to you. There is no cure for goblin fruit."

But Isabella was already thinking. The glimmers of an idea were converging in her mind. Fragments of things seen in the pages of the *Gramayre*. More confidently, she rose up to her full height and planted her feet in the poisoned earth.

"I shall cure him," she said.

It was Gwendolyn's turn to be dumbstruck. "Cure him?" She looked down again at Mr. Nagg. "You don't even like him. He abandoned you for an afternoon snack." She laughed pointedly. Accusingly. "He's not even fit for grunt work anymore. What would be the point?" She held the lantern higher, getting a better look at Isabella.

Isabella locked eyes with Gwendolyn. Somewhere, under all that bravado, was genuine anger. And under that anger, artfully concealed and tucked away in the smallest corner where her eyes met her soul, was . . . confusion. This Gwendolyn Gooch, whoever she was, did not understand why Isabella would want Mr. Nagg back. She'd, correctly, deduced him to be of little intelligence. Mean-spirited. A poor husband, and weak in character. He was the type of person that Gwendolyn treated as set dressing, or as something to hang fur coats on.

And she was right, of course. Mr. Nagg was all those things. And Isabella knew that whatever life she returned to, it would not include Mr. Nagg. Her rational mind told her that it would be easy, even understandable, to retreat without him, to let the market have what was left of him. They'd spent two decades avoiding each other as best they could.

But he wasn't Gwendolyn's to take. Isabella was not done with Mr. Nagg yet. It wasn't Gwendolyn's right to charge into East Grasby, trample over decades of scrupulously cultivated grudges, and steal closure from under Isabella's nose. Had Gwendolyn washed his filthy socks? Had Gwendolyn boiled his scrunge whilst his first wife moldered in a shallow grave barely a hundred yards away? This Gwendolyn Gooch had no right to be Mr. Nagg's executioner. She hadn't earned it.

"I will be taking Mr. Nagg." The surety in Isabella's voice surprised her. She held up the wonky poker. "And you will not stop me."

The smile that spread across Gwendolyn's perfectly made-up face indicated she'd been waiting for the right moment to execute a dramatic reveal. "I'm afraid I can't allow that. I don't think you've met my partner."

Behind the strange woman, something rose large. A shadow that lumbered into the light. It was a corpse, headless and fair-skinned, with a lithe torso and waxy dead flesh. Isabella recognized that handsome, strong body, somehow unchanged for over twenty long years.

Gwendolyn crowed triumphantly, but cut herself short as the body stepped fully into the light. It was wearing a pot of basil on its neck, where its head should be. The pot was broken now, a broad crack in the front spilling out dirt and giving the appearance of a screaming mouth. Underneath, bleached bone peeked out. The tendrils of basil waving in the night air gave the strange appearance of hair.

"Body," Gwendolyn snapped at it, "what in the seven hells are you doing? Remove that pot of basil at once, you look ridiculous."

Isabella was thunderstruck. It was her saving grace that Gwendolyn Gooch did not tolerate whimsy from her employees.

"That is not Gooch-approved headgear," she rounded on it.

"Isabella!" the pot of basil piped up from where it sat atop the body, held in place by the thrumming of Gramayre. "Isabella, I am beautiful again! You can be mine! I shall have you, you shall be a thing that belongs to me, that is mine!" More dirt fell away from the opening, showing the skull's rictus grin.

"You what? Her? You will remove that plant this instant and go back to the boudoir."

The grimalkin, as softly and stealthily as if it were a real cat in a coal cellar at midnight, touched Isabella on the leg with its nose. This was enough to break the paralysis.

She had a choice to make. She could run, abandoning Mr.

Nagg in the mud. This Gwendolyn would likely not pursue, and Isabella would be safe from danger. The monstrous basil would remain behind, also. She'd have to leave both of them here, in the filth of the market. Or she could stay, and risk almost certain capture (and perhaps even death) at the hands of this woman and her goblins. A choice she did not want to make.

She was at a crossroads.

Isabella reached inside her shirt and removed something small.

"Now you listen to me, you horrible corpse," Gwendolyn spat at the body, all imitation of affection having vanished on contact with resistance. "My goblins surround you on all sides. No one crosses a Gooch, do you hear me?" A horrible smile etched itself across her face. "In fact, you'll both be staying here. Our work has barely begun."

A white flame sparked to life in the darkness, like a distant star. Isabella dropped the tinder, which fell to the dirt, shining ever more brightly.

"Sorcery!" wailed Gwendolyn. "Body, hold her! Stop her!"

The body made as if to fulfil the command, and then jerked backwards as if it were being pulled in the other direction by its own head.

"This body is mine," cried the pot of basil. "I must have it, for Isabella!"

Gwendolyn raged at the body.* The body swung about as it tried to fulfil both her commands and the cacophonous will of the pot of basil.

As the white light faded, a hound materialized in the shadows in front of Isabella. It was hulking, prowling, larger than a horse. It had glowing eyes as big as dinner plates.

---

* It did not occur to her that she should intervene personally. Not when there were employees who could be coerced into it.

"You have called me with the tinderbox, sorcerer," it growled. The voice was low, and unfriendly. "And so I must serve you. You may ask a boon of me, the Second Hound, greater in strength than my sibling the First Hound. Tell me what it is you wish, and if it is within my power, I shall give it."

Isabella grabbed hold of Mr. Nagg by the shoulders.

"Hound," she whispered, so quietly only she could hear it. "Take us home."

A wind picked up in the valley, carrying with it stray goblin fruit and scraps of awning. Fiercely and quickly it blew, drowning out the protests of Gwendolyn Gooch, snuffing out all lights but the burning of the tinderbox and the twin eyes of the Second Hound. Darkness wrapped itself around Isabella and Mr. Nagg, enveloping them in velvet and sulfur.

# 33

## GOBLINBALL

HE GOBLINS were gathered around Gwendolyn's tent, in the darkness, a restless horde of green and rubbery skin, and they were going to kill her. The evening had started normally enough, with Lady Gooch busy doing more of the boring scribbling she was so fond of, and so the goblins had the evening to themselves. The same way they did every night. Once the game of giving goblin fruit to villagers had become dull, the goblins increasingly found themselves with nothing to do. And so, at the end of their patience, they had turned to a game of goblinball.

The rules of goblinball,* scrawled with chalk on a large stone at the edge of the market, were deceptively simple:

1. *There are no rules.*
2. *The second rule had been smudged during a game of goblinball, and no one could remember what it was. There was speculation amongst the goblins as to whether*

---

* Goblins adore lists. They go out of their way to make them. They love them almost as much as they love sorting things into piles, and then destroying those piles.

*it had been deliberately erased, but nothing had been proven, because goblins have little patience for proper investigative procedure.*

According to the *Gramayre*, no one wins a game of goblinball, except perhaps anyone who wagered in favor of high civilian casualties.

The goblinball itself was made from matted goblin hair wound over and over again into a semi-spherical shape. Goblin hair has exceptional tensile strength, and when repeatedly stressed, it slowly gains that distinctive rubbery quality which makes for an excellent (and lethal) goblinball. The problems began when the goblinball ricocheted off a half-finished wall and out past the boundary of the worksite. The goblins were explicitly forbidden by Lady Gooch from exiting the site at night, and so they gathered along the edge of the boundary staring wistfully into the dark.

A meeting was called, and the goblins, over one hundred strong, gathered to discuss their options. Initially, it was a cacophony of shrieking yelps and loud complaints (as was tradition), eventually settling into more of an informal symposium. Ideas were mooted, with each goblin standing to hoot in the goblin tongue. The suggestions were compiled and arranged, as goblins love to do, in order of which smelled the best. This took a further half an hour. Several robust runners-up were noted, such as building a bridge made entirely of goblins so that none of them technically set foot outside the grounds (rejected on account of goblin aerodynamics), and training some of the chickens to hunt down and retrieve the goblinball (rejected in case the chickens should develop any funny ideas about who was in charge).*

---

* It might seem odd to you that goblins, which are (after all) only offshoots of a single hive mind, would argue at all. Think of it like playing solitaire.

About half an hour into this process, a large snake began to eat goblins around the camp. It had legs, which made it more of a wyrm than a snake, but the nuance was lost on the goblins. The creature casually walked into the symposium, cried "bapplez" in hissing tones, and started swallowing goblins whole. Chaos erupted, with goblins fleeing in all directions.*

Now, goblins are patient creatures. Forbearing. As a fungus, they are keenly aware that they only need wait long enough and the entire world will be theirs. It doesn't matter if there are some road bumps along the way, in theory, as in the long term the tactic of distributing goblin fruit to spread the mycelium layer was working just fine, thank you very much. That being said, the collective mind of a goblin colony is incredibly sensitive to potential threats. They can identify, for instance, a wildfire. Or a cyclone. These are dangers significant enough that the colony might be compelled to act in self-preservation.

It was the release of the linnorm under her watch which finally upgraded Gwendolyn Gooch from Entertaining Nuisance to Existential Threat. Deep below the surface of the valley, the network of fungus which composed the collective goblin brain revised its calculations. Gwendolyn Gooch had proved an effective innovator in the spread of goblin fruit. The villagers gathered this year would make for excellent fertilizer for next year's goblin crop. She had, however, outlived her usefulness, and was now clearly attracting dangerous sorcerers and serpents.

As one, the goblins reached a resolution. Gwendolyn Gooch must die.

---

* This is a tried and tested defence tactic common to goblins, small birds, and career politicians.

# Fetch ◆◆◆◆◆◆

## (Mirabilis mirrorbilis)

OTHER NAMES: SHADE, DOPPELGÄNGER

The fetch manifests without warning or ceremony, and is a sign that death is close.\* It appears in every way to be a copy of the onlooker, and is seldom visible to others.† Some fetches have been said to follow the viewer for days before death occurs, moving through walls and curtains with equal abandon, which can be quite bothersome if you rely on them for privacy. Fetches are docile in demeanor, instead displaying a peculiar empathy that implies sentience, but no way has been found to convince one to communicate in words. Not all those doomed to die will see a fetch, and in some exceedingly rare cases, a creature having seen a fetch is spared death for unknown reasons.‡ It is common courtesy to thank your fetch for their service if you see them, because even if they do have something to do with your imminent death, one should strive to go to one's grave with dignity.

*from the Mount Pelican copy of the* Household Gramayre, *volume IX*, Of Spiritual Properties and Ethereal Real Estate, *section XXIV*, *"Fetches"*

# 34

# GWENDOLYN ESCAPES
# THE MARKET

GWENDOLYN GOOCH did not know the meaning of the word *lose*, but she knew when her plans required a rapid readjustment. Back in her tent, nursing her ego, she clutched a tall glass of wine* and thought about her next move. The body was gone. It had lurched off into the distance as if it were being controlled by a demented puppeteer. This whole evening reeked of sorcery and nonsense. She downed the wine and poured herself another. This was turning into as much of a disaster as Gooch's Bar & Grill, or (she hesitated to remember) Straight-to-Gooch Deliveries.

Poring over her fiscal projections, which were not positive given the sudden downturn in productivity amongst the village workers, she began to plot her next move. Alas, the numbers didn't lie. It was time to start thinking about new ventures.

---

* Experimentation had revealed that distilled goblin fruit produced a dry alcohol which was not at all poisonous, and which tasted faintly of surprise. She called it goblin wine, which gave a false impression of the alcohol percentage.

The wretched Nagg woman was a sorcerer, and revenge would require the kind of Daedalian planning that only a business-woman with an extremely long lifespan could afford to indulge. No, this Isabella Nagg had not heard the last of Gwendolyn Gooch. She took satisfaction, however, in the fact that her Mr. Nagg would be dead in mere hours by the look of him. She'd written him off in the Deprecated Assets section of her accounts book.

Her accounts book! Best not to forget that. She picked it up and started to pack a large holdall. Always leave the party early: that was one of the mantras she liked to repeat to herself when a business reached the Abandon Ship phase of its development. Her pit was full of goblin bodies, and the fruit-charmed villagers were proving about as useful as a glass hammer. She shoved her market plans into a part of her mind where she kept all her schemes, saving them for another day. Maybe she could get into crickets. There was supposed to be quite the lucrative market in morally superior insects in the southlands, across the straits. A farm? An advice farm? She'd workshop it on the way.

She turned, already moving for the door, but found her path blocked by a trio of goblins wielding the very serrated knives she had insisted they acquire to deal with the bloodthirsty trees. They were eyeing her with a hungry look.

"Lady Gooch must be tired," said a goblin, dragging the knife along the floor.

"Lady Gooch must rest," said the second, with a low chuckle.

Gwendolyn had been on the board of directors for no fewer than seventeen companies in the past century, and she knew a violent coup when she saw one.

She tipped the nearest table. Tablets, oils, and perfumes scattered everywhere. The goblins were engulfed in a choking smog, and Gwendolyn made for the back of the tent, grabbing a fruit knife. It had a pearl inlay, and she'd stolen it from a close friend on their birthday, which made it sentimental. Executing a swift series of cuts, she forged a Gooch-shaped hole in the back of the tent and stepped through.* As she slipped into the darkness, she heard the shocked noises of goblins all around. They hadn't expected her to come out alive, that was clear, so she seized the element of surprise and attacked.

Gwendolyn Gooch was many things. Leader in commerce. Notorious criminal. Wanted in several countries for economic crimes including but not limited to arson, fraud, and inventing the concept of embezzlement. These were things she had taken for herself, identities she had forged. Underneath all this, however, Gwendolyn's blood was touched by Gramarye, all the way back to Great-grandmother Gooch. Pointed ears she possessed, yes, but grace and swiftness were her birthright also. She was more dangerous in high heels with a letter opener than the average warrior with a broadsword, and the goblins realized their mistake too late. Numbers would not avail them here, as for the second time that evening the assembled horde was routed by a middle-aged woman wielding an improvised weapon. Step by step, she cut her way through the crowd, using the other hand to grab goblins by the throat and hurl them twenty feet in the air.

It was a long way from her tent to the boundary of the market, and even as she carved and diced and filleted, she could see more glittering teeth appearing in the light shed by the lanterns. There were so many of them. Had she . . . had she miscalculated? Even elf flesh must tire, and her knife-wielding arm, covered in goblin goo, seemed heavy. She wasn't as young as she had been once, though she tried not to think about that. A century or two ago, she'd have cut these creatures to ribbons with a single hand, and had energy to spare to do a few laps of the perimeter. She

---

* She was intimately familiar with this procedure.

flagged just a little. A goblin lunged past her guard and gave her a savage bite on the ankle. Enraged, and in shock, she stepped on its head, which exploded into foul-smelling gunk. A flesh wound, but a nasty one. She didn't remember the last time she'd let an enemy get the upper hand like this. The goblins circled around, slowly tightening the noose on her position.

Gwendolyn Gooch raised herself up to her full height. Was this the end for Gwendolyn Gooch? Did she have regrets? Knives and teeth closed in on her all around, and in her last moments she closed her eyes and thought about how, if she could do it all again, she'd have made more money.

But the killing blow never came. Instead, there was a thump, and a squeal. A braying sound, and the sickening crack of goblin cartilage stamped underfoot. She opened one eye.

Goblins are suffused with numbers and enthusiasm, but these qualities are more than counterbalanced by their lack of physical strength, and their tendency to scatter in the face of danger. Danger, in this instance, was represented by a donkey, which was using its hind legs to throw goblins into the air with a remarkable disregard for its own self-preservation. Behind it, bringing up the rear through a confused sea of toothy faces, was a pony which appeared to have manifested a bag of snakes around its neck, which were slithering off into the crowd and causing yet more panic.

"Is this business?" asked the donkey, reaching her as the pony cantered around distributing snakes and the goblins ran about in a blind panic. "Are we doing business?"

Gwendolyn smiled. She could make something of this. A scheme was already starting to germinate in her mind.

"How would you like," she said, in her most convincing voice, "to be an employee?"

# 35

## THE CURE

I N  T H E single bedroom they hated to share, Isabella watched as Mr. Nagg wasted away, ranting feverishly. He strained against his bonds, the belts securing him to the bedposts, and his skin burned with a terrible inner fire. Sometimes he seemed lucid, begging for water, and other times he burbled nonsense sounds or screamed. All the while, Isabella studied the *Household Gramarye* for some fragment, some tidbit of lore that might save him. The grimalkin paced at her feet, trying to get her attention. It had arrived at the house missing its tail, another sacrifice made to the hounds of the tinderbox. "Isabella," it said to her, though the words barely penetrated her awareness, so absorbed was she in her dark thoughts, "Isabella, the licce will come for us, we must flee." She did not answer it. She could not. There was no time. Thoughts of flight were useless—where would she go? There was nowhere. Only her house, her kitchen, her valley. And it would hunt her, tirelessly. She knew that to be true in the depths of the Common Sense, which kept her mind from smashing to pieces like the giant which carried the skies on its shoulders.* No, Isabella would not flee. And she would deal with one problem at a time.

She stared at what was left of Mr. Nagg, tied to the bed. She'd seen this before, this withering of flesh, this terrible curse. She'd buried the memory, long ago. Lorenzo. He'd had the same look in his eyes, the same death rattle caught in his throat, even as she'd cut his head from his shoulders. She hadn't been able to help Lorenzo, but she was different now. She had the *Gramarye*.

As she worked, turning page after page through wirrikows and hellwains, bugbears† and hobhoulards, she did not allow herself to pause. There was no time. Yes, Mr. Nagg was a coward. A bully. A bad husband, and a poor excuse for a companion. But he was hers, and the goblin market would not take another from her. She would not allow it. She could not allow it.

Out to the garden she went, in the throes of Gramarye, and she pulled from plants as she walked, those plants she had spent her years cultivating and of which she now demanded a service. Chrysanthemum she gathered, to stay those on the threshold of death. Angelica she plucked from the root, to repel sorcery. Althaea she crushed between her palms, to soothe the ravages of goblin fruit. Fumitory, a bitter scent to banish evil. Witchwood for strength. Hoodwort for fidelity. Winterbloom.

---

* This was a fact, surely as the beetle drove the sun across the sky, and the devil was an estate agent. The giant didn't do much, which was just as well, because when he shrugged or sighed, it resulted in extreme weather.

† The common or garden bugbear finds itself drawn to bright lights and food, and can be found hovering inside concert halls and museums with ceilings big enough to accommodate it. The *Household Gramayre* recommends that on meeting a bugbear, one should try to make oneself seem as large and intimidating as possible, but to avoid looking like a platter of untended leftovers.

Marshbane. Through the moonlight she stormed, gathering her life's work to bring it to bear against the sickness.

The recipe came to her not from the *Gramayre*, but from somewhere beneath the layers of Common Sense, under the grief and anger that had fueled her for so long, from below the person who called themselves Isabella, from deep inside the heart. From someone who had always been there. Someone beautiful.

The final ingredient was obvious, in the end. The answer was so simple she could almost weep. Standing in the moonlight before the Nagg Stone, her gaze travelled downwards to the mandrake plants at its root. The yearly mandrake cuttings Mr. Nagg brought to Bagdemagus. The mandrake he must have used, autumn after autumn, to keep the goblins at bay. Useless, hideous, extraordinary mandrake that was anathema to the very toxin she was attempting to purge. It would work, she knew it in her soul.*

Back to the small house she marched, under the broken gables, to the fireplace. "Cook, little pot, cook!" she commanded, and the pot obeyed, flames springing to life beneath it. Herbs she cast into the cauldron, muttering to herself as she pulled yet more volumes of the *Gramarye* to her side. They came to her gladly, as they would to a master of their craft, and she did not notice that they hovered inches above the table as the pages fluttered open to the spells she needed. As she worked, the grimalkin danced about her, glutting itself on the sight, all words of warning subsumed by the ecstasy of Gramarye. It whispered secrets to her above the bubbling hiss of her

---

* Specialists in the Gramayre are divided on the existence of the soul, and experiments to catch or detect one have run the gamut from gentle questioning to laying down bear traps in an art gallery.

elixir as she delved ever deeper into secret lore, preparing this one possibility. This one miracle. Her cure.

Up the stairs Mrs. Nagg went, carrying her pot of steaming porridge. Mr. Nagg writhed and rocked in the bed, face drawn and pale. Already he seemed to be fading, skin stretched tight over his bones. Grasping him firmly, almost cruelly, she forced her cure down his throat without so much as a word of comfort. He would live, if she had to kill him to do it.

Then, she waited. Seconds turned to minutes, and slowly, glacially, his contortions began to lessen. His eyes started to see once more, and he turned to face her, voice hoarse. "Isabella," he said, recognizing her. She felt his head. The fever was subsiding, under the surface. How much time had her concoction bought her? He was skeletal, his face grey with fatigue. She must prepare another draught, for energy, or he might not make it until morning. She rose to leave, and a hand grabbed her wrist. Wiry, now. Weak. But pity stayed her, and she turned to face her husband.

"Isabella." His voice was feeble. Perhaps he would live, now that he had tasted her cure. He was helpless as a babe, and yet he seemed almost . . . pleased. "I knew you would save me."

Yes. Of course he had. Isn't that what she did? Isabella pulls Mr. Nagg out of a scrape. Isabella cleans Mr. Nagg's plates. Isabella fixes the messes he makes. She searched his cadaverous face with her eyes. What was she looking for? Why had she dragged him from the market? Even now, she struggled to find the answer. He reached out for her, and in his expression was an echo of that feeble, sickly smile which had shackled her to his house, to this place, for so long.

"I found Edith." It was all she could think of to say. "I found her, Henric."

Was he frightened? He seemed confused. Eyes darting to the door. He made to rise, but he had no energy for it. The goblin fruit had wasted his flesh almost to the bone.

"You killed her." She said it softly, but it was not a question. Somewhere between leaving home to find him and bringing him back, she had changed, and she could say now what she had been afraid to consider before.

"Yes," he whispered. "I had to. She was going to leave, Isabella. I wanted her to stay. I thought if she was sick, then she would stay."

Her expression must have held some aspect that frightened him, because he kept spluttering as if trying to grasp some explanation which would suffice.

"I didn't mean her to die, I only used a little. You know I can't be by myself. I needed her to stay. I need you, Isabella."

He reached out a hand to her, but she instinctively pulled back. Her thoughts were racing. Poison? Where had Mr. Nagg—

Mandrake. She looked down at her hands, still coated in residue from her potion working. Mandrake was poison, and no one knew that better than Mr. Nagg. How had she never seen that before?

The words of the *Household Gramayre* came to her, unasked. *Smaller doses may result in lethargy, anxiety, and confusion . . .*

Oh, Mr. Nagg. Hopeless, mediocre Mr. Nagg. Sly enough to capture a bird, cruel enough to keep it in a cage, too stupid to know he would be the death of it.

His smile was manic, a crazed death mask. "You understand, I know you do. I was there in the valley that night, when you killed that man." He gurgled, and a little blood leaked out from between his front teeth. "You cut his head off. We're the same, Isabella, you and I."

And just like that, she let him go. Let go of her need to save him from disasters of his own making. Released herself from his grasping, greedy claws. It was like she had been carrying him on her back for so long that she'd forgotten why everything was so heavy. It was time for that part of her which was called Mrs. Nagg to die. Oh, Mrs. Nagg! Ever suffering, wondering how to salve her pain, never realizing that she was pain. Isabella forgave Mrs. Nagg, and she shed her to the bedroom floor like a serpent leaving its old skin behind.

Mr. Nagg curled up on the bed, reached for her with both hands.

"Isabella"—he wept openly now—"you won't leave me, will you? You'll stay?"

She approached the bed. Freed from Mrs. Nagg, she could see more clearly. It was time for this story to end, and Isabella was the only one who could end it. One last mistake to fix on Mr. Nagg's behalf, in honour of who Mrs. Nagg had been. For Edith.

# 36

## REAPER

THE UNSEEN entity which called herself Reaper came for Mr. Nagg the same way she came for everyone: whenever she felt like it and wielding a gigantic pair of scissors. Gently, she snipped the thread of his life, and it was over. Reaching past the still form of Isabella Nagg, who was cutting off her dead husband's head in a practical manner, she took the thread in her hands and cradled it the same way she did all the others. With care, she examined it, raising it up to her cataracts so she could perceive the fine details of it. It was, like most lives, neither good nor bad. Those were not terms she really concerned herself with, nor understood. She put the thread away neatly in her pocket.

In better days, she wouldn't have had to fetch the threads herself. She thought about it often, those many years ago when she and her sisters had sat in a field filled with still flowers under a tree that never bloomed, spinning, measuring, and cutting the threads of mortal life to fulfil the grand design. Alas, no longer. Spinner still sat under the tree, feeding her hair into the wheel and creating wanton life. Reaper wandered the world, putting an end to mortal life when it seemed apropos. And Measure? Beautiful, wise Measure. Measure who determined the length of a mortal life, who kept the seasons turning one after another, who maintained that delicate balance on which all the world's laws were founded. Measure was nowhere to be found. Without Measure, the sun wandered across the sky without purpose. Without Measure, that which should be dead rose from the soil in a grim mockery of the living. Without Measure, nothing was as it should be. Reaper didn't know how long a life should be, not without Measure to guide her, and yet in her sister's absence she did her best. She gave them all the time she could spare. Whenever she cut a thread, she wondered if things could have been different. She wished for her sister's guidance, for the comfort of knowing how things were Meant to Be. And yet their parting had been bitter. Final. In Measure's absence, Reaper didn't understand anything anymore, such as why Isabella was cutting the head off a corpse.

Reaper reached into her pocket and retrieved Mr. Nagg's thread, feeling the bumps and twists of it, winding it around her fingers. Then, she left.

# 37

## THE BASIL'S EVIL PLAN

I N THE end, Mr. Nagg died the same way he had lived—a
disappointment. It was not her first time removing a man's
head, and so it didn't take as long as it had for Lorenzo. It
was poetic, she thought. Edith was long gone, and justice was
beyond her reach now, but if there was to be any in this world,
then Mr. Nagg would return more life to the world than he had
stolen.

"Isabella," said the grimalkin, freshly awake from its nap, "is
that what I think it is?"

She looked at the head she was holding in one hand. "Mr.
Nagg is dead," she proffered by way of explanation.

"Yes, I can see that." It stretched a little. "But what are you
going to do with his head? Please tell me you're not going to—"

Moving to the windowsill, she found her second-largest
plant pot, currently holding some begonias,* and gently lifted
out the plant as best she could. Then, she placed Mr. Nagg's
head inside and covered it in soil.

"You," said the grimalkin, sourly, "are going to get
a reputation."

---

* The begonias resented this, but that is a story for another time.

"Grimalkin," she said to the famulus, "you must watch the body until dawn. It has already been left alone too long."

"Isabella," it said, staring at the severed head in her hands, "what about the licce—"

"If you do not watch over Mr. Nagg," she said firmly, "we shall have two on our hands. Go, and I shall deal with the basil. Now!"

She commanded it more firmly than she had intended, but it had the desired result. The grimalkin pattered over to the stairwell and took a look behind it, as if memorizing her face. "Try to stay alive," it said, attempting a dry tone that failed to mask its concern.

Finally alone, she set the cauldron down in the hearth and sat on one of the cold wooden chairs that made her back ache. The fire had burned low by now, and shadows were everywhere.

Pushing aside the tomes of the *Gramayre*, she slumped across the table's broad, comforting surface, and she wept. Not for Mr. Nagg, and his piteous, racked body, trapped forever in his last moments of suffering. But for what Mr. Nagg was to her, what he had failed to be, and for what she had discovered. The tears were angry ones, and she resented them even as she grieved what had become of her. All the wasted time, all the lost potential of her years, sitting in this house, searching for the strength of poor Edith, who had paid the ultimate price for her bravery.

And she waited. Across the table from her, ephemeral as a shadow, her fetch waited with her. You didn't see your fetch unless you needed it. Unless the possibility of your death was close at hand. It looked like her, just as tired, just as old as she felt. It smiled, a kind smile, and reached out a hand across the table, and she placed hers there, though she could not touch it.

"Isabella." The voice of the pot of basil, just as she had always imagined it. Her constant companion. Her comfort.

"Wise, beautiful Isabella. Do not weep, Isabella. All shall be well."

It took a moment for her to realize that the voice was real. She raised her head from the table.

In the doorway to the kitchen, a horror loomed. The corpse of Lorenzo, dead these twenty years, assumed a lopsided posture, hunched over as if it didn't remember how to stand. The pot of basil, perched on the neck in the manner of a head, was broken at the front, revealing Lorenzo's skull, where she had buried it all those years ago.

"Lorenzo." She had worked her spellcraft all the day, and through much of the night. She was too exhausted to run, and yet she stood. She would face this creature on her feet, in her own house. A licce. He had not died that day. And now he was here for her. For revenge?

"Isabella," the pot of basil crooned. There was a vestige of Lorenzo's voice in there. "Now that I am whole, we can be together as we planned. You can be like me, Isabella. Immortal."

Was Isabella surprised? No. She had known this confrontation was coming from the moment she had seen the body in the goblin market. But there was nothing to be done. No time to study, no working of Gramayre available to her that she had not expended in the rescue of the poor, dead Mr. Nagg. It was almost funny. To spend her entire life cleaning up after Mr. Nagg, and now to die because she had insisted on, yes, cleaning up after his death throes. It was poetic, in a way. Isabella's life, wasted. She laughed, and it was hollow.

The pot of basil bristled.

"Why do you laugh?" It seemed annoyed. "This is all you and I have ever wanted."

She wiped the tears from her eyes, which were sore from rubbing and stung from the herb smoke of her cauldron.

"I don't want that anymore," she said to it. There was no

harm in the truth now. It was going to kill her, and she would rise as a licce to haunt this empty valley until the end of time. "I don't need you anymore, basil. I was wrong to keep you, I was wrong to leave you in the dark."

The body jerked, and the basil muttered darkly. The two seemed at odds.

"Do you remember," she asked it, "the night we met? How much of you is in there, Lorenzo?"

It had started innocently enough. A walk in the moonlight with the passionate, the dangerous, her darling Lorenzo. It wasn't the done thing in East Grasby for a young woman to fall for a stranger, but oh she had doted on Lorenzo. The perpetually confused expression. The winsome smile. He'd stumbled into town, describing himself as a mendicant bard looking for somewhere to sleep for the night, and she'd found him hiding in her father's barn. It was a romance of the kind she'd read in the legends, where a dashing knight chances across a lonely maiden in the forest. Lorenzo was as smooth a talker as he claimed to be in the saddle, and they met each night in secret. He would speak to her of his grand plans for their future together, and she had been swept up in the illusions he conjured. They'd planned to run away, to elope somewhere new. But she'd needed time, and she'd told him to stay in the barn while she laid hold of what coins she could from the family home and said her goodbyes. Three days, she'd asked for. It hadn't seemed too much to ask. But on the third day, the first day of autumn, she'd returned to the barn to find him gone, his trail leading down into the valley. She'd never run so fast as she had that day, all care and thought of subterfuge gone as she raced to save him from himself.

But she was too late. When she arrived, Lorenzo was sitting there, goblin fruit dribbling down his chin. The first fruit of the autumn was always potent. She'd done him a mercy, in the end, not that he could have resisted in his stupor. She'd wanted to stay with him, but if the fruit was already in bloom, then goblins were afoot. It hadn't been safe. She couldn't carry him, but she couldn't stay until dawn. In her desperation she'd done the only thing she could think of—she'd chopped off his head and taken it home, thinking it was impossible for a licce to rise from a corpse so badly damaged.

That rest of that night was a blur, time had healed old wounds in the only way it knows how, but she remembered carrying the head to the largest pot she could find. Digging at the earth with her garden tools, tools that were supposed to be used for growing, for making, she'd filled the pot with soft earth. Atop the soil she planted the first herb she could find, to disguise what she'd done. Her pot of basil.

"I remember," said the pot of basil. "I remember waiting for you, Isabella. You told me to wait. And I have waited all these long years. You are finally mine."

"No, Lorenzo." The air fell still between them. "You are dead. And I do not want the same things I once did."

The pot of basil ignored the words it did not want to hear. "Do not weep, kind Isabella. You are confused, but your troubles are almost over. You will think more clearly in the dark. In the eternity we shall spend together, you shall come to love me again."

"Basil," she used the name readily, for to her this creature was closer to the pot of basil than the Lorenzo who had died so long ago.

She was so very tired, and the wickedness of the basil seemed to fill the room, guttering the candles. Triumphantly, it stepped into the kitchen, ducking so that it did not knock its own head on the ceiling. For a moment Isabella considered giving up, of slipping into unquiet dreams.

But there is no rest for the wicked, nor for wizards.

"Ah!" the pot of basil rejoiced. "Moments now, and we shall be together in death. We shall be immortal, you and I. Undying. Never ageing. Isabella and her pot of basil, as it was always meant to be."

As it moved, the fire leaped in the hearth, and something glinted. Something she had forgotten. The tinderbox was where she had left it, on the other side of the table. It had one use remaining, one last and most terrible hound left to conjure. But by the time she managed to light it, the basil would have her. She needed time.

# Hob ◆◆◆◆◆◆

## (Arachnida domesticus)

OTHER NAMES: HOBHOULARD, BROWNIE

The hobhoulard, or hob, is a common species created on laying the foundations of a house, and is bounded thereby.* Fond of dark places, such as under sinks, in attics, and behind stacks of bags in cupboards, hobs are best known for their willingness to engage in household chores in exchange for gifts, such as a saucer of milk or a plate of delicious frozen crickets.† The many arms of a hob allow it to complete tasks with great speed, and to scuttle across ceilings with little difficulty. Hobs despise being perceived,‡ and go to great lengths to avoid being seen. Seldom has a hob been successfully interrogated to ascertain why they tolerate living in symbiosis. Hobs can be changeable in their opinion of co-inhabitants, even going so far as to hide items belonging to residents they despise, but their loyalty to the house itself is unshakeable. To intrude on a domicile protected by a hob is a poor choice indeed, if one values one's limbs.

___

*appearing in the second Verdigris Tabernacle copy of the* Household Gramayre, *volume II*, Of Things with Too Many Legs, Things with Not Enough Legs, and Things with the Correct Number of Legs, Which Is More Than One but Less Than Five, but Also Not Three, *section VIII, "Eight"*

* (tidy block capitals, annotated by the legal scholar Antimonides) The common hob's inability to leave the domicile extends to the land around it, up to the boundary of the property. This boundary is not always transferable by legal means, meaning hobs can often be found in unexpected places where titles have been split into multiple properties.

† (unknown commentator) Hobs unhappy with the offerings may write rude messages in dust or cobwebs such as CLEAN ME or CHEAPSKATE instead of cleaning.

‡ (attributed to Anastasia of Rebolt) It is speculated that the hob is a manifestation of the house itself, and that should a hob be harmed or slain, the building will suffer or meet a tragic end soon afterwards.

# 38

## THE DEATH OF
## ISABELLA NAGG

THE HEADLESS corpse lurched across the room with an unsteady gait. Lorenzo had been an intimidatingly large man in life, and the licce spawned from his corpse was wide enough to block any easy escape from the kitchen. It reached for her.

"Back!" she cried, grabbing a ladle from nearby. If only she could reach the tinderbox! But it was farther away than she could reach, and it might as well have been leagues away for all the use it was to her without a few moments to light it.

"Isabella," the pot of basil crooned. "You need not struggle, kind, gentle Isabella. We shall be together for eternity, once you are dead and cold."

The licce drew closer, hands outstretched, and the basil laughed, a deranged cackle of betrayal.

Facing the end, Isabella prepared to fight, squaring up to the corpse. So this is it, she thought to herself. These are the last moments of Isabella Nagg.

But in their fixation, all present had forgotten there was one piece left on the table, or (more accurately) underneath it. A furry hand reached out from under the kitchen table and grabbed the licce by the ankle, yanking with incredible force that threw the abomination off balance. The lights flickered and then a cupboard door slammed open, smacking the licce in the chest. It staggered. The Nagg Farm hob had sensed an intruder. Cutlery levitated from the sideboard, stabbing into the licce as it struggled to regain balance, swatting away projectiles like flies. Isabella took her chance and darted past the other side of the table, snatching the tinderbox as she dived for the door.

Enraged, the licce smashed at the kitchen surfaces with powerful fists, shattering the table she loved so much. To her it was like the sundering of an altar. The volumes of the *Gramayre* were hurled to the flagstones, pages creased and spines buckled. Isabella paused halfway through the door, turning back to look for the hob. Could she leave it? It had saved her. Crockery smashed against the floor as the licce raised its hands reflexively to protect the pot of basil, but the hob was running out of things to throw and, as the licce pulled a cupboard from the wall, places to hide. "You fool," shrieked the basil to its body as Isabella retreated through the back door. "She's getting away! Follow her!"

Isabella plunged into the night, squelching in the mud. The moons were hidden behind a cloud, and the night was dark, but she fled out into the fields by touch and scent alone, down these paths that she knew better than any living soul. Behind her, she heard the door of the house slam open, and still she ran. She'd never realized she could sprint like this, with the wind at her feet and hair tangled in her face, she ran until she could run no more, heading for the pathways out into the moors. There, she could hide. She needed to get as far away from the farm as possible. When she finally reached the road leading away from the farm, she paused.

Could she abandon the grimalkin? The hob? Could she really escape into nowhere with just the clothes on her back? Fleeing would not deter the licce. It was dead, and it would never tire in pursuit. She hesitated, unsure what to do. What decision to make.

A crossroads.

She fumbled inside her pockets for the tinderbox. Iron and flint she struck. Once. Twice. She heard the shuffling of long strides in the distance, crunching down the path towards her.

On the third attempt, the tinderbox finally produced a spark.

*I am the Third Hound, greatest and last of my siblings.*

The voice spoke to her, inside her, all around.

*You have summoned me with the tinderbox, sorcerer, and so I must obey. Ask a single boon of me, and I shall grant it, if it is within my power.*

"Help me," she asked. Where was the hound? She could not see it. She could hear the licce approaching. Her time was running out, even as the sparks from the tinderbox began to fade away.

*Very well,* said the hound. Then, the night itself moved. Clouds parted, revealing the twin moons. No, not moons. Eyes. The shadows above coalesced into a vast hound that seemed to fill the sky. Two vast eyes stared down on the world as the twin moons blinked, and the horizon yawned. The world dissolved into velvet and sulfur.

Moments later, the darkness retreated as the moonlight shone on Isabella's surroundings, and as she gained her bearings, her heart sank in despair. She knew this place. The hound had moved her, swept her up and deposited her at the back of the farmstead. Back to the cursed Nagg Stone, to the field of godforsaken mandrakes. The basil screeched in the distance, an inhuman scream of rage. Why had the hound sent her here? It had bought her mere moments at best. She threw the tinderbox at the stone in anger, and it bounced off into the dark. "I asked you to help me!" she yelled at the sky, but the twin moons stared down uncaringly.

The gate opened at the end of the field. "Isabella"—the basil's voice sounded more distorted with each passing moment—"you cannot run from me."

Why had the hound sent her here? She looked around her, swiveling left and right, searching for the answer. But she was out of time.

The licce bounded towards her across the field. The creature had picked up a cleaver on its way out of the house, and it swung the tool at her with great strength. It was aimed for her neck, there was nothing that could stop it now.

With a clang, the cleaver struck stone. It had missed, impossibly.

"What?!" The pot of basil seemed just as confused as Isabella.

The body raised the cleaver again, and gave it another swing. The arm descended, quivering, and halted an inch from Isabella.

"Body!" the basil shrieked. "I command you! You are my body, and you will do as I say!"

The body shuddered, shaking as if being pulled in two directions at once. It had laboured too long under its own devices, and it had gained its own feelings, wants, and desires. It had spent the many years of its isolation without its memories, and it barely remembered Isabella. The life it knew, the life it wanted, belonged to a corona of golden hair, and an imperious voice. The body didn't belong to Lorenzo anymore. It didn't want to be here, and it strained against the domination of the head, digging its feet into the soil.*

---

* The body could not possibly have known that, several miles distant, the object of its affections was putting together plans for the Menagoocherie

Swinging its limbs erratically, the licce stumbled over its own feet and crashed neck-first into the Nagg Stone, on which Isabella was leaning. The pot of basil dropped free of the neck and cracked against the base of the obelisk.

Isabella finally exhaled, only now realizing that she'd been holding her breath since the first swing of the cleaver. The sheer bad luck surrounding the Nagg Stone had bought her a few moments, but it couldn't last forever. Even now the body was scrabbling to find its feet.

"Isabella"—the basil was furious. Roots pushed their way from the soil of the broken pot, extending like legs in an attempt to push itself upright. The skull, nested in a cage of twisted roots, screamed in a voice tainted by death and madness. "This is pointless! You cannot resist me! I am immortal, and you will join me whether it is tonight or a thousand nights from now!"

The basil was right, of course. It would chase her until the stars went out, if it had to. She could run from here, but it would find her. And yet, what could she do? How did you kill a creature that was already dead?

She placed a hand on the Nagg Stone, looking for strength. Looking up at the moons, she begged them silently for the answer. Why would the hound have sent her here, of all places? The body was now back on its feet, and the pot of basil was dragging itself towards her using its roots like sinewy claws. Through the soil. Through the mandrakes.

Kneeling at the foot of the rock, she reached into the gnarled roots gathered about the base, fingers curling around the largest plant she could find. Then, she pulled.

---

of Talking Beasts, having forgotten all about goblins and walking corpses. Behind her, a donkey and a pony pulled her cart in happy silence, content in each other's company, and the promise of the open road.

*Those who hear their given name called by the mandrake plant and find it true know that . . . in these cases death will surely follow . . .*

She pulled.

As the mandrake left the soil, she felt its shape in her hand. It was alike to a person in form, a bulging pale root with trailing arms and legs. Between the folds of plant flesh, a tiny mouth opened. It screamed, and the noise pulsed like a shock wave through the still night air.

An unnatural voice rippled through the air, contained within the scream. The cry of the mandrake, which brought certain death.

*Isabella.*

The voice called to her, called her by the name she had been given. In the darkness, under the light of the twin moons, Isabella wavered. The door of death yawned wide, inviting.

But something wasn't right.

*Isabella*, it called to her.

That wasn't her name. Not anymore.

Rising to her feet, she dropped the mandrake to the earth.

The licce thrashed on the ground, beating the earth and clawing at it with its bare hands. It had no head and could not scream, but the contortions of its muscles as it bucked to and fro made it seem like a dying spider. The basil plant contorted as well, roots grasping at the soil, clawing for a hold on the living world. What remained of Lorenzo, hearing that name it had never questioned, never outgrown, was called to that true death from which there is no escape. Soon enough, both torso and skull stopped moving. The basil plant, no longer animated by Gramayre, withered away into ash.

Then, the wizard whose name was not Isabella dusted the mud from their clothes and walked back to the house.

# EPILOGUE

T HE *Household Gramayre* refers to the Need Fire in volume II, *Of Elements*, as "a working of last resort" and
describes the process for making one from the ruins of
your own house. A Need Fire can only be made in this way, as
a marker of the life you intend to leave behind. The passage in
the *Gramarye* makes sure to mention, as do several footnotes in
most copies, that the flames produced by a Need Fire burn for
as long as they must, and cannot be extinguished.

Nagg Farm burned more easily than one would have
thought. The wizard had used the tinderbox to light it, tossing it onto the pyre, though no hound had appeared this time.
The buildings were founded in old stone, but wooden walls and
ambitious* thatching made the place a powder keg just waiting
for a spark. They'd laid the hob's body to rest on what was left
of the old kitchen table, and in its furry hands the keys to the
cottage it had doted on.

Accompanied by the grimalkin, they stood on a hill over-
looking the farm as roaring flames consumed the place they'd
once called home. Down into the valley, the jaunty tents had
caught alight and the fires were raging just as merrily. Flames

---

* in places, non-Euclidean

were the safest way to waylay a goblin threat, at least for now. Next year the goblins would re-emerge in the valley, and someone would need to be ready.

"The valley still needs a wizard." The grimalkin had one eyebrow raised. Both eyes were closed forever now, the price demanded of the third tinderbox hound. The famulus seemed to navigate the world as quickly and quietly as it ever had. ("I see in many different ways," was all it would tell her.)

Wizard. That had a nice ring to it. Whoever Isabella Nagg had been, she was dead, slain by the mandrake as surely as if her head had been severed from her shoulders. This new person? This new person was a wizard.

"You'll need a wizard name, naturally," continued the grimalkin, already wandering off. "How about Balthazar? I always liked Balthazar."

The new wizard of the valley shook their head. That didn't feel right at all. "I quite like Alfred," they said, pensively, picking up the bags.

"Alfred?" the cat scoffed. "No, you need something a bit more arcane. People aren't going to take an Alfred seriously, they'll be asking you to juggle or find missing socks before you know it." The grimalkin furrowed its brow in thought. "Isaac? That's a classic. Everyone loves an Isaac."

They sat in silence a while longer, watching the farms return to smoke and ash.

"What did you do with the body?" asked the grimalkin, quietly.

"I left it in the house," said the wizard. "Let the Need Fires take it."

The creature nodded, and the silence continued.

Several minutes passed in quiet companionship.

"What about something like Æthelred?" suggested the grimalkin. "Very mystical. People love a diphthong."

"Maybe Isaac isn't so bad, after all."

The cat rolled its milky, unseeing eyes. "You're as bad as Bagdemagus was, you know that? Took him a week to pick a new one. A week! Indecisive, though I suppose if you live as Geraldine as long as he did, you want to make sure you get it right the second time around."

Smiling, the wizard reached down and gave their familiar a quick scratching between the ears.

"Sentimental, the lot of you." The grimalkin kept talking. "Don't know why I even truck with wizards, you're all the same. Well, as long as you clean that shack he called a house, I don't suppose I care. Are we having fish for dinner? Let's do fish."

It was still complaining as they went down the hill and started the long walk home.

# The Tree ✦✦✦✦✦✦

*(a tale of the* Gramayre*)*

Long ago, under a grey sky that never changes, there was a field of ashen flowers. In the middle of this field, there is a tree that never blooms. Under this peculiar tree, there will one day be a spinning wheel, and at that spinning wheel you may find an old friend. You met her once, when you first came into the world, and you will never meet her again. Spinner is her name, and she sings as she feeds her hair into the wheel, from which springs all that is, all that could be, the many ways in which our lives intersect. Beside her sits Reaper, who cuts the threads of life so that they may be woven into the tapestry at her feet. She takes from all equally, and without regret. One chair remains empty, however, and this chair belongs to Measure, who was lost very long ago. Measure, who gives our lives meaning. Where did Measure go? What can the world hope for without Measure? And yet, fear not, gentle one. We have never known her, and yet she will return to us. We will know Measure again.

*from an apocryphal page found in the East Grasby copy of the* Household Gramayre, *untitled*

# ACKNOWLEDGMENTS

No-one in their right mind would have accepted this book in its first draft, so we must all be grateful that John Ash at CAA likes a project, and that he didn't /act/ like "I'll pivot to fiction" was the crazy leap that we both knew it was. There will always be a touch of Gwendolyn that is undiluted John, though her earliest origins can be traced back to an abortive *Pathfinder* game (thank you Joey for the gift that is Gwendolyn Gooch). Tom Mayer at W. W. Norton took the book and ran it through more edits than St. Sebastian had arrows stuck in him; his patience and diligence turned it into something wonderful, and I'm grateful for his work (and that of his team) in making Isabella Nagg something I am proud of. Sophie Grunnet did a fantastic job on the internal artwork, crafting wonders from my half-baked ideas. Special thanks to the Boys: Porthos for reading this when I could trust no one else, and Tenser for his all his thankless design work (and for making dinner when everyone was tired). Lastly, my husband is unfailingly there for everything from 3 a.m. advice to keeping the house in shape, all whilst I bitch about silly author problems from the comfort of my desk—my obsession with you will probably always be deeply unhealthy, but I won't apologize for that.